KISS OF THE FALLEN

KHARMA KELLEY

ISBN: 978-0-9981573-5-1

ISBN: 978-0-9981573-6-8 (print)

www.authorkharmakelley.com

Wicked Bayou Press

www.wickedbayoupress.com

info@wickedbayoupress.com

ACKNOWLEDGMENTS

Special thanks to my editors, Evelyn S. & Margaret B. for helping me bring out the very best in this kickass tale of a sword-wielding horny femme fatale and her reluctant vampire Romeo. An unlikely partnership while the world burns is my cup of tea and I'm so glad you saw this in the story with me. I have a lot of bad habits, so thanks for calling me on my BS. You ladies make me wanna be a better writer!

And to my husband, Micah, who never fails to carry the torch for me. My cheerleader, my coach, my love; forever.

THE DARKEST NIGHT

"Sooner or later, Mr. Darkness comes for us all," Tristan said through his earpiece, "and you will be no different."

He stood fixed and unstirring on the stone platform on the church roof, waiting and watching the world from a grim, bird's-eye view. The old Byzantine cathedral was and always would be his place to watch the world unfold. Or unravel...whichever one made the most sense. In New Orleans, it was a fifty-fifty chance.

"Yeah, yeah, I get it. We can die again, and this time it's awful. It's not necessarily like our second lives are fleeting, Tristan," a rich, Manhattan accent retorted, dismissing him through the earpiece. "So tell me, why hasn't Master Darkness come for you yet?" Gregory asked, perched atop another building at least twenty clicks away from where Tristan was posted. He groaned as he stretched his lean body upward, glancing at the night's cloudy, storm-brewing sky. "I mean, it's not like you haven't walked up to his door and knocked on occasion."

Tristan sighed. Though Greg was being cheeky, there was a grain of truth to that. He had died once, and ever since had longed to test the boundaries of death. How many times had he jumped into frays between other supernaturals, heavily outnumbered? How annoyed was Tristan when he came back victorious? If others already deemed him reckless when he was a human, what the hell was the term for what he was now? The blood, and the sin along with it, was all he had these days. It made a date with Master Darkness a tempting one.

"Maybe he's saving me for one more dance, Greg. If The Three keeps giving us jobs like this, he might pick up my dance card a lot sooner than later."

Greg scoffed at his brooding partner. "Geez, Tristan. You need to get more positive, old buddy. You should think about getting a companion, you know?" He laughed to himself. "Have someone to hunt with, live out eternity with... Bang it out when eternity gets frustrating. I'm actually quite tickled at the sheer thought of your four-century-year-old ass being whipped over some companion. That'll be the fucking day."

Tristan grunted. "Yeah, well, I like my freedom. Besides, I have you to hunt with. I'm fine with eternity on my own, and the other thing—let's just say I can find it when I need it. No need to have it chained to me."

"Yeah, why not, when you've got two fully functional hands, right chief?" Greg smiled until he didn't get a confirmation. "Tristan?"

Tristan tensed as he zeroed in on a young, dark-haired woman in a frosty gray dress who popped out of a bookstore and hurried down the sidewalk. He couldn't take his eyes off her and the brown, paper gift bag she grasped in her right hand.

"Heads up, Greg. I got a visual. Green Girl heading northbound towards you. She's carrying a brown bag full of goodies."

Tristan continued to watch her. He had to be certain she didn't make any exchanges with anyone. If there was a grimoire in that bag, their job was to retrieve it.

Greg frowned hearing Tristan's warning and hopped down onto a ledge to get a better look. Finally seeing the woman

KISS OF THE FALLEN

power-walk through a crowd, he nodded. "I see her. I'm gonna tail her."

"Hey," Tristan warned. "You just tail her, all right? Don't approach her or spook her."

Eagerly, Greg leaped to the other building, running parallel and trying to keep up with her. "Tristan, I'm not afraid of some fucking witch, all right? I got her!"

Tristan hopped down from the roof onto a stain glass ledge. Being the more seasoned hunter, he always took the low road, while a watcher took the high. They always hunted in pairs, and no one ever broke protocol—not if he wanted to live.

"Don't underestimate Green Girls, Greg. Just let me know where she is, and I'll get to her on the ground."

"Yeah, yeah, Tristan. Let's bag this Green Girl and go home!" Greg continued to leap from building to building, watching the dark-haired girl move through the crowds of people on the sidewalk. She looked around in a frenzied search, the hint of suspicion clear on her face.

Tristan vaulted down fifty feet onto the steps of the cathedral and burst into a run across the street, catching up to her. "Greg! Give me coordinates! Where is she?"

He bumped and pushed people out of his way, sending pedestrians flying against walls as he moved through, his eyes searching for the woman.

"Greg!"

Greg leapt down from the building and landed only a few feet from her last steps. "She's past the music shop," he huffed. "She still has the bag. I'm right on her tail."

Tristan ran faster, knowing where Greg referred to. "Stay right there, Greg! I'm coming! Don't do anything until I get there!"

Greg snorted and continued to follow the woman even as she turned to meet his eyes. He was way closer to her than Tristan. He could take her down.

"Tris, no worries, I can still see her with the bag." He moved through the crowd, continuing to focus on just her and the brown satchel.

Finally cornering her against the gate, Gregory stood at the opening of the alley, smiling. Their little cat-and-mouse game finally drew to a close, leaving them both panting.

"Double, double, toil and trouble! What do we have here? What's in the bag, Green Girl?" Greg ran his fingers against the bricks on the wall. "I hope it's treats, being so close to Halloween and all."

The dark-haired woman with eyes like fireflies leaned against the gate and pulled the bag to her chest. "None of your business, vamp!" she barked. "You have no right to harass me here. Now let me go!"

"Give me the bag and I'll let you walk outta here." His dominating voice echoed in the small alley. "Refuse, and you'll be lucky to crawl outta here. Your choice."

The dark-haired witch shook her head in violent and vehement denial, little tears flinging off her young face. "No! You'll have to come take it!" She stood like iron even in the midst of her terror, conjuring bravery through her mind when her body felt anything but brave.

Greg smiled and licked his fangs in anticipation. Witches were the bane of his existence. He always felt they regarded themselves higher than many other creatures, but in the end, they were just like any other human—food.

"Ohhhh, an invitation!" He moved with such speed, he appeared to have teleported right in front of her face.

The witch screeched and tried to back up. "Please! Don't hurt me!" Tears trailed down her cheeks as she clutched at her bag, clinging it to her.

Greg leered down at her, disgusted at her crying. Weaklings tasted horrible. "Now, I can drain you dry, but I hear your kind's blood tastes like shit and takes forever to rinse out. I don't see the big deal with your kind anyway. Bunch of sniveling, spell-bending sluts if you ask me. But if you give me the book, I will spare you. You have my word. Now, reach down like a good girl and pull out the book."

Tristan saw Greg cornering their target in the alley and rushed forward. "Greg! Don't!"

Greg looked back at Tristan with a smirk. "It's all right, Tris. I got her!"

The witch, slowly with a sneer, reached in and pulled out a small, silver orb. As Greg turned to face her with a gaping smile exposing his fangs, she quickly stuffed the orb into his mouth.

"*Ab intus illuminet!*" she shouted, throwing her hands toward him.

Greg roared and convulsed as the silver orb within him lit up with brilliant light, casting blinding streams through his eyes and mouth until he burned to a pillar of ash.

The witch tossed more orbs out toward Tristan, who quickly shadowed before she could detonate them.

Horrified, she looked around, bouncing her eyes from one side to the other, clutching the brown bag in one hand, her last orb in the other. "Show yourself! Or leave me alone! I'll toast you just like I did your friend!"

"I'm sorry he terrorized you," the deep voice of Tristan echoed, "but I'm gonna need that grimoire. If you relinquish it to me, I will not harm you. You have my word."

She scoffed. "What good is a vamper's word?" She clutched the orb tighter. "You are no ally of witches. You seek to watch us burn! I'll kill every one of you lying, monstrous, parasitic vampires as long as there's a breath in my damn body!"

"There's no way I can persuade you to give me the book?" he asked again.

"No!" She threw the orb down. "Illustr—"

Before she could complete her spell, Tristan appeared behind her and covered her mouth.

"Fine, have it your way, Green Girl." He dropped his other arm with force on the back of her neck, knocking her unconscious. The witch sunk to the pavement like a sack of potatoes. He peered down at her and shook his head. "Now I'm down another partner, thanks to you."

Tristan cast his eye on the ashy remains of his fallen comrade. He should kill her. After all, she did kill a vampire, and to keep the peace it was really 'eye for an eye' in the supernatural world. You kill my brother, I kill your sister kind of thing.

But what did it matter? The witch had a right to protect herself, and Greg was foolish to underestimate her. Witches never were what they seemed, and they played the victim well, but they were, no pun intended, quite crafty. They used that perceived weakness to their advantage. Killing her would only bring more unhappy discourse between his kind and the Green Girls, the usual slur for witches.

He walked over to the brown bag and pulled out a thick, red and black covered book and examined it. The red paint on the cover was not paint, but old blood stained to color the hard cover. He smelled it and sighed. That made the book truly bonafide. The creator of the grimoire always colored it with their blood, letting the thick, red liquid of life stain the fibers. There were many wannabe witches and frauds out there who made grimoires, but he felt the power on this one. It definitely was legit.

The Three would be happier than a vamp in a blood bank to get this, as it would be an invaluable bargaining chip to hold over the witches. Granted, that was why they found it necessary to dispatch him and Greg to retrieve it on such short notice.

A rumble through the night sky signaled a storm, and no sooner than he dragged the witch's body under the eve of the nearby building, the ominous clouds opened up and began to pour down. Tristan stood for a moment as the rain began to wash Greg's ashes away.

Greg had no companion, nor was he very established in the vampire ranks. He was just a young, often overzealous vamp. He didn't deserve this, to have his existence literally washed away in some alley. But then again, Mr. Darkness couldn't care less. It appears a vampire's life can be fleeting all the same.

What did all of this mean in the end? Vamps, witches, were-shifters—they all had some bone to pick at the other. He'd lived his whole life fighting battles, and one thing he'd learned—the end never justified the means. The vampires were no different. They were struggling to keep their dominance up in a world that hated and feared them.

Tristan was eager to deliver the grimoire to The Three, so he could finally bow out of this ridiculous war.

ON NEUTRAL GROUND

*H*ow long should a vampire continue to reap the rewards of immortality without consequences? Tristan had asked that question to his mentor, to his friends, hell, even annoyed upper management by addressing it to The Three.

No one knew the answer. In fact, many said there were no consequences, which meant they lived to run amok and watch the world burn. Some just called him crazy and tried to convince him to go under, which sounded more tempting every time he heard it. Becoming a living, dried up corpse locked in a tomb for a minimum of 100 years may seem like a pathetic vacation to the recently resurrected fledglings, but to a war-torn, long fang like him it often seemed like a heavenly idea.

Let's chunk this fucking book at The Three, and then we can discuss a much-needed vacation from the world.

Approaching the oversized, black leather doors, Tristan stopped at the entrance and eyed the two guards. The Sergeant at Arms sucked his teeth and kept his eyes trained on him.

"I'm here for The Three. I've got what they were asking for." He opened his long, dark coat to give the Sergeant at Arms a peek at the red book. With recognition, the man nodded and opened the door for him to enter.

Tristan inched into the grandiose chamber adorned with royal blue, silver, and black curtains and carpet. The colors of The Three. There were no windows, just large, classic murals depicting battle scenes of old supernatural wars. Many were fought in parallel of human wars, such as the Peloponnesian War, the Battle of Hastings, and, Tristan's favorite, the French Revolution. That one was truly witches, demons and halflings pissed that the rich and haughty vampires left them in squalor.

He trekked up the small set of stairs to the three empty wooden thrones that stood before him and stopped, awaiting their arrival. Glowering the chamber, he scoffed. He had seen this place far, far too many times, had come to The Three's beck and call far, far too many times. Now, he was ready to let it go.

His attention moved to a side door that opened on the far left of the thrones and watched a woman in a long, dark blue dress step out. With a welcoming smile and a smooth sway of her hips, she could only be Ivana.

She made a beeline straight to him, and Tristan offered her a polite smile.

"Hello Ivana."

Her silver eyes flashed with her charming smile. "Hello yourself, Commander." Her sultry tone echoed through the empty chamber. She stopped just short of him and raked her eyes over him. "Good to see you, Tristan. How long has it been?"

She crossed her arms, still smiling.

"A long time, Ivana. And if Javen didn't kick over every rock to dispatch me for this recent job, it'd probably be longer still." Tristan's tone was a touch warmer than his typical voice, most likely for Ivana's sake. With the face of a nubile seventeen-year-old, he could still see a century of wisdom behind her reflective eyes.

"Well, in either event, I'm happy to see you have not got under. Still finding some reason to rise into the night, it seems."

"It gives me something to occupy my time."

Ivana smiled as if she had x-ray vision. "You and I both know, Tristan, that couldn't be further from the truth. You've always been a crusader. A fighter." She stepped closer, her aura just as palpable as her words. "It's in your blood, despite your cynicism. Javen admires it, as do I." Despite being a vampire, Ivana had a brightness to her, a vivacious life force which seemed uncommon for their kind. Javen claimed to have turned her to save her from 'a fate worse than death', which amused Tristan because he always believed that being a vampire... *was* a fate worse than death.

Oh, the excuses one makes to have a gorgeous young woman indebted to you for eternity.

"Have you seen your companion?"

Ivana nodded. "He's here. They just finished another meeting in the back. They know you are here, as they asked me to check on you."

She walked around him gracefully, like a dance, with her hips swaying. Watching him as he stood, she inhaled his scent and eyed him like prey. "I came to see if there's anything you needed," she leaned in to press her dark red lips dangerously close to his ear and the soft puffs of her breath against him stirred his focus "while you waited."

Tristan tried not to be phased at Ivana's very open invitation to him, but it had been a long time since he'd indulged. Unfortunately, his cock knew it. In fact, it reminded him physically, jerking a bit before he sighed and took a step back from her.

Christ, I just wanna get outta here before I end up staked for trying to 'stake' Javen's protégée. Is that too much to ask?

"You drive a hard bargain, Ivana, but I'm fine just waiting here."

A man would have to be a fool to pass up a roll with Ivana of

Bainesborough, but a vampire would know better. Ivana didn't rub up to just anyone and Tristan knew that, but it didn't give him an excuse to be with her. Protégée, companion, it didn't matter to Tristan. In the old days, that meant she belonged to Javen, and he wasn't a vampire who shared.

Ivana grinned as she sensed Tristan's muted excitement. Oh, how she loved to get a rise out of the stubborn Commander. He was deliciously tortured and ridiculously a rule-follower. It was why Javen often referred to Tristan as one of his most dedicated soldiers. Everyone listened to him, and he was an unrivaled warrior. She wasn't all that surprised to see the dark vampire commander grace The Three's chamber again.

"Very well, Tristan. You know, I long to see you *comfortable*." She moved from his side to face him dead on, a mischievous gleam in her eye.

Tristan nodded. *Yeah, I bet.*

He desperately needed to change the subject. "I hear you've been forming alliances and peacekeeping meetings between various Supe groups like the Were-shifters and the Green Girls," he touted. "Is that true?"

Ivana sobered but still smiled at his question that tugged at her passion. Her eyes lit up.

"It is. Remelia has been opening to talks regarding the witches, and rumors have it that Gannon may be as well. Now, we're just in small talks and negotiations, but with a little time and patience, we can probably form some treaties with at least a few."

Tristan scoffed. "That is, until they find another reason to tear out each other's throats." He shook his head. "You're wasting your time, Ivana, if you think you can bring all of the Supes to join hands or wings or paws or whatever and sing some 'We are the World'. That's just not in their nature."

Ivana's smile slowly morphed to a frown. "It's not a waste of time if we can stop killing each other and stop wasting vampires' lives fighting." She pointed at him. "A life like yours, Commander." She crossed her arms. "To how many battles and frays have you been dispatched in your lifetime, Tristan?" When Tristan stood silent, she nodded and asked a rhetorical question. "Where's your partner, Greg?"

Tristan sighed. He understood what she was saying, but he was a lot older than her. She didn't realize that this shit would never change. It was ingrained in them all, and they were no better than humans.

We hated and fought in our fear just like they did. We were failures. Some supernaturals felt they were superior to humans, but how could they, when the same greed and hatred fueled their decisions as well?

"Ivana, I'm not shitting on your efforts. Frankly, I think it is commendable. But do you honestly think we would really stop the bickering and plotting, considering I just went on a stealth mission involving witches?"

Ivana's frown deepened with concern, visibly surprised Tristan would say such a thing. "What do you mean? What happened with them?"

Before Tristan could say anything, the side door opened again, and three vampires stepped out.

Javen, Valette, and Kostya were collectively known as The Three, prided for being three of the oldest vampires to date. They each came to the table many years ago with their own following and broods, hungry to join forces when vampires were being hunted and killed. They were the vampires all the others flocked to for leadership when The Three ruled equally, even sharing the throne.

Javen glanced at Tristan and Ivana, then smirked. "Good to see you, Tristan. I take it Ivana was helpful and made sure you were comfortable while you waited for us?"

Tristan nodded. "Yes, she did."

When he watched Ivana, her face still held that frown. Her lip trembled as though she were itching to say more to him, but she swallowed and turned to her mentor.

"Well, one does what she can, Javen." She walked towards The Three. "Some vampires are just rough around the edges." She gave him a wink and a smile, washing away any angst she'd worn just seconds ago.

Tristan didn't know what to make of it, and he wished he could just ask her what was wrong, but seeing her clam up around The Three told him this wasn't the time or place.

Javen took her hand to help her up the steps then pulled her close when she reached the top, letting her hands brace against his biceps. He gazed into her eyes and smiled.

"I told you Tristan was a hard nut to crack. No doubt he stood like a stone block the entire time."

He kissed her on the lips.

Ivana smiled politely at Javen and squeezed his arm. "Well, I'll leave you all to your meeting." Without another word, she stepped through the side door and closed it shut.

"Apparently, he gets more *stubborn* as the years dredge on," Valette interjected with a grin.

With wide brown eyes, she fixed on Tristan before sitting on the throne to the right. She let her dark dress flutter down, but not before gracing him with a view of her ivory gams and the fact she wasn't wearing any panties.

Jokingly referred to as The Virgin Queen, Valette played bashful and chaste, yet loved sex so much she put nymphos to shame. Many vampires said she must have been the world's first cock tease. Looking at her now with her smug expression and crossed legs, Tristan figured the other vampires may have been right.

"Hello Valette."

She grinned. "Hello, Tristan."

Javen moved towards Tristan and shook his hand. "Good to

see you, Commander Castillion." He browsed around behind Tristan. "Where's your partner, Gregory?"

"I'm afraid Gregory was killed during the mission, sir." Tristan took the grimoire from his coat and handed it to Javen. "The Green Girl who possessed the grimoire attacked, and Greg was unfortunately vaporized by white light."

Valette gasped. "I thought they decided to ban white light?"

Kostya shook his head. "Remelia and the Green Girls would never allow that; you know better. They understand how effective it is against vampires, and they can even manipulate it to fight Were-shifters. They would never let it go without a fight." Kostya's thick, Slavic accent put emphasis on the word 'fight'. He tensed on his throne.

Kostya, the most reserved of The Three, had always been a bit surprising to Tristan since he had the bloodiest past of them all.

Javen examined the book and smelled it. Grinning, he shot his eyes to Tristan. "The witch you took this from, did you kill her?"

Tristan answered with a tic in his jaw. "No."

Valette scowled. "No?"

Javen raised his hand to silence her, still assessing Tristan. "Good. There is no need for more bloodshed and while we're at this stalemate with the witches, every life counts."

Valette leaned forward, her face still twisted in a scowl. "But she killed one of our own!"

"Valette, that's beside the point. Haven't you been listening to anything Ivana has been evangelizing? Killing eye for an eye is a vicious circle. One that will never end with peace." Javen ran his fingers over the grimoire. "You did right, Tristan. Thank you for retrieving this for us so quickly. I will make sure you are paid handsomely." He turned to the other member of The Three. "Kostya, make sure he gets Gregory's cut."

Kostya nodded, standing to his feet. "It is done. We will also hold a vigil in the great hall to mourn his loss."

Javen walked the book up to the stone table and set it there.

"Yes, something else that Ivana has been working on with Valette. Making sure we mourn the fallen."

Tristan crossed his arms. "Ivana has been working on a lot, lately. You must be proud."

Javen smiled. "She has, and I am. She's young and an idealist, but Ivana could never be talked out of anything. I love her for her impetuous behavior."

Tristan smiled politely. "Impetuous, indeed."

"Yes, but it could also be dangerous." Javen walked toward Tristan. "She's been ruffling a lot of feathers with her drive to bring unity with the supernatural creatures. Some are open, but many are not. They don't like change, and some don't like the idea of a vampire leading the charge."

Tristan nodded as the theory made sense to him. "Supes don't like alterations in patterns, you know that."

Javen frowned. "I have one more job for you, Tristan. It's important."

Tristan shook his head. "Javen, I was clear that I am done with all this. I want no part in what's to come. I just want to live out my days away from bickering and discord with the Supes." He sighed. "Hell, these days humans are less problematic. Doesn't that say anything?"

Javen got up to his face and stared at him, his eyes soft. Emotional. "I know, Tristan. We are all tired of the fighting. But we need you, and we're trying to build a better relationship with the Supes."

Tristan did not share the same sympathy. "Is that why we're stealing little books from Green Girls?" He stood confident and still as Javen wrestled with the question in his eyes.

"That is entirely different, Tristan. I'm talking about Ivana. She's been getting death threats."

"From whom?" Tristan scowled. It was the first time he'd ever heard of such a thing. "How long has this been going on?"

"Around the same time Ivana met with the Were-shifters a

few weeks ago," Valette interjected. "We've been keeping her here, safe—which she has *not* been too happy about! Little ingrate!"

Javen stepped back. "This is why we need you, Tristan. I can't keep her cooped up here while she's trying to make a difference, but I can't let her go to this next meeting with the witches, Were-shifters, and heaven knows what without someone to protect her." Javen pointed at Tristan. "One of our own. Trusted, respected, deadly fighter. We need you, Tristan."

Tristan raked a frustrated hand through his hair. He knew Javen would try to pull something out of his ass to make him stay. Screw this, he was done. He'd told The Three he was done after this crap job. The job that took yet another partner.

"There are other night fighters in your charge that can take care of Ivana for you. Ones just as seasoned as me, Javen."

"I don't want them!" Javen shouted in an outburst. He stepped back and took a deep breath to calm down before he spoke again. "Do you realize how important Ivana is to me?"

Tristan nodded.

"Then you know. You know how those naysayers will hurt her just to get to me and to us, The Three. It could be just smoke, or they could really mean to hurt her."

"She now represents our entire race of vampires," Valette interjected. "She's the key to finally achieving peace."

Tristan scoffed. "Cut the bullshit, Valette. You three don't want peace..." He cut his eyes to Javen. "You want dominance. I told you I want no part of this shit. You guys can fight for world dominance—oh excuse me, world peace—-without my help. Thanks, but no thanks."

As Tristan began to walk away, Javen blocked him. Tristan frowned.

"Javen, I told you I was done. I meant it."

"You're going to turn your back on your leaders?" Javen asked. "Your race?" He crossed his arms, fury swirling in his eyes. "This is not the Tristan I know. Cowardice does not become you."

Tristan met his eyes with anger. He clenched his fists so tight, the nails dug into his flesh and he felt the stickiness of blood in his palm.

"Javen, you're my governance, and I respect you. But don't *ever* call me a coward again if you want to keep it that way."

Tristan ached to strike him, if not out of revenge for the comment, then out of pure frustration for the situation he was in. He just wanted out and to be left alone. But Ivana didn't get to choose her mentor, and she wasn't like the rest of them—bloodthirsty, hypocritical snobs.

Maybe there was some truth to what Valette said. If Ivana was viewed as a positive force for unity, then she needed to be protected.

He should do his part to protect her.

Javen stepped to the side, unblocking Tristan. "That was uncalled for. I apologize for attacking your reputation. My companion is important to me. I could've made a string of them in my lifetime, but I didn't. I held back because I didn't want to know the pain of losing them. But with Ivana, it was right for me. She's my only, and I don't think I will want another."

He turned to Kostya and Valette. "You can feel however you want to feel for us and the cause, but please do this for us. You're the only one we trust."

Valette and Kostya walked up to the stone stairs, their eyes trained on Javen.

"This will officially be your final job with us before your retirement, Commander Castillion," Valette said as she pulled a pin out of her hair that had held it up. "The Three will bloodswear on it."

Javen walked up to meet them on the stone. "Agreed. It will be official, Tristan. It's not our intention to jerk you around. We just need you to get her safely to tomorrow night's meeting. Then your allegiance and duty to The Three will be fulfilled. You'll be able to do whatever you'd like, and we will never call on you again." Javen stood in the middle of Valette and Kostya. "Do we have terms, Commander?"

Tristan stood for a moment, running it through his head. A blood-swear was a legitimate and formal agreement. It would mean The Three would officially retire him, and he would finally be free from all this. All he had to do was what he was good at, fighting and protecting. Seemed fair for a change.

Slowly, Tristan walked up to the stairs, stood before them, and extended his hand. "We have terms. I accept this final job based on the agreement that I will be released from service to The Three and any duties pertaining to your order."

Valette took the long, pearl dropped pin, and handed it to Javen. "So be it."

Javen pierced his hand with the pin. "So be it." He then handed it to Kostya, who also pierced his hand. Kostya nodded. "So be it."

Tristan took his stiletto from its sheath and punctured the center of his right palm, watching the blood trickle down onto the stone in little starburst droplets. He shook Valette's hand, then Kostya's, and finally clasped hands with Javen, who smiled, exposing his fangs.

"So be it."

Tristan released his hand and watched as his wound slowly began to heal. "I'll be ready to chaperone Ivana to her destination. You can count on me she'll be safe."

Javen nodded. "Of that, I have no doubt, Commander."

Tristan stood there and couldn't help but wonder if shaking hands with The Three was akin to shaking hands with the devil. Heaven help them if they reneged on their agreement.

ONE LAST MISSION

The following night, Halloween approached under a blood moon. It had everyone up in arms, and The Three pleaded with Ivana to change her mind. Samhain was a night where dark shit just seemed to happen. The Green Girls owned the night and the humans were out in droves dressed like the creatures they would run from if they only knew most of them really existed. A blood moon was like a freak show beacon which cranked every faction that conjured and slashed to DEFCON 3.

But the call soon came to Tristan that she was still meeting with him, so he arrived at the Great Hall early to talk to a couple of other night fighters who would join him in escorting Ivana. He liked to ride close to the person he was protecting but needed eyes out to see trouble before it ran into them.

The first Supes meeting that Ivana had scheduled to attend would be on the edge of town, and Tristan needed to organize the motorcade. No one knew the route they were taking except Tristan and the driver. The fewer people who had access to Ivana's movement, the better. If Were-shifters and others were threatening her life, they may try to strike whenever she was out of The Three's watchful eyes.

He liked to hand pick his crew, and the two other night fighters that met his tough criteria were Christophe and Dashiell. They were tough and didn't have an ego to stroke. Especially Dashiell, who trained under Tristan. He was a fast learner and often complained about the ridiculous missions he had to take for The Three.

Tristan worked with Christophe many years ago when Tristan first turned, but from what he remembered, the old Jesuit priest-now-vampire was a force to be reckoned with. Christophe professed himself to be quiet and timid in his human life, holding strong to his faith. A lot must have changed the old vampire because he didn't believe in much these days except that the world had only two beings: the strong and the weak.

Heaven help you if you were weak.

Tristan waited by the outside stone steps, which led to the armored limousine. He calmly checked his watch for the time. Then, Tristan pressed his earpiece. "Okay you two state your positions."

A voice with a thick German accent broke the silence first. "Christophe here. I'm taking the west flank. Eye in the sky."

"Acknowledged," Tristan replied. He never searched for his partners because it was poor form to inadvertently give away their positions. If enemy Supes were watching, he didn't want to give them any free intel. "Okay, how about you, Dashiell?"

A cough rumbled through the earpiece. "East flank. Down n' dirty, Commander. Do we know who we're watching out for? Were-shifters? Witches? Demons?"

Tristan shook his head. "We don't know. Anonymous threats have been made, so just keep an eye out for anything suspicious from *any* Supes, all right?"

"Shit, Tristan. The Three has us out here looking for a needle in a haystack. You know that, right?" Dashiell groaned. "They

KISS OF THE FALLEN

would have us adios a drunken coed in a costume to save their little Ivana. This is bullshit, dude. I'm not a fan of drawing attention from the blood bags. Human authorities are like a dog with a bone once their kind is killed and we really don't need that kind of heat."

Tristan sighed. "I know. It's shitty, but it is what it is, fellas. Keep your eye out. There could be Green Girls out and about, shifters, and who knows what else. And watch the Green Girls!" he warned. "Don't get too close."

"Gotcha. Some of those bitches have white light," Dashiell replied. "Greg, that poor bastard."

"Well, he's no longer suffering." Christophe said, standing on a nearby rooftop looking at the moon. "This is a bad night, Tristan."

"Don't' tell me superstitions got you too, Christophe?" Dashiell asked over the earpiece. "You guys fuck me up. It's a great reminder why I'm not either of you guys' partner."

"Why? Afraid you'll learn something?" Christophe asked.

"No, afraid I'll be another notch on Tristan's partner belt!" Dashiell laughed. "What number of partner was Greg, Tristan? Number four?"

"No, no, I think that one was number six, *ja?*" Christophe interjected.

Tristan groaned. "He was number three, assholes."

His earpiece communication exploded in laughter from both Christophe and Dashiell.

Tristan shook his head. *I don't know why I bother.* "Oh, both of you can go fuck yourselves. It's not my fault they can't listen."

Dashiell tried to sober, laughter still laced on his words. "You should spread them out over the centuries. Have some patience, man. If you didn't want to split your commission, just say so."

The large door to the mansion began to open, and Ivana, dressed in a long black lace gown, proceeded down the steps with Javen holding an umbrella over her.

Tristan felt saved by her arrival; it signaled it was game time.

"All right guys, shut up. The precious cargo's here. Everyone keep your position," Tristan commanded over his earpiece. "When we head out, keep your flanked positions until we've gotten out of town. I hope you guys fed because I need hyper-speed tonight, gentlemen. Fade if you have to but keep up. Only me and the driver know the route."

"Affirmative," Christophe replied.

"Ditto," Dashiell replied, popping bubble gum.

"For the love of all that's holy, Dashiell, *please* maintain radio silence," Tristan warned, at the same time giving Ivana a friendly nod as she approached him.

As always, she was all smiles, staring at the Commander. His dark hair was wet from the constant mist of rain encroaching on the Halloween night. His black coat outlined his tall, lean figure that was terribly masculine.

It was moments like this, admiring Tristan's handsome existence, Ivana wished they had met in another time, another life perhaps, before she was taken by Javen and made his. Tristan seemed so isolated and apathetic lately, and she wished someone could make him care about something again. In another life, she wished that someone were her.

"Hello again, Commander," Ivana greeted with hooded, smoky eyes. Her ivory face was a strict contrast against her dark clothing.

"Hello, Ivana," he politely replied. He turned to acknowledge Javen with a nod. "Javen."

Javen smiled. "Commander, I can't begin to express my gratitude for this service." He turned Ivana's face towards him and her smile faded. "You be safe, my love." He gave her a kiss on the lips that wanted to be more, but Ivana pulled back. Clearing her throat, she gave a forced smile that faded again as soon as she spoke.

"Thank you, Javen. I'll see you soon to report the news on how everything went." She took the umbrella from him and continued to walk past Tristan, where he opened the limo door for her to get in. She scooted to the other end and sat quietly, looking out the window.

Tristan nodded at Javen. "I'll report to you once we get to the destination."

"Thank you. I know she's in good hands with you."

Tristan slipped into the limousine as the door closed behind him. Finally in the safety of the car, Tristan opened his coat and pulled out his route plan. He passed it to the driver.

"Here, plug that code into your GPS, and it will load our route plan to this meeting. Do not deviate from it under any circumstances. Understand?"

The driver reached back and took the slip of paper. "You got it, sir."

Ivana kept quiet as they began to pull out of the semi-circle driveway and to their destination.

Tristan observed her emotional face. He wanted to ignore it, because who knew what kind of drama he was threatening to unleash by inquiring, but he did want to know why she had clammed up the other day. It was like the issue with the witches had been news to her.

"You're gonna be fine, Ivana. They just want to make sure you get there safe. You won't even know I'm around."

She scoffed. Tristan couldn't be ignored even if he tried. The vampire had an intimidating presence.

"That's not what I'm concerned about." She stayed facing the window. Her fingers traced at the misty raindrops on the glass, trying to distract herself.

"Then what is it?" Tristan asked. "Does it have anything to do with your silence the other day and the cold shoulder you just gave Javen?"

"You're very observant, Commander," Ivana responded softly. She didn't know what to do, and who to trust, but she knew something was strange with Javen. Their fight last night had proved it. "Javen is hiding something from me," she added.

"Like what?"

Tristan wondered if the secret was his last mission of getting a grimoire from a Green Girl. He never discussed his missions with anyone except The Three, who commissioned him. That was a rule he almost broke the other night when he saw her, and he wasn't trying to make the same mistake twice. If she brought it up, he would simply deny it.

Ivana turned to look at him, her bright eyes watery. "I wish I knew, but it isn't good. There's too many missions going on. Things that are affecting my conversations with the other Supes. I feel like I'm fighting an uphill battle."

She wanted to believe she was making some sort of difference, but it seemed Javen didn't care as much for her ideals. As if his needs came first like a spoiled little boy.

"Why didn't you tell me about the death threats, Ivana?"

Tristan held a scornful expression, his eyes searching hers. There was something she wasn't telling him. He could see it in her eyes. She wanted to, though. Just like she did the other night when he met with The Three. He didn't know what to do to get her to trust him, but, then again, why would she? He was hiding something from her as well.

Ivana frowned. "It wasn't a big deal. It's not like I have tons of threats, Tristan. Javen and the others are just creating a big issue out of this. I was making progress."

Tristan shook his head at her naivety. "*Any* amount of death threats is cause for concern. You know Javen would lose his shit if anything happened to you. If the other Supes planned to hurt him by hurting you, all hell would break loose."

Ivana gave him a pitiful attempt at a smile. "It's not the other Supes I'm worried about."

Tristan turned to face her again with concern at her statement. "What do you mean?"

Suddenly, the driver slammed on the brakes, and both their bodies surged forward.

Tristan frowned. "What the hell is going on?"

"Sorry, freaking asshole in a damn Hummer blocking us up! Move, you fucker!" The driver honked as other costumed pedestrians walked by. The crowd was making it difficult to move around.

Tristan's eyes trained on the Hummer, and he froze when all the doors opened. "Shit! Get down!" He covered Ivana, pushing her down to the floorboard as masked assassins jumped out the Hummer and sprayed their limousine with gun fire.

Ivana screamed and shielded her face as silver bullets zipped and ripped through the car. She peeked up to witness the driver's seat riveted with holes and his body still and limp. Blood seeped through the punctured leather. She closed her eyes shut as cushion debris fell on her.

"I thought we were safe in this armored limo? What's happening? " Ivana asked, yelling in tears.

Tristan winced as a bullet grazed his hip, feeling the intense burn as the hot silver passed through. They were using armor piercing rounds, most likely from a significantly large caliber as the bullets' hits sounded and felt like elephants kicking the car.

This told him the assassins were well prepared, and he had to get Ivana out of there. Fast.

He turned on his earpiece, hoping to hear from either Christophe or Dashiell. "Dashiell? Christophe? We're getting heat from all sides here and we're ambushed! State your position! I need you guys to cover us as Ivana and I are trapped in the limo." A moment passed, and all he heard was static. "Christophe? Dashiell? Report your position."

Nothing.

Tristan yelled. "Acknowledge!"

Nothing still. Just static.

They were on their own. "Shit," Tristan hissed.

He met Ivana's worried eyes. Her mouth was slightly open, exposing her fangs. She was beginning to panic, but now he really needed her to focus if he had a chance to get her out safe.

"Ivana, listen to me, okay? Are you hearing me?"

She quickly nodded. "Yes."

In a heated rush, he began instructing her on what to do if she had any chance of getting out of this alive. The car wasn't going to provide cover for them for much longer.

"We can't stay here, or we're going to die. But the assassins have to reload. That's when we'll move. Either they'll try to get the doors open to take you or wait us out. Neither are acceptable. I gotta get in a position to see who I'm fighting, but when I do, I'll start shooting. Okay?"

She violently nodded again, clutching his coat as she hunkered down to the floorboard.

Tristan lifted her chin, so she could face him and meet his eyes He needed to see her expression, needed to know she'd understood him.

"When I start shooting, I need you to run out of here as fast as you can to that church. Fade if you can, but *do not stop*. Make it inside, and I'll cover you, then follow," Tristan said.

"Okay." Ivana swallowed. She took deeper breaths to try to calm herself as Tristan began to move away from her.

Tristan stopped when a tug on his coat alerted him to the fact that Ivana still gripped it. He gently put his hand on hers and pushed it away.

"We're going to be all right, Ivana. Just remember what I said."

Tristan pulled the seat back to the escape hatch in the trunk and checked both his Desert Eagle pistols in his holsters. He wasn't sure what they would be up against, so he made sure he had at least two other clips of silver bullet blessed rounds, double impact to kill *most* of the type of Supes willing to attack, including Were-shifters and naughty little Green Girls.

When the sound of shots firing slowed, he pushed up close

against the trunk, looking through the space between the tail lights to see three masked assassins in full tactical gear, standing in front of another black Hummer.

Christophe and Dashiell were nowhere in sight, dead or alive. He examined the scene, and fuck it—the mystery kill squad had set a death trap for them, blocking the motorcade in the front and the back so they were ambushed. The assassins probably thought after breaking down the motorcade, it'd be easy pickings.

Tristan had news for them. This wasn't going down without a fight. He huffed a breath, then cracked the lock on the trunk.

"Go!" he yelled at Ivana.

As the trunk lifted, Tristan began unloading fire at the masked shooters, hitting two of them while the other ducked behind a vehicle. The barrage of bullets continued as Tristan turned and leaped on top of the car, firing shots at the gang of masked assassins in front of the limousine, returning fire.

Ivana opened her car door and sprinted towards the church as instructed while Tristan continued to lay down cover fire, taking care not to strike any frightened, scattered humans as they ran out of the way.

On the roof of the limousine, he took full advantage of the 360-degree view, and the distance from their assailants from his location gave him the advantage to hear the hum of each bullet coming his way before they could reach him. This allowed him to dodge and maneuver in a way that any less experienced vamp would be incapable of. From there, he was picked off a few assassins who ducked behind cars and one who was trying to catch up to Ivana.

When two assassins in front of the limousine stopped to reload, he slid down the front of the limo and grappled with one until he jabbed the assassin's face. He pinned the would-be killer down and brutally snapped his neck. The other shooter popped off a round that hit Tristan's right shoulder. The force of the caliber pushed him to the ground. Seeing him momentarily subdued, the shooter waved at another on a motorcycle.

"Get the girl! Get the girl!" a muffled, male voice yelled as two riders took off towards Ivana. She ran with superhuman speed to the doors, but they wouldn't open. Desperate, she ripped the giant door free, broke its the locks, and ran inside.

Crying, she pushed a Virgin Mary statue against the door and backed up. She grabbed the flagpole by the door and broke it across her knee in three places, selecting the middle piece as a weapon. Ivana gripped it tightly. Then, the wood and steel of the large church doors splintered.

Tristan flipped up his back to his feet, but he staggered a moment from the silver eating into his flesh. He came up behind the distracted shooter, but the element of surprise was broken as the masked assassin turned around and aimed his gun at Tristan's head.

"Say goodnight, vamp," the muffled voice demanded.

"Goodnight," Tristan said with a shrug as he pulled out his silver, stiletto blade tucked behind his back and quickly sliced into the assassin's heart.

With a grunt, the assassin dropped to the pavement like a pile of bricks. Dodging gunfire from all angles, Tristan kept moving towards the church. Two assassins ran up the steps. Tristan leaned against the Hummer and dropped his empty clips, loading a fresh magazine in each of his .44 caliber pistols.

Ivana, hearing the beating as the assassins began busting their fists through the wooden doors, looked to the back of the church. If she could get to a different exit, she could have a fighting chance to get away.

Running towards the back, past the altar, she gasped as a lone figure stepped out of the shadows. The mysterious person's face was covered with a ski mask, and he slowly walked towards Ivana. Her face wet with tears, she held up her hand with the wooden stick like a shield and backed away.

"You don't have to do this," Ivana pleaded. "There can be peace between all of us. Let me fight to make that happen. Please, I don't want to kill anyone."

The shadowed assassin stopped and slowly pulled off his mask, revealing a familiar face to her.

Ivana's lips trembled, holding back tears, completely shocked at who stood before her. She dropped the stick, all will leaving her body. She stood still but almost defiant, ready to accept her fate. Ivana shook her head, defeated at the revelation of her killer.

"*Why?* This won't stop or change anything. We were making progress." Tears ran down her face. "There can still be peace."

The shadowed assassin pulled out a long, silver stiletto blade, watching it reflect against the church light. Then advanced towards Ivana. With a deep voice, her killer revealed the truth to her:

"No peace."

"Where's fucking friends when you need 'em?" Tristan spat aloud to himself, still backed against the Hummer. He shook off the wound in his shoulder, hit the slide release lever on both weapons, and racked the slide forward, ready to rock.

He had to make a run for it quickly and get to Ivana in the church. They were sitting ducks out there and needed better cover. As two more assassins came out of the frantic, running crowd, he quickly fired at them both, watching one drop, and he made a break for it. He dashed toward the church and continued laying down fire, clipping assailants whenever he could.

As he reached the steps, he felt the force of a bullet strike the flesh of his left leg, forcing it from under him. Struggling to get up, he fired at one assassin breaking down the church door when another bullet struck his arm.

That was when the other killer at the door threw a familiar, silver ball in his direction.

As it began to charge up, Tristan's eyes widened and with a curse, and he tried to shield himself with his thick, black coat. The white light flashed, and Tristan growled as his exposed hands and the side of his face burned. He squeezed his eyes shut a little too late, and the light singed his pupils. His body throbbing, he struggled to get up when the assassin at the door went up to him and put a foot on his throat.

Tristan raised his gun and pulled the trigger, but there was nothing but the click of an empty chamber.

"Oops," the assassin said through his mask with a muffled but masculine voice. "Looks like someone's out of rounds. That sucks."

Tristan choked out a laugh. "Yep, it does. Guess I'll have to kill you the old-fashioned way."

With blinding speed, he grabbed the assailant's foot and turned it so that he flipped and plummeted to the concrete next to Tristan. Yelling a gut-wrenching wail, Tristan brought his left arm down with his blade. Simultaneously, he broke the assailant's neck and stabbed him in the chest, ensuring the assassin's death.

Multiple motorcycles sped off in the distance, as they fled among the chaos they caused in the Quarter.

Pulling himself up, he watched the deceased assassin, still masked and mysterious.

Leaning down, he pulled the mask off the assassin's face and fell once more onto the steps. He stared down at the black-clad corpse and realized he had seen that face before. A long time ago, perhaps during his training.

Claude was his name, an old Parisian executioner from the French Revolution. But it couldn't be.

Claude was a *vampire*. Why would vampires try to kill Ivana?

Panting, he got up and studied the church door. It was beaten and punctured, but still holding. She had to still be safely inside.

Tristan used all his strength to move as the silver slugs still in his body began to burn intensely and slowly drain him. He scrambled to the door, beating against it.

"Ivana!"

No answer.

He backed up, and with all his might, heaved at the weakest area of the door to finally break through. His haphazard momentum threw him down onto the cold marble of the old church.

"Ivana!" he called out.

A pang in his gut formed at the returned silence as he called out to her. The moonlight from the blood moon cast Tristan's shadow ominously against the floor and church wall, which were dimly lit with gaslights.

Bracing himself on the stone font of holy water, he finally got fully to his feet again and peered ahead down the rows of pews to the altar.

He froze as he saw a familiar figure in a black gown laid on the altar table.

His breath caught in his throat, and he quickly started a combination of running and hobbling to get to the altar, which now felt a million miles away from him and only got longer.

"Ivana!"

When he finally reached the carpeted steps stained in blood, he slowed and turned his head at the sight. He was too late.

Tristan stood over the altar and lifted up Ivana's vacant, ashen face. A pentagram was drawn in blood on her forehead, and her once alluring black dress was soaked with blood; it dripped from the train of her gown.

He gritted his fangs as he witnessed her laid out like a sacrifice with several wounds in her chest. The execution was brutal and unforgiving. He sighed in remorse as her once lively features now seemed more like gray stone. Her body was limp, all life removed from her. This time, forever.

"No!" Rage building within him, he slammed his hand down on the altar, the marble cracking at the force. He had failed. He'd failed miserably at his mission, and now Ivana was dead.

It all fell apart on him, and he had no idea why or how. Something wasn't right. *This* wasn't right. She didn't do anything to deserve this. It was all he could think of as his strength diminished and he collapsed on the floor.

I'm not going to die, he commanded of himself. *I'm going to live just so I can find out who's behind this and make them fucking pay. I'm not done yet, Mr. Darkness. Still more hell raising to do.*

Tristan passed out as feet ran towards him.

FALLOUT

*T*ristan's eyes shot open, and he gasped for a breath as he sat up. He felt the chill of air on him and the biting smell of bleach as he tried to focus on his surroundings.

Bright hospital lamps blazed on his pale skin, forcing him to hold his arm up to shield his eyes. He could only see, but didn't feel the needle and line in his arm that was most likely used to flush the silver remnants out of his body.

His torso was bare, a sheet covering the nude lower half of him. He leaned forward, trying to get himself moving again.

"Take it easy, Tristan!" A familiar voice broke the silence. Tristan felt a hand on his shoulder trying to push him back down, and he quickly shoved it off with a deep frown.

"*You* fucking take it easy!" he yelled at Dashiell. He put the heels of his palms in his eyes and groaned.

Everything came rushing back to him. The ambush. Ivana. He turned to his right to see Dashiell standing next to him, whose face was solemn. Dismal.

Good. Just as it should be.

Tristan, with bared fangs, grabbed Dashiell's shirt and pulled him close, anger erupting from every pore.

"Where the fuck were you? Huh? What the hell happened to you and Christophe! You were supposed to be watching our back. *Her* back!" He violently shook him, and Dashiell pushed him away, releasing himself from the struggle.

"Now she's dead," Tristan finished.

Dashiell ran a hand through his thick, brown hair, keeping his distance from the angry Commander. The failure was indeed his to share, and Tristan had every right to be pissed, but it was beyond his control.

"We were tailing you until we got cut off suddenly. You changed routes, everyone we saw started to look suspicious, and I couldn't communicate with you or Christophe. We all fell apart, and about the time I caught up to you, it was too late. Christophe is MIA."

Tristan slammed his fists against the cold, steel table. He had thought of everything for this plan, working hard to properly take steps to deliver Ivana to her destination safely, but it was all for nothing. Nothing he did seemed to matter. She was dead, and he had to answer to his failure.

"Assassins were waiting for us. They knew we would be there. We were set up."

But it was more than that. Someone wasn't telling the whole story. He knew what he saw, that vampires were part of that attack. It didn't make sense, but he saw it with his own eyes. They were trying to kill Ivana. Why? He wanted to tell Dashiell, but considering he no longer had any idea who was friend or foe, he just nodded in agreement.

"Has anyone picked up the scene yet?" Tristan's eyes trained on Dashiell as he stood at the foot of the steel table.

"Cleaners have come and gone. There were a lot of witnesses given Halloween, so they had to pose as local law enforcement, then tag and bag as many Supe bodies as possible and clear the hell out of there. That's how they found you."

"Did they find anything strange or peculiar about the hit? Nothing that could help identify who the hell pulled it off?"

Clearly, if bodies were being picked up, the cleaners would have discovered the dead vampires among the collection and started asking questions.

Dashiell shook his head. "If they did, they haven't said anything to me. The cleaners are sorting through the bodies and said they would give The Three a report as soon as they were done. But no word yet. What did you mean by 'strange or peculiar?'"

Tristan stretched his torso as he sat up, feeling the crack of his bones as they continued to heal. He imagined a mob of angry vampires, led by The Three, waiting for him when he opened his eyes. Nothing was more certain than the fierce retribution Javen would demand due to the loss of his one and only companion, the woman Tristan was charged to protect, even if that was at the risk of his own life.

"I don't know what I mean. Everything's fucked. Where are The Three?" Tristan rubbed his temples, already knowing the answer.

Dashiell sighed. "They are waiting in the throne room for you. No one is allowed in there until they talk to you. Livid would be an understatement at this point, and Javen is beside himself with anger. He knows the whole thing went FUBAR, and he wants answers."

Yep, he figured as much.

So do I.

Tristan had failed to protect the life of his companion. He didn't expect Javen to ever forgive him, and to be honest, Javen had had vampires killed for a lot less.

Rest assured, The Three probably had a torture chamber waiting for him, regardless of his explanation. Crazily enough, that didn't frighten him. Hell, he'd been tortured before.

No, his fear seeded from the unnerving ache in his brain that vampires had something to do with Ivana's death. He didn't yet know what level in the event they played, but the fact that they played in it at all was enough for the grotesque snake of suspicion to slither within the loyalty he had for those around him.

Tristan ripped out the IV line and slid off the steel table, situating his bare feet onto the cold marble of the floor.

"Where are my clothes?" he asked quietly.

Dashiell grabbed the bag sitting on the stool next to him and tossed it to Tristan.

"Thanks. Go tell The Three that I'm awake and ready to seek an audience with them alone." His eyes cut up to Dashiell as he stepped into his pants and pulled him up the length of him. "Considering the circumstances, I'm sure that won't be a problem. I'm sure they are just dying to see me."

Dashiell scratched his head. "Of course, but if you're trying to spare me from their wrath, I wouldn't bother." He was just as accountable for the failure, but The Three already had plans for Dashiell.

"No. I need to face them alone. There are places we need to go in this discussion that should only affect me and The Three. So, yes. I guess I am sparing you a bit."

Tristan buttoned up his black shirt, still slightly wet from blood, some of it his, some the blood of the assassins, and some the blood of Ivana.

The dark memory of her ashen, bloodied face invaded his thoughts, and his heart sank. She didn't deserve to die like that. Tristan knew she was no angel because none of them were, but if there was ever such a thing as a 'good' vampire, Ivana would've been it. She wasn't bloodthirsty or conniving. She hadn't tortured humans for fun and hadn't sought political domination. As far as Tristan was concerned, Ivana was fucking Glinda, the Good Witch among the vampire race. She believed in harmony and followed her passion.

And look where that got her, he thought to himself. *Slaughtered by those who felt her passion to unify as a threat.*

And who found it a threat? Unfortunately, nearly everyone. Supernatural beings opposed societal changes.

The confused crinkle in Dashiell's forehead suggested he wasn't totally okay with Tristan's rationale, but, in either case, he'd rather not spend more time in front of The Three for them to tear him down at his part in the disaster. "Fair enough. Sync up with me once you get out. I wanna help get the bastards that did this. Ivana didn't deserve death, no matter what kinda asshole Javen can be."

"Will do." Tristan grabbed his coat off the back of the chair by the door, flung it behind him, and slipped his arms in. His long-line, black, wool coat flapped like a dark cape as he walked out of the doors.

The long corridor was a bridge between the covert operations facility and The Three's mansion. Eager to talk to Takeshi, the head of the of cleaners, Tristan headed deeper into the facility, looking for him. His need to see if the theories running around in his head had any validity fueled each step he took. The clomping of his boots echoed through the hall as he headed to the last room from the furnace.

Entering the room, Tristan paused at the row of black body bags, each laid out on their own steel table. The overhead fluorescent lights hummed over the tranquility of the dead lying in Takeshi's care.

Tristan stepped in and looked around. He and death never seemed to be far from each other, and today was no different.

"Takeshi!" he called out into the room of the dead. Continuing to walk further in, Tristan stopped at one of the body bags and slowly unzipped it. He watched the zipper trail down until a face was visible. Pulling back the thick plastic, Tristan frowned as he recognized the face staring empty back at him.

"What are you doing down here, Commander?" Takeshi asked as he walked up to Tristan.

He was dressed in an all-black, tactical jumpsuit, which covered most of his pale body with the exception of his arms. The vivid tattoos that adorned his arms were exposed from his pushed-up sleeves and seemed to rise off his alabaster skin.

A former member of the Yakuza, Takeshi was quiet and didn't speak much about his past life or much in general. He was fiercely loyal to The Three and worked for Valette exclusively before she became part of them. Because of his reputation of silence, many saw him as a keeper of secrets as all he ever really spoke to was the dead. He knew how to 'clean up' messes and bodies a fallout like tonight left behind, until no one was sure anything had really happened at all.

Tristan snapped his eyes over to Takeshi and then to the familiar corpse staring up at him. "I wanted to ask about the bodies cleaned up from Ivana's murder. I killed some assassins during that scrap but didn't identify them." He shook his head as he recognized her as the witch that killed Greg. The one he had spared. "Was this Green Girl at the attack?"

Takeshi walked up to the body and nodded. "Yes, she was. Her body was taken in as well as a couple of other Green Girls found." He cast his reflective eyes to the row of bodies in the black bags. "It's been quite a busy night."

Tristan eyed Takeshi. "So, the hit was all witches? That doesn't make any sense. They don't have the muscle to pull something like this off."

Takeshi moved to the other body next to the deceased witch and unzipped the bag. "I didn't say that. We found some Were-shifters too."

He studied the male Were-shifter, whose face was semi-morphed between human and beast. It was normal for a shifter to die in 'limbo', a combination of their beast heart and human one. It made it easy to identify their bodies but very painful to hide from the human world—one of the many reasons no one was a big fan of the Were-shifters. They were the most monstrous and impulsive of the Supes, all with the thinnest veil of secrecy. No wonder the cleaners had to work fast. Luckily, the assassins were masked to reduce the risk of prying eyes.

"What the hell were Green Girls and Were-shifters doing, pairing up to kill Ivana?"

Takeshi shrugged. "Very good question. It's confusing, really. She was in talks with their people."

Tristan sighed. This was even more perplexing than he thought. So, there were vampires, witches and Were-shifters at the attack.

That's impossible.

Tristan feared to share what he saw with anyone until he met with The Three, but he had to confirm something. He had to, because the way things were shaping up, Tristan was beginning to feel a bit like a lunatic.

"What other Supes were involved?"

Takeshi shook his head. "That's all my cleaners found. A few human bodies got jumbled in the mix since there were so many bystanders, and the guys were in a rush, but that's it. No other creepies or crawlers of the night were found."

"No vampire bodies?" Tristan finally asked. "Except for Ivana's, that is?"

Takeshi's was confused, but rather curious of his question. "No, Commander. Are you talking about vampires as part of the attack? As in *vampire* assassins?"

"Yes."

Takeshi stepped back as if Tristan had blasphemed. "No. There were no vampire bodies. I would have anticipated as much, wouldn't you?"

Tristan frowned. "I would not have asked if I felt that way, Takeshi. So, you're saying no other vampires' bodies were found among the assassins? Not even ash, where it was suspected a vampire was present?"

Takeshi folded his arms. "Yes. With the exception of Ivana, the driver, and your half-dead, beaten body when my crew found you, we turned up no vampire assassins."

Tristan felt the tension build between them. It was clear that Takeshi was picking up what Tristan was implying, and whether or not he felt the implication valid, Tristan was growing tired of feeling crazy. He closed his eyes and saw Claude's face.

I know what I saw.

"One of the assassins attacked me, Takeshi." Tristan crossed his arms. "And he wasn't a Were or a Green Girl. I saw his face. He was vampire."

Takeshi scowled at Tristan, then further unzipped the bag to the dead Were body.

"Impossible. I told you, there were no vampire bodies other than Ivana and her driver."

"Perhaps your cleaners didn't get everyone," Tristan replied. "There was a vampire I killed, and he attacked me and Ivana."

Takeshi's eyes were not as stoic as usual. Irritation loomed in their silver reflection. "Perhaps you saw a Were who didn't fully transform. Kept his fangs, but not much else?"

Tristan shook his head, finding the irritation contagious. "No. He wasn't a *Were*. He was vampire. I'd seen his face before, a long time ago, and I know the fucking difference between a Were and a vampire, Takeshi. Do *not* test me!"

Takeshi stepped back into a fighting stance. His face was crumpled into a deep frown. He was ready to either defend himself or inflict pain if need be.

"Testing you?" His deep, staccato voice pattern resonated in the hollow room of the dead. "It is you who tests *me*, Commander. My team are honorable vampires and quality cleaners. Now you insult them?"

Tristan wasn't trying to burn bridges, but he needed answers.

In the ten minutes he'd been down here, new information had been flipping his entire world upside down.

"I didn't insult them *or* you. I'm trying to find out what the hell I saw when there were bullets flying everywhere, and I was out there with my ass hanging out trying to save Ivana! I know what I saw, and I'm asking if you know something!"

Takeshi zipped up the Were body with haste. The sound of the zip was more of a curt screech against the plastic.

"I told you what I know. You are chasing shadows, Commander." He shook his head slowly at Tristan like a father scolding a child. "To lay a claim on vampires being on the fighting side of this attack is a poisonous thought. A thoughts I hope The Three will not entertain, at least not without proof."

Which I have none of. Apparently, I'm the only asshole who saw Claude's body. So, either he got up and walked away, or someone removed him. Did I imagine it?

Takeshi relaxed his body a bit and then zipped up the witch, shielding Tristan from her lifeless gaze. "Please leave, Commander."

Tristan still had questions, but he could tell that Takeshi no longer had the patience for it. He'd taken a gamble, and he'd lost. He should have known that Takeshi would not have entertained such an accusation, being the loyal vamp he was.

Tristan wasn't finished with him, but he needed to talk to The Three anyway and continue to kick over stones that pissed off everyone around him. Without a word, Tristan backed away, then turned and left the morgue.

Takeshi was right. Saying that vampires were present was toxic but not as crazy as Green Girls and Were-shifters teaming up to attack.

Ivana had been in talks with both of them, and she had last told him things were progressing. Why would they burn down the bridge between the vampires? Especially since the witches and Were-shifters were immortal enemies.

Witches were the key to the Were-shifter origin, as their magic and sorcery were rumored to have created them eons ago. The Green Girls denied it, of course. However, in doing so, the Were-shifters hunted, tortured, and studied them, trying to figure out what powers they possessed and how it could protect them.

Tristan would feel sorry for the witches, except he knew they did the same to the Were-shifters, trying to figure out how to hurt them. It was all one big shit show.

Throughout the mansion, areas were decorated with white lilies and roses in memory of Ivana. The royal blue banners of The Three were tied with a white ribbon, a symbol of mourning.

As Tristan turned the corner to the throne room, several vampires stood outside the door, waiting for an audience with The Three. They were talking amongst themselves until Tristan walked past them to the guarded entrance. Standing inches from Maurice, the guard on duty, Tristan gave him a nod.

"I'm here to see The Three."

Maurice's scarred face frowned. "They have been anxiously waiting to speak with you." His pale grey eyes didn't hold much emotion, but what little of it Tristan was able to pick up held great distaste.

Tristan didn't let it phase him. He never was one for popularity contests, and if he had to be *persona non grata* to get the job done, then so be it.

Maurice stepped aside and allowed Tristan to walk into the Chamber. Immediately, the scent of fresh lilies invaded his nose as he continued to move into the vast room.

In front of the three thrones was a mahogany platform with Ivana's body covered in a royal blue shroud. Valette and Kostya stood around the corpse and peered up as soon as large door closed shut with a slam behind him.

Moving at lightning speed, Valette lunged out at him, striking his cheek with her long nails that dug into his skin. Tristan felt the tear of his skin, followed by the trickle of chilled blood running down his cheek.

Numb and already healing from the strike, he stood complacent of the insult. He wiped the blood off his face as she glared at him with fiery eyes, blazing with contempt.

"You were asked to do one thing! One fucking thing! And that was to look after her for us! Look at what you've done, Tristan!"

Almost spitting his name, Valette pointed her finger at the table where Ivana's body laid, covered. She lunged for him again, but this time Kostya quickly caught her wrists and pushed her back.

"None of this is going to bring her back. I'm not interested in maudlin displays of loss. She's not coming back, so what more can we do?" Kostya's thick Russian accent echoed through the room. All I want to know is what happened."

"As do I," a deep voice shot through the silence. Tristan sought past them to find Javen next to the thrones, the planes of his face partially hidden in the shadows.

Tristan stood quiet as Javen slowly stepped away from the thrones and closer to him. His body taut, Tristan waited, alert, thinking the vampire would attempt to strike him. In fact, he decided to stay frosty until he spoke his piece.

As Javen got closer, Tristan could see the simmering rage in his mannerisms. His stiff walk, his pupils like pinheads, he could essentially feel the old vampire's disdain for him as he approached.

"Tell us, Tristan. Please, tell us how just a few hours ago, I was kissing Ivana goodbye, and now we are going to burn her body tomorrow night?"

Valette stood with arms crossed, watching with tear-stained eyes. "What the fuck happened?"

Tristan took his military stance and locked eyes with Javen. "I am deeply sorry for Ivana's death, Javen. I know she meant the world to you, and I respected her, greatly. I want you to know that I took great care in planning transport for her, but somehow, that plan was discovered."

Kostya cocked his head. "What you mean?"

"I'm saying that someone knew we were coming and set a trap to ambush us," Tristan replied. "They were prepared for a strike to kill Ivana. This was not luck, Javen. Someone *knew* exactly when we would be there, and we were horribly outnumbered."

Javen frowned, his movements uneasy. "Do you know who?"

Tristan shook his head. "No, but I'm looking into it. Dashiell told me that Christophe is missing. I need to find him too. Maybe he has some answers."

Valette scowled. "You're not implying that one of our own is involved in this, are you?" Her wide eyes shimmered tears that soon resembled turbulent waters as she blinked them away. "This was clearly the work of the Green Girls! Takeshi showed me their bodies."

"That and the Were-shifters, apparently," Javen added.

Tristan shot his eyes to Valette. "I'm saying that Christophe may know something we don't. But yes, I did encounter something during the attack that raises more questions."

Javen continued to move closer to Tristan until he stood merely inches away. "What is it?"

Tristan frowned. "One of the assassins after Ivana was a vampire."

The moment the statement rolled off his tongue, he felt a wave of silence grip the entire room. For what seemed like a full minute, only the sound of desperate gasps was heard. Tension soon began to mount and stack between the four of them until finally, Javen broke the painful silence.

"A vampire?" He shook his head dismissively. "There's no way." He stepped back and turned to Valette. "The cleaners said they found witches and Were-shifters, that's it. What vampires would try to kill my Ivana?"

Valette threw her hands up. "You were seeing things in the

heat of battle, Tristan. Vampires would never hurt our own, and they sure as hell wouldn't try to kill Ivana, of all vampires. You have any idea how insane this sounds?"

Tristan took a step forward. "Yeah, I realize how this must sound, but I know what I saw." His eyes did an arc from Javen to Valette to Kostya as he spoke. "Something isn't right about this whole ambush. I fought several of the assassins, some hand to hand, but I know when I'm fighting a Were, and I wasn't fighting a Were. There may have been witches. I mean, one did carry white light, but I didn't lift their mask to confirm. And finally, I killed one of the assassins, face to face, and pulled off their mask. He was a vampire named Claude. He was there."

Javen's eyes squinted, and his face lowered in shock as if he were trying to digest what Tristan was saying. He bucked at the thought and grabbed Tristan by his coat.

"You're a liar, Tristan! You'll say anything to remove yourself from the blame of my Ivana's death. Even shitting on your own race." He growled and shook until Tristan finally shoved him off, knocking him a few feet back.

"Of course, I'm to blame! I accept that. But I'm telling you the truth, Javen. Something stinks about this whole thing. I've worked for hundreds of years for you and have done pretty fucked up shit. Why would I need to lie about this? Vampires were there, Javen, and they attacked your companion. Now, why would they do that?"

Javen snarled. "Because they wouldn't! You're insane! We've been fighting the witches and the Were-shifters, and they have continued to turn against us, don't you see!"

"They saw Ivana as a threat, and they decided to team up to send a message." Valette walked over to her throne and plopped down. "And *you* let them send that message. You don't even give a shit about this war anyway, Tristan. You'd rather bow out with your tail between your legs."

Kostya moved from Ivana's body. "Where is this body of the vampire you saw?"

Tristan sighed. "I don't know. Takeshi said his team didn't find anything like that."

Javen scoffed. "So, we're supposed to just take your word for it on something this damning? The same word you gave that you would protect Ivana and keep her safe?"

Tristan's eyes flickered amber and he felt his fangs descend on impulse. He was growing weary of this denial and lack of faith in him. "I had done everything in my power to protect Ivana, nearly dying to try to save her. Now I live with the failure of losing her, but I will *not* be your whipping boy for this. Now I'm telling you, vampires were there, and I'm not going to stop until I find out what really happened!"

As Tristan turned to walk out, Javen moved in front of him. His eyes were cold, and fury that once simmered was boiling now.

"Until you have proof, you will not spout such lies and rumors about Ivana's death, or I will have you excommunicated from the vampire society and exiled for your treasonous inclinations. Something like this could tear us apart, just like our enemies would want. Do you understand, Commander Castillion?

Tristan's face was stoic, as tired as it was, as he glared at Javen. "I think you're forgetting, Javen. This was my last mission commissioned under The Three. I couldn't give a rat's ass of your society. I've been trying to get out for years. Like I said, I'm tired of the war, and apparently some things never change."

With that, Tristan pushed past him and continued to leave the room.

Fuming, Javen took a few steps toward him, but Valette ran to him and blocked him with her hand on his chest.

"No, don't," Valette warned, her voice soft. "Let him go. There are other ways to deal with him."

Tristan tore the large door open so fiercely, it splintered and cracked against the wall as he walked through. The other vampires quickly moved aside as he moved past them with determination.

He wasn't crazy. He knew what an accusation like this could do, but it was the truth. He knew what he saw, and whatever it meant, it told him that all of this was bigger than he'd imagined.

And far from being over.

MYSTERY GIFT

*O*ne drink. Two drinks. Three. Tristan shot the warm, dark liquid into his mouth, enjoying the sting and burn of the liquor as it trailed to his stomach.

He decided that alcohol-infused blood was the greatest vampire invention since the inception of vampires, especially on nights like tonight. He was certain that it had to have been an old-school vampire like him, a warrior who missed the numbing effects of wine and alcohol after a battle, who created the vamp-friendly drink.

For reasons unknown, a vampire's body rejected typical, distilled alcohol. It didn't affect them the same way it would a human. However, when infused with human blood, it proved to be the ideal vehicle for the alcohol to finally get a bloodsucker shit-faced.

What a brilliant asshole that pioneer vamp was. Tristan could only imagine how many failed experiments the vampire had done to get that much potent, grain alcohol into human blood. It was rumored—and Tristan imagined it very plausible—that many humans died a horrible death, essentially being drowned in grain alcohol like giant Ortolans or forced to drink large quantities of it until they eventually died of poisoning.

Of course, there was no way to get to 20 proof, let alone a proper 80 proof, if the humans were topping out at a mere five percent.

Who were the main people selected for such experiments just for a vampire to get hammered? Green Girls. They were, after all, used to being drowned in something, and between them and the transient humans, it was enough to conduct several years of atrocious trials until The Three demanded it was time to stop. This hadn't been the straw that had broken the camel's back for the witches, but it hadn't helped win them over in the wars.

Tristan remembered Ivana being terribly disgusted as he had told her the origin of the drink, aptly called 'Sangri-La'. She had vowed never to drink it, and said it was a shining example of how our species were just as cruel as the humans.

He slammed another drink down his throat at the thought. She had been so naive.

Of course we were just as cruel, if not more. How easy was it to pluck the wings off a butterfly when your hand was a hundred times more powerful?

But she had seen things differently, and even though he hated to admit it, Ivana had made him want to believe that the war could end. If ever an ember sparked within him on that sentiment, it definitely had been extinguished the moment he'd seen her dead body.

Such a hope like she had harbored simply had no place in the world of monsters and men. It had just been folly.

Dashiell pulled up a chair next to him in the dimly lit bar, picking up the bottle of Sangri-La and examining it. "Quite an expensive drink, Tristan. Celebrating or mourning?"

"A little of both, actually," Tristan said quietly. "I'm free from the chains of The Three, but, unfortunately, I leave dishonored, with a FUBAR final mission on my record."

It was all bullshit to him. He spent years fighting for a cause he'd barely wanted to believe in anymore. What did it all matter? Green Girls, Were-shifters, fairies, ogres, vampires...Let's face it: they were *all* assholes. None of them were the 'good guys' of the world. They were all just fighting for dominance in a shadow world, away from the eyes of fearful man.

It was pathetic, really. Too many of his friends had gotten swallowed up in this game over the years. The same friends who had hope. The ones who wanted to believe things could have been better than all the bloodshed.

Those same friends were all dead. Perhaps the only reason he was still alive was because he didn't buy into the crap anymore.

Mr. Darkness loved a good martyr, and fools were born every day to keep him company.

Dashiell smacked his lips. "C'mon, Tristan. You can't blame yourself for Ivana's death. You did everything you could. In the end, the protection of a vampire like Ivana belonged to her companion, and where was he?"

"He was asking *me* to look after her. And I failed. I've asked around for Christophe, but no one has seen him." He looked to Dashiell. "You?"

Dashiell shook his head and opened the bottle to take a swig. "No. No one has seen him since before the motorcade. I've been backtracking the route of the motorcade downtown, but I haven't seen a damn thing. No blood. No sign of struggle. It's like he just disappeared into fucking thin air."

He winced, the blood drink burning down his throat, and set the bottle down with a mild slam against the table.

"Ack! Fucking Type A positive?" He pushed the bottle to Tristan. "Might as well be drinking piss. Good thing you don't get smashed often. You have *shitty* taste."

Tristan gave a wry grin and poured another shot. "Well, don't worry. I'm gonna hit the ground running tomorrow night. I'm going to find Christophe, and I'm going to prove what I saw tonight when Ivana was murdered. The Three are hiding something, I know it."

He kicked back the shot of blood alcohol, this time savoring the burn.

Dashiell scoffed. "Tris, they're elitist vampires. When are they *not* hiding something?"

Tristan frowned. "This is different, Dashiell. I think they know more than they let on about what happened tonight. Takeshi didn't even seem himself. I think he knows something, too."

"What the hell does that mean? Takeshi is a freak. You've seen his tattoos? Yeah, he's got them on his fucking dick." He raised his hand up as Tristan cocked a curious brow. "Don't ask me how I know that, but all I'm saying is, he's always been a fucking freak, so don't let him get to you."

"I killed a vampire tonight, Dashiell."

"What?" Dashiell's eyes widened. "When?...*Who*?"

"During the fight. I think his name was Claude or something. He was attacking us and was about to try and kill me." Tristan's tired eyes were fixed on Dashiell. "So, I killed him."

Dashiell couldn't process what Tristan was saying. It couldn't be possible. It just couldn't. "You're saying that *vampires* were involved in Ivana's assassination?"

Tristan nodded as he kicked back another shot, finally starting to feel a buzz. "Yep."

Dashiell scanned around, concerned if any suspicious ears were hovering about, possibly overhearing Tristan's revelation. He blew out an exasperated sigh, still processing what he'd just said.

"That's...that's...*crazy*."

Tristan's face was deadpan. "Yeah, so thought The Three. They didn't take my report very well, as you can imagine."

Dashiell shrugged. "It doesn't mean they're guilty, Tristan. You know I hate The Three. They're fucking show-boaters, elitists, and manipulators. But they never took kindly to vampires who killed their own kind. You know that. They've done some sick shit to vampires who broke that law, just to set an example."

Tristan grunted in frustration. "He was vampire, Dashiell. I know what I saw."

Dashiell gave Tristan a quelling glare. "Look, I'm not discounting what you saw, Tristan. I don't think you would be mistaken about this." he whispered. "But think about what this means. You're implying that The Three had something to do with the knowledge of a vampire being involved with a vampire diplomat's death. That's some heavy shit." He scanned around. "It's dangerous, and there are ears and eyes about."

"You think I don't know that?" Tristan scowled at him, his voice escalating from inebriation and anger. His eyes, like daggers, cut into Dashiell. "You just keep *your* ears and eyes open. And don't believe everything they tell you."

Tristan stood up from the table and shrugged his coat on. He glared at Dashiell as he threw a few bills on the table. "Something fucking stinks about all of this. Now, you can either help or stay the hell outta my way." He whipped around and stormed out of the bar, pushing vampires out of his way to get to the exit.

He heard Dashiell call for him, but he kept going. He wasn't in the mood to explain himself anymore. He knew he was in this all alone, and that was perfectly fine. Him against the world was just how he liked it.

TYPICALLY, Tristan would pace the ledge of the old Byzantine cathedral and think about what the hell he was going to do next. It was his place to reflect when life just got too out of hand. However, as he passed the structure with the boarded doors, all he could think of was how Ivana made her stand and died there.

Her death had marred everything decent he had. He looked

up to the top of the cathedral where he usually would be and sighed. There was nothing but demons there now on that ledge, so he continued to head to his home, knowing dawn was coming.

Tristan no sooner entered the foyer of his home than he heard the rustling of metal upstairs and began to bare his teeth to attack. His gun drawn from his holster, he snarled at the thought of someone invading sanctuary.

Someone has the gall to invade my home after the shit I've been through today?

His body tense, he leapt to the top of the stairs, checking around the hall until he focused on his bedroom door, closed, with light shining from under it. His senses still buzzing from the alcohol, he paused to get his bearings, letting the adrenaline stomp down his inebriation.

Ready to eliminate the threat, Tristan lunged and kicked down his bedroom door. With his gun drawn, he froze as his eyes met with the stark, violet eyes of a woman crouched on his bed.

His mouth gaped open as she pulled against glowing chains that were shackled to her wrists and ankles, the metal brushing against the bare flesh of her stomach and lace-covered breasts. Her abundant auburn hair cascaded down her back as she struggled to get to her knees as she faced him. She was breathtaking among the black satin of his bed, and Tristan's eyes lingered over her, from the full pout of her lips all the way down to the lacy black triangle at the meeting of her thighs.

Okay...It wasn't his birthday...and what was in that fucking drink?

Her scowling face was less than pleased at Tristan's ogling. She pulled against the chains with a loud clink that brought Tristan back to earth.

"Take this off me *now*!" Her eyes were thin slits as she glared at him.

Tristan moved closer to her, looking around the room for anyone else who'd decided to drop in on him. The only anomaly there was the woman wearing nothing but strange chains and underwear on his bed. There was an otherworldly aura about her that he couldn't quite place. Maybe she was a supe, but nothing gave him a real hint.

His gun still drawn and aimed at her, he finally responded. "Who the hell are you? And why the hell are you here? I didn't order a blood-bag stripper."

The woman sneered at him viciously. "I'm not a stripper, you asshole! Now turn me loose or I'll rip your heart out!" she barked out through gritted teeth.

Tristan gave her a smirk. "Woohoo, strong talk for a woman who can't move three inches from where she is." He chambered a round in his gun. "Now, I'll ask you once more. Who the hell *are* you?"

He paused as she suddenly took a deep breath and inhaled him and the air around him.

"Damn it," she cursed beneath her breath as she realized what he was.

Her senses reeling, she desperately tried to focus on her lucidity as her body primed itself for the hunt.

No! Not until I find out why I'm here in this jerk's room, she pleaded with herself. *Focus. Focus.* But it was too late. He was so close now, so very tempting, and her body would not listen to reason. It was the nature of her kind, and yet she despised herself for it.

Tristan tried to shake the cloudiness from his head as he stared at her. All he could think of was ripping that delicate fabric from her body and plunging deep into her, then sinking his fangs into her lush, radiant skin and sampling her life force. He moved closer to her as she leaned back against the bed, her ethereal eyes seductive and enchanting. Tristan stopped at the edge of the bed, nothing but the iron rail to stop him from moving even closer.

But something in the back of his mind urged that it wasn't

right. The need to sate himself with her made him want to tear the heavens down just to have her. This maddening, clawing sense of urgency that was so hot, it threatened to burn away all sense of reasoning.

Even him stopping against the railing made his body burn for her. An insatiable need to taste her, to take her, like some unknown force drove him to her like a rabbit to a snare. The feeling was so innate and primal, Tristan felt he could eagerly walk through all the flames of hell just to taste her now. It was what some would call pure insanity.

He lowered his gun.

She crooked a finger to him to come closer, and he obeyed, moving to the side of the bed, finally dropping his gun to the floor. Reaching for him, she closed her mouth on his, pressing her body against him.

Tristan growled at her bare, almond flesh rubbing against the folds of his clothes. He could feel all of her now, as if there were no clothing between them. It made his body hard, throbbing. Never had he wanted to be inside someone with every fiber of his lost soul with such a hunger. Her full lips plundered him, greedy and lustful. He was already painfully erect, pulling at his coat to remove it as her mouth assaulted him in the most sinful way possible.

Zoë, you have to get a grip. She called within herself, as her tongue darted into his mouth, brushing against his fangs. He had the metallic taste of blood on his tongue, as if he had just come from feeding.

The ripple of his flesh beneath his clothes begged her to strip him to see all of the sinew he hid from her gaze. When his erection poked against her stomach, she groaned at the promise of it. Every molecule in her body was honed to seduce him. To take him and make him hers...

The bastard deserves to die. He had just fed, probably off a human. Kill him now!

She shook her head, trying to dismiss the huntress in her, clawing to get out. If she let it take over, this vampire was as good as dead. If she would reject it, the enthrallment would tear her soul to pieces. But this was not a 'stake the vampire, ask questions later' kind of situation. He was the only one who could help her out of the chains and probably out of this mess she'd somehow found herself in. She hated to admit it, but she needed the stupid vamp.

Just a little more, then you can kill him. Bite him!

"No!"

Hissing, Zoë broke away, pushing him away from her. "Get away, damn you!"

Tristan shook the haze from his head as he saw her writhe on the bed in pain. His bedroom suddenly filled with the tortured screams of the woman as she convulsed and shook on his bed. He started to reach for her when he saw her back as she pressed her stomach against the bed, screaming. Then she collapsed.

He went cold at what he saw.

Tristan stepped back as he saw the elaborate tattoo on her back—wings so gorgeously crafted, one would have sworn the black feathers on her bare skin were real. But he knew exactly what those wings represented.

Oh, fuck me!

They were the symbol of the clipped wings of the league of angels who chose to fall to protect mankind.

Vampires were never at the top of the food chain, as much as they'd like to think so. They had slayers as well, stronger and more gifted than any Buffy or Van Helsing a human could conjure up in their fantasy world.

They and they alone were the *true* rulers of the night.

Black Blood Slayers, demons that had the power to lure a vampire from miles away if they chose, could draw anything without a soul and bend some of those creatures to their will. They were the supreme angels of death to vampires and the lesser demons on earth. They were enchanting, cunning, and lethal. Vampires unfortunate enough to encounter one did not live to talk about the experience.

Yeah, the night just kept getting better.

Here was one, right in *his* bed.

KILLER LOOKS

Z oë's eyes eased open to focus on a single lamp burning on the nightstand across the room. Groaning, she felt the sharp stabs of aching that penetrated every time she moved. Her face flushed on the mattress, she rose with apprehension to scan the room, gasping as pain shot through her neck like someone had their two-ton foot pressing down on it.

It made her nauseous, her stomach in knots. Moving her hand, the clink of the metal reminded her she was still restrained.

Suddenly, she froze as she heard the cocking of a gun in the dark of the corner.

"Rise 'n shine, princess," a cold, deep voice cut through the dark silence.

Breathing through the aches, Zoë peered through the darkness to see a figure sitting in the darkness next to the lamp. Restrained and hurting, she was at the mercy of the stranger in the room. "Who...who are you?"

"That's my question, not yours," Tristan replied, his gun aimed at the beauty on the bed. Slowly, he turned up the light on the lamp to reveal his grim and tired face. It was the middle of the day, and he hadn't had a wink of sleep. What vampire in their right mind would feel comfortable shutting their eyes with a Black Blood Slayer in the same fucking area code, let alone same room?

Staying up past dawn really sucked, because all it did was suck the energy right out of a vampire. Some more than others, of course, and, luckily, it was more bearable with age. Living for over four centuries had its perks; however, he couldn't tell if his crappy feeling was a result of staying up too late, getting drunk, or finding a half-naked Black Blood Slayer in his bed.

"Let's do us both a favor and cut through the bullshit. I don't know who you are, but I sure as shit know *what* you are. So, who sent you?"

Zoë tried to think back but couldn't remember anything past waking up in chains on the bed. Whoever put her there knew just how to subdue her. The chains would not allow her to phase out or break them on her own. She slowly, painfully shook her head.

"I don't know. I can't remember anything, but—"

Tristan leaned closer, allowing her to see the desert eagle pistol staring her in the face. "I'm done with liars, biters, and manipulators, so you'd better start talking or you're going to be in for a world of pain."

She frowned at his threat, finding herself staring at the barrel. "You're really gonna shoot me in the face?"

Tristan gave a quiet nod. "Right in your fucking face."

She glared at him. "Well, if you know what I really am, then you know that gun won't do you any good."

"The rounds are blessed."

Zoë scoffed, trying to call his bluff. "You *sure* about that, Vamper?"

Tristan leaned closer with the aimed pistol barrel to her wide-eyed face. "Only one way to find out."

She stiffened at his earnest suggestion. "Look! I told you, I don't *know*! I don't know how I got here, and I don't know who hell you are! All I know is that you're a blood sucker, and I'm sully-chained to your shitty bed!" She sighed and lowered her voice. "Look, I mean *you* no harm. Please, free me."

Tristan shook his head. *'I mean you no harm', said no Black Blood Slayer, ever*, he thought to himself. "What's sully-chained?"

"If I tell you, will you release me?"

His voice chilled even more. "No, but I'll be less likely to test that hypothesis on whether one of these bullets to your face will end you. Now, what's sully-chained?"

Tristan eyed the chains which seemed to have inscriptions and symbols etched on the links. They glowed right off the chain.

Zoë sighed. "Normal chains can't hold my kind, obviously. These chains are enchanted with spells to keep us in our solid state and restrain us. They are used to punish a Black Blood who's led astray, not to deliver us to our target!"

No Slayer would ever present themselves in such a vulnerable position. No weapons, no clothes. Just chained up like some animal. Only a few beings were able to do something like this, and none of the suspects made any sense to her. None.

"You're still sticking to the story that no one has sent you here to kill me, right? Despite the fact you're a fucking Black Blood Slayer in a vampire's bed. Doesn't that strike you as kinda odd?"

Tristan didn't like this one bit. Ivana was killed by vampires. No one saw said vampires, but when he told others he saw them, all of a sudden, he's greeted with a Black Blood Demon in his home? She was just waiting to enthrall and kill him.

Zoë growled and racked against the chains.

Tristan cocked an eyebrow. "Careful, don't bruise yourself, princess."

"Argh! Of *course*, it's odd!" Zoë exclaimed, seething. "I don't know how I got here! When we are sent to this plane to kill the soulless, we come of our own free will. We don't come gift wrapped, chained like some tiger, trying to seduce our fucking target in a bedroom!"

Zoë breathed in deeply, slowly exhaling the air from her

lungs. It pained her to even breathe, and despite the ache, it wasn't long before another wave of enthrallment would come.

She could feel it. But if she tried it again restrained, he'd either get smart and kill her, or she'd kill him and never get free from the sully chain.

She couldn't give two shits what he thought, but she was telling the truth. None of this was authorized, and even though no one found it out of line to kill a vampire, she really had no orders to end him.

She cut her green eyes to him. "I'm going to *very*, very slowly sit up, okay?"

Tristan kept his eyes locked on her. "Very, very slowly, please."

He quietly watched as Zoë eased herself up from her palms, the soft roll of her body reminding him of a wave. The curve of her shoulders, down to the dip of her tattooed back and back up, cresting to the delectable curve of her round, bare derriere, threatened to charm him like a snake in a basket.

Her long, curly hair flipped to her back as she settled on her knees, sitting on back of her legs. Her caramel skin had a radiant glow, almost ethereal as his eyes followed the line of her against the lacy, black underwear.

It didn't leave much to the imagination, but, sometimes, an imagination was overrated. Tristan had had other women grace his bed, but none quite like this one. He had to hand it to whoever had delivered her to him, she definitely was Satan in a *beautiful*, Sunday hat.

He couldn't help but to think how close he would have come to death if he hadn't had his guard up. Even with it, he vaguely remembered tasting her lips as if they had held the last drop of water in the wake of a dying world.

Zoë could feel his eyes on her, his deep stare hidden under the cover of darkness. She should have been used to it—the staring. After all, that was what she was designed for.

Their beauty was supposed to be magnetic and hypnotic,

always drawing the soulless to their will. Her people were the fallen angels that dedicated their lives to protect the souls of man from the soulless, especially from dirty vampires. Shut out from the divine light, Black Blood Demons dwelled between two planes. One was earth, the other, *nothing* like heaven.

"Despite me being chained earlier, I could have killed you. I was *going* to kill you...but I didn't. I didn't because I was not assigned to hunt you. I was chained here, but I wasn't given orders to kill you, don't you understand? I'm not going to hurt you, so please release me."

Tristan sat back and sighed. He should kill her. It's all he'd thought about since he had come to the realization of what she was.

Like their angel brethren, Black Blood Slayers appeared on earth for only a few reasons: to avenge, slaughter, or punish.

Who had sent her? Black Blood Slayers were rare on earth, but when they came, the streets ran red with the blood of vampires. Blood and ash—it was all they left behind. They didn't even have to work hard, as they were able to enthrall vampires, just like vampers were able to enthrall humans.

It was what she had done to him earlier, making him want to mount her and taste her like a crazy dog in heat. It was the ultimate trap to spring on a vampire. The smell of their blood was intoxicating and their bodies so enticing and full of life. No blood sucker could resist.

Apparently, not even Tristan. But that was what had been holding him up from putting a bullet in that gorgeous face staring at him.

She pushed him away.

She was right. She could've killed him. He was there in her grasp, barely lucid, totally in her enthrallment, but she hadn't killed him. Black Blood Demons weren't known for mercy, so something else had to be wrong for her to purposely fight her nature.

"If I let you go, there will be no protection for me whatsoever from you. What if this is a trap, just to get me to free you? Whether you were told or not, the people who sent you only had one intention, and that was for *you* to kill *me*."

Zoë shook her head. "I'm not under any orders, I swear it. I was stolen. I shouldn't be here, but someone or something put me here." She blew out a frustrated sigh. "I will not harm you. You have my word."

Tristan sat quietly for a moment, eyeing her for any moment of doubt or suspicion. Whoever did this failed, but regardless, if he let a Black Blood Slayer go, he would be considered insane. He didn't even know how to really kill one, so perhaps letting her go would remove her as a threat while he tracked down the sick shithead who had delivered her.

With a tic in his jaw, Tristan finally spoke. "How do I break these chains, demon?" he asked, standing up to his full height.

"They are inscribed for me, so only I cannot break them. You can touch them and remove them without much effort."

Tristan walked over to the bed, his gun still aimed at her. "Just so you'll know, I'm not easy prey. If you betray me, I *will* use all my power to try and kill you. I'll leave my mark on you with my last breath, understand?"

He slowly lowered his gun, holstering his weapon.

Zoë glared into his bright eyes and pushed back her frown. Her teeth clenched tight at his threat, but she merely nodded. "Understood."

Tristan moved on the other side of the bed, slowly and methodically moving to her side, trying to find a place where the chain met her ankle to the bed. Carefully, he snapped the shackles off, watching Zoë flinch at the sound of the loud metallic clunk against his hardwood floor.

He stood quietly, staring at her as she slowly shifted her body to raise her other long, toned leg upwards to his chest. Her eyes stayed locked on him as his hands carefully took her foot and then slipped his fingers between her silken skin and the shackles.

With a grunt, Tristan quickly broke the shackle, letting it fall on the bed. The silence between them was thick as all that connected between them were careful, intense stares. Neither was willing to look away. Whether it was from lack of trust or something else was beyond either of them.

With freedom minutes away from her, Zoë held up her hands to him, the shackles biting into her wrists, but she made no sudden moves.

She could tell that every word he spoke, he meant. She could tell by the heady smell of his blood, he was an older vampire. His scent reminded her of frankincense, oak, and leather...everything that was woodsy and masculine.

She clenched her mouth shut as she felt it water for an antici-pated taste of him. Her nipples tightened, and warmth radiated from the core of her body.

Panic started to run across her face as she watched her unoffi-cial captor quietly grab the shackles from both wrists and snap them off. If she didn't get away from him soon, she'd trigger another enthrallment, and that wouldn't be good for either of them. Maybe this time, she wouldn't control herself.

Tearing the vampire apart in more ways than one was undoubtedly what her body wanted, but not her mind. She gave her word she wouldn't harm him, and she was *nothing* without her word. Even if it was to a shitty, parasitic blood-sucker.

The break of the metal shackles gave her a quick sigh of relief. "Thank you. I'm Zoë."

"I don't care *who* you are. If you meant what you said, and you had no intention of harming me, then you should be leaving, *now.*"

Tristan backed away from her, pointing at the door. The sooner he got her away from him, the sooner he could find out who the enthusiastic gift giver was. Someone clearly wanted him out of the way, and now he had to follow the breadcrumbs to find out who and why.

Zoë slid off the bed and stood to her feet. The chilly breeze through the open bedroom door made her body tense. She felt raw and exposed standing there before him, only wearing a thin demi-bra and lace thong.

Her face crinkled into a scowl at his cold demeanor, shoving her out like some pest. She began to open her mouth to say something, but clamped it shut.

Just get out, before you kill him.

Her inner thoughts, for once, made sense. Zoë needed to leave. Staying would only make the situation worse. She had her own mission to figure out what the hell had happened to her. Essentially, she felt kidnapped, and whoever thought doing that was a good idea would soon find themselves on the business end of a sword. No one made her a captive and lived.

Nobody.

Zoë quietly nodded and proceeded to will the portal open to her dimension, so she could leave. The deafening silence in her ear as she focused yielded nothing. Panting, she refocused, only to see Tristan staring at her.

She closed her eyes shut and tried again, focusing hard enough to hear the once muffled sound of her heartbeat now clear as day. Her limbs trembling, Zoë tried to will the portal open, but instead felt a sharp pain slice through her head. Screeching at the intense pain, she lost her balance and dropped back onto the bed, clasping her skull.

Tristan stood on guard as he watched the Black Blood Demon writhe in pain. Unsure of what she was doing, he kept his distance, curious of her reaction and sudden pain.

"What's going on with you?"

Zoë sat up and began to feel the slow trickling of warm liquid from her nose. Trembling, with the back of her hand, she wiped her nose to reveal her thick, midnight blood smeared against it.

Willing the portal open was something she had done a million times. It was as easy as breathing, yet somehow, she couldn't get it to open. Panting as the ripples of pain moved through her head down to her feet, she turned to him.

"Something's wrong. I can't move from this dimension. Something's blocking me, and I don't know what it is."

Tristan frowned, despite the grumbling of his stomach at the sight and smell of her blood. "Seems pretty convenient, *demon*."

Zoë hissed, both from pain and sheer annoyance. "You think I *want* to stay here?" She scoffed as she slowly pulled to her feet again. "Don't flatter yourself, blood-sucker; you're lucky I have bigger shit to deal with than you, or else I would've had second thoughts."

Tristan stretched, cracking his neck. His eyes still trained on her, daring a challenge from the half-naked demon. "Same here, princess." He pulled his gun. "Now, kindly use the traditional method to get the hell outta here. Use the *door*."

Zoë's skin flushed with anger. She stormed past him, shoulder checking him as she blasted by and through the doorway.

Tristan watched as she ran down the stairs, all her curves bouncing with each step as she unabashedly moved through his house in her underwear. Her clear, green eyes squinted with anger as she descended the old stairs. He definitely couldn't say he wanted her to stay, but it was, however, at least entertaining to watch her leave.

Getting to the foyer, she snatched a black coat from the rack and shrugged into it. Zoë went to yank open the front door to the brightness of the day. The deep contrast of light forced her back for a moment until her eyes adjusted.

The sidewalk led to the street that was already bustling with humans going about their day. Stepping out, she slammed the door shut and proceeded to move hastily away from the house and into the Garden District where the wretched vampire apparently resided.

Tristan, hearing the door slam shut, took a sigh of relief as he too descended the stairs. *One nightmare gone but definitely not forgotten.*

A Black Blood demon appearance sure as hell wasn't a coincidence. Not after all that had been going on. Someone wanted him gone, and he was going to find out who. Luckily, the list wasn't long, and, with the death of Ivana, he had an inkling who was on that list eager to shut him up.

His thoughts were interrupted as a high-pitched yell and a loud, booming crash came through his front door. The door erupted with a body flying right through it and into his home. The cracking and splintering of wood exploded throughout the foyer. With sunlight blasting through the opening, Tristan leapt back up to the top of the stairs, shielding his eyes. The sting of the sun threatened to blind him, and he leaned back against the wall, into the shadows, hissing at the intrusion.

Peering forward, he slowly looked down to hear the groans of a figure in black on the floor. It was crumpled in fetal position, but slowly stretched to reveal scratched, bare legs. Rolling over, Tristan began to recognize the dusty, cut face that belonged to whoever came crashing through his front door.

It was the demon, Zoë.

Hissing a curse, he drew his weapons and aimed them at her. "What the fuck are you doing here? Are you *trying* my patience, demon?" He must've been the biggest asshole to even let her walk out of his place alive. "Answer me!"

Pulling to her feet, Zoë felt the same slicing pain in her head as she did earlier when trying to escape through a portal. She couldn't get far from the house without a force as powerful as the sun's gravity pulling her back, sending her flying across streets and through walls until she came crashing here again.

She felt splinters and glass push themselves out of her skin and begin to heal, but the horrible pain in her head throbbed and threatened to make her retch.

Zoë spit out a bit of blood from her mouth, trying to catch her breath. "I've...been...*grounded*. I can't leave this plane and I can't leave..." She cut her eyes up at Tristan and the two pistol barrels staring down at her. "I'm somehow bound."

With squinting eyes, Tristan frowned, his fangs bared, and growled at her. "To what?"

Zoë sighed and surveyed her surroundings, angst building in her as she realized the new situation. "To *you*."

RAPTURED

*T*ristan stood in his position, nearly motionless as Zoë glared at him. Was she fucking serious? His eyes burning, sensitive to the intruding daylight around the corner, Tristan didn't dare take his sight off her.

"What the hell are you saying by *bound*? I see no chains between us." His fingers literally itched to squeeze. Something had to give, and today the choice was looking to pick either his life or hers. "I don't have time for games, princess. You have 30 seconds before I light you up. Speak."

Zoë held up her hands, still lying on her back, staring up at him. She sensed no fear or twitchiness in the vampire's icy, reflective eyes. One wrong word or move and the blood-sucker was going to pop one off. There was no denying it, and no sense risking it.

"I don't know how this happened! Someone has bound *you* to *me*, meaning wherever you go, *I* go."

She shivered at the thought. Binding was done only on missions where a Black Blood was sent to protect someone. It was a way to keep the individual close to their protector. If an assailant wanted to kidnap the target, it wouldn't be long until a

Black Blood came trailing behind like an invisible tether ready to exact justice.

But never had she heard of a vampire being bound to one of them. Ever. Definitely not for protection.

Hell no. Someone really hated her, and this vamp, obviously. She hadn't expected the forceful pull of her body reigning her back to his proximity again. Back to his cold gaze and where he pointed a gun in her face.

I should make him eat that gun, her inner voice called to her. *Or turn this house into Swiss cheese and let the sun get him.*

Then the binding would *have* to break.

Tristan, still exacting his aim at her head, began to laugh. His sinister tone was laced with sarcasm as he watched the bright-eyed Black Blood Slayer lie amongst the rubble of his doorway. The sunlight was washing against her scantily clad body. Cuts and bruises from her collision were already healing before his eyes. He could tell by her breathing pattern that she was perturbed. Good, so was he.

"I can't wait to meet who sent you here, princess. Apparently, they are fucking brilliant."

"I told you, I don't know—"

His twisted laughter sobered, and he quickly cut her off. "It doesn't really matter, now does it?" Tristan's face turned to stone again. "So, humor me for a moment. Let's say you, for some reason, have no earthly idea why you're here and why you're bound to me. A Black Blood Slayer being bound to her prey."

He arched his eyebrow at her "Black Blood Slayer..." He raised his right hand slightly. "... Prey."

Zoë slowly shook her head, her eyes thin slits. "I know this all sounds like bullshit to you, but I'm telling you the truth. Something's going down, and I have a feeling we're in the middle of it."

Her eyes cut to the doorway. With daylight burning outside, the vampire had no choice but to stand his ground. Zoë stopped and tried to remember the last thing she did or saw. Though the haze of her mind, all she could dig out was a word. A name.

She opened her eyes. "Remelia."

Tristan froze at the name of the missing Supreme witch. "What do you know about her? Huh? What does she have to do with all this?"

Zoë sat up as her fuzzy mind played a broken scene that didn't make any sense. It was like someone took a chunk of her memory, only leaving pieces out of context. "I don't know. All I have is a name. Who's Remelia?"

"She's the Green Girls' leader. The one they hail as their Supreme. There were rumors she disappeared, so if you know something about it, then you'd do best to tell me now."

Zoë began to ease her way up to stand.

Tristan coughed and spat out a clot of blood, which didn't prevent him from firing a warning shot at Zoë's feet. "Don't. Fucking. Move."

Finally on her feet, she kept her eyes trained on him and remained still even as she felt the wood splinters hit her feet from the nearby shot.

"If I wanted to hurt you, vampire, I would've done it by now."

She eyed his tense body that held a slightly unsteady sway. It was very late in the day now and his body was beginning to break down.

"Look at you. You're blocked between me and the blazing sun of the day. It must be pushing midday by the looks of the shadows outside, and even for a vampire your age, it's taking a toll on you. You've already begun to bleed."

Tristan kept his aim on her, even as he felt the cold trail of blood trickle past the top of his lip from his nose. "I like pushing boundaries. Now tell me about the witch."

She shook her head. " If you haven't figured it out by now, you're no good to me dead."

"Wish I could say the same for you."

Zoë bared her teeth, her chest heaving from reigning in her growing anger. *If you lose it, he'll try to kill you.*

"Look, you want answers, and so do I. But we can't get anywhere like this. Neither of us. Can we at least agree on that?"

Tristan raised an eyebrow and stifled a cough. There was a long, pensive pause before he spoke again. "Yes."

Zoë sighed. She saw the lovely day outside past the rose bushes out front. Then, she regarded the sunlight spilling through the house. She kicked off her heels and felt the creaking of the floor beneath her. Finally, her eyes cut back to Tristan.

"I never thought I would say this to a fucking vampire, of all Supes, but it's important you don't drop dead on me here. I don't know what is happening, but we've obviously been screwed, and with us bound together, it doesn't make it any easier. We're natural enemies, it's true, but we *have* to work together. Or we're both dead."

Tristan hissed under his breath. Trusting a Black Blood demon? He may as well have walked right into the sunlight right then and there. At least the pain would have been brief.

But there was a problem. Every passing moment, it became harder to keep his focus. If he kept at this standoff, he would eventually pass out. Then he'd be fair game to her.

Maybe if he killed her, the bind would be broken? Couldn't imagine being tethered to a corpse, but magic was a bitch. It was worth a try—but, still, she had information he needed. If the demon knew what happened to Remelia, chances were she probably knew about Ivana as well. That was valuable enough to keep her breathing.

"Tell me what you know."

"I can only do that with your help." She pulled the coat tighter onto her body. "I need you to help me get my memory back."

Tristan wiped the blood from his mouth. "And how do you suppose I do that?"

Zoë looked away. She must have been mental for even

thinking this was an option. But that was the problem: there were no options.

"There's a way. But I need to get to a church, and there's no way you can go right now. I need you healthy to pull this off. Now, where's your den?"

Tristan's eyelids began to feel like they had 20-pound weights on them. "My den is none of your concern, Demon."

Zoë took a small step back and felt her toes rub against a small, metal loop bolted to the wood floor. A small smirk on her lips blossomed as she eyed him.

"I'm standing on it, aren't I?" She tapped her foot against the trapdoor. "Now get that gun out of my face and get into your fucking cubby while you can still stand. We don't have much time."

He straightened his aching body, but only for a moment. "You try anything, princess, and I'll put a bullet...in your—"

Before Tristan could finish, he blacked out and fell against the stairs, falling to the floor.

Shit! Zoë quickly bent down to open the trapdoor to his den, then with unnatural speed ran to catch Tristan before he tumbled onto the sun-drenched floor at the base.

She pushed him against the wall at the second step and checked his face. His eyes were closed. He was panting but alive. She scanned around. The door was exposed to sunlight, and as old as he was, right now he wasn't strong enough to take too much exposure. Just great.

Zoë took off the coat and put it over Tristan's face. Tucking herself under his arm, Zoë got him up, nearly dragging his body to the open cellar door. She smelled a tinge of burning flesh along with hearing a faint hiss as Tristan's arms got burned by the sun.

"Hold on, almost there." Staring down at the dark hole, she threw him down into the darkness and climbed after him, closing the door above her. Her eyes immediately adjusted to the darkness.

The den was extremely minimalist and only consisted of a wooden crypt lined with dusty satin and pillows and an electric lamp. She attempted to turn the lamp on, but it was dead.

She turned to find Tristan, an unmoving heap, next to her feet. This guy was old school, but Zoë also suspected he didn't sleep down there. His bedroom seemed more lived in than the den. In any case, he was safe from light and could sleep until nightfall.

Rolling him over onto his back, Zoë pushed away the coat, then the dark hair and dirt from his face. When she could see all of him better, Zoe found the vampire quite attractive.

He had a strong jaw and defined cheekbones. Gentle, soft lips rounded out his features against his pale skin. He had a soldier's body. Ridged, toned and sleek. She didn't notice before, as a gun staring you in the face tended to change priorities.

Leaning over him, she began to breathe him in. That essence of his was unique, dark and arousing. Her fingertips gently hovered over him, and she leaned down inches from Tristan's face to taste the blood that lingered on the corner of his mouth.

Just a taste, she thought. *I've earned it.*

Enthrallment called to her as she desperately pressed her face to his, letting her lips trail across his mouth, hoping to taste a bit of his blood. She darted her tongue at the corner of his mouth. As she licked her lips, a shockwave of excitement tingled her body and shot down to the center of her.

She gasped as her body roared to life. He tasted sweet. More sugar than salt, but more pain than pleasure was how she would describe it. Old vampires always had the strongest, sweetest blood. And this one had a warrior's heart—she could feel it.

Zoë couldn't push herself away, but she had to. The temptation was far too strong. She could drain him dry right there, and it would all be over. Her sleeping prince would shrivel like a rose in the heat, and the bond would be broken, freeing her to seek out the truth.

Do it. It would be so easy. A long kiss goodnight. When her fangs grew and grazed the corded muscles of his throat, Tristan groaned, briefly but barely opened his eyes to her.

Like a spell broken, Zoë's eyes widened as she realized her body was priming itself for another victim. Tristan. She had to get away from him, or she'd kill him.

At that point, some distance was better than no distance. The more she stayed around him, the more often enthrallment would trigger. Tristan was right; whoever bound them together only wanted one thing to occur: the death of the vampire by a Black Blood Demon.

She scrambled backward as Tristan passed back out. Not taking another chance, Zoë went back up the trapdoor and got out of the den. She slammed the door shut and sat on top of it with a sigh. Her body cramped, knotting at the rejected promise of being fully sated. She retched, but there was nothing to release.

"I truly cannot remember ever working so hard *not* to kill a vampire."

She shook her head at the irony of it. There she was, a Black Blood Demon sitting in her underwear, alone in a vampire's home, protecting him until nightfall. No portal access to go home. No weapons. No clothes.

She scoffed aloud. "This is bullshit."

After a few minutes of seeing some folks on the sidewalk staring at her sitting down in full view, Zoë finally decided to get up and give herself some semblance of privacy. She picked up the half-split door and dragged it to the doorway to prop it up. It was by no means safe or secluded, but it didn't draw as much attention as a door-free home with a half-naked demon in it.

Her eyes traveled upwards to the upstairs bedroom she found herself chained in hours ago. Being bound to Tristan the vampire, she couldn't go far for what she needed, but at least she could start in his house first.

Zoë checked the wall clock. It would be several hours until sunset, so she had to use her time wisely, starting with finding some clothes. Then, when sleeping beauty woke up, it would be time to go to church.

～

VALETTE MARCHED out of the throne room, her black dress fluttering behind her like sordid wings failing to take flight. The smell of lilies everywhere was nauseating and also the final straw in getting her to leave.

She pushed through the group of vampires who hovered, waiting for an audience. "Move, assholes!"

She ignored the peanut gallery's mumbling as she continued past them. The clicking of her heels against the hard linoleum was the only sound echoing out as she made her determined strides through the hall.

Everyone was preparing for tonight's memorial and Union Address as The Three were to present what had happened with the death of Ivana. This would be the memorial for her tonight, and all the royal blue banners had been dropped and tied with red sashes, signifying the death of a fallen vampire in the upper echelon of their society.

Walking through the hall, Valette could still smell the oil lamps which burned brightly in Ivana's honor.

Good riddance, Valette thought to herself as she pushed more people out of her way that didn't move for her.

Javen's little pet was nothing but a ball and chain on the rest of them. Her idealism was simply toxic to the true nature of the vampire race. It was cute at first, but, honestly, vampires submitting to the other Supes for peace? How long did naive little Ivana expect Javen to entertain such ridiculousness?

But if the masses want a martyr, we will make her a martyr.

Finally reaching the outer doors of Javen's private chambers, she pushed through to find him alone. He stared out into the moonlight, his eyes fixed out towards the night sky.

His tall, muscular frame stood solemnly, all in black with the exception of the blood red tie. He used one of Ivana's swan brooches as a tie tack. It didn't take a genius to figure out how he was feeling at that moment, but regret was not a welcomed emotion for what they had to accomplish.

Valette purposely slammed the door behind her, immediately jarring him from his brooding. He turned to look at her for just a moment, then back into the night's void.

"What are you doing here, Valette? I wish to be left alone."

She rolled her eyes and scoffed at his maudlin display. "The benighted widower can mourn later for the masses. What are we going to do about our little problem?"

Javen didn't flinch, didn't move. "And which little problem is that?"

Valette walked swiftly through the chamber, coming towards him. "What problem? Just the only one that could jeopardize our plans. Everything is depending on the belief that Ivana's untimely death was the result of Green Girls and the Were-shifters going renegade and attacking the vampires."

"I know."

"Good. Because there can be no question. And your wayward commander, Tristan, is asking questions he should not be asking. Why didn't we kill him during the attack?"

Javen finally turned to meet her eyes. His pupils black and hyper dilated, he sneered at her. "I wasn't expecting your squad to be so sloppy. Besides, we needed a witness to confirm what happened. Tristan was supposed to believe the same as everyone else. I clearly underestimated his prowess, just like I overestimated the squad and their ability to carry out a simple job, even when all of the odds were in their favor."

"Admit it; this was your fault. No one told you to put Tristan on this detail to begin with!"

Javen rubbed his head in annoyance. "It was my decision to make. No one was going to believe that I would put anyone but Tristan on a detail as important as Ivana or us for that matter. If I'd chosen someone lesser, it would've raised suspicions."

Valette folded her arms, frowning. "No one was sloppy." She pointed her finger at him. "*You* waited too long to make this decision in the first place! Kostya and I told you this should've been done months ago, but instead you coddled and toyed with Ivana until she'd already made significant contact with Remelia, Otto, and whoever other Supe leaders remained in the mix. How can you expect we climb to the top of the food chain when your pet was trying to be head of the fucking supernatural ACLU?"

His teeth grinded against his jaw. "Shut up, Valette. What do you want from me? What's done is done." Javen glared at her. "What sacrifice have you made to this cause?"

"Don't you dare tell me to shut up. And this is not about sacrifices. This is about cleaning one's mess. A mess you made into the grand scheme of things. I know you loved Ivana, but she was a casualty. And a liability."

Valette reached out and gently caressed his face like a consoling lover. "This was what we wanted. What we *all* wanted. Our people need to know we are rising. War is coming, Javen, you said it yourself. Be thankful. Your little bird managed to build a legacy of peace, and we can use that to our advantage. But first, we have the stop the other little bird in our midst from singing."

She ran her finger past his jaw, then down to Ivana's diamond swan brooch. "So, what are we planning to do about it?"

Javen turned away from her, his hands behind his back as the moonlight shadows cast gray against his midnight attire. "Where's Remelia?"

Valette smiled. "Behaving, but she still won't talk. She had done a powerful cast before we found her, I know it, but she won't talk. And frankly, with the power that bitch has, we keep her gagged and salted as often as possible."

It may have been seen as overkill for an average witch, but there was no taking chances with a Supreme witch. They knew far too much to where even their tongue could be a weapon against vampires. Kostya even demanded they buried her up to her neck in salt, the weight of it suspending her without motion and nullifying her powers as much as possible. Even then, it took quite a bit of convincing to stop Kostya from simply cutting out her tongue.

Javen straightened his sleeves. "Doesn't matter. We also have the grimoire now, so I doubt it was anything epic she did. The Green Girls are up in arms and on high alert to find her."

Valette shrugged. "They really don't realize how fucked they are now in this fight. Too bad we don't have good leverage on Otto and his Were-shifters like this."

"No matter." Javen began to pace. Turning and walking towards Valette, he finally stopped and folded his arms. "The Green Girls want someone to stand accountable for their madam's disappearance. Let's give them someone to pick a bone with, then." He looked out into the night and gave a smirk.

"What are you thinking?"

Javen checked his Rolex and saw the time for Ivana's memorial and address was near. "Let's let our enemies take out our other enemies. After the address, tonight, message the Green Girls we have a renegade vampire on the loose." He turned to face her and smiled. "And he may have been responsible for Remelia's disappearance."

Valette smiled, her devious attitude oozing out her pores. "The Green Girls will go ape shit and probably kill him on sight, they are so riled up, but I worry putting a vampire in the path of being even remotely responsible proves a risk to us."

Javen began to walk towards the doors. "What risk? They hate us and probably suspect us anyway. The best way to divert that energy is to a scapegoat. And after the speech to our people tonight, any victory they feel after killing Tristan will be short-lived. The vampires are hungry for dominance and respect, so let's give them a reason."

SHADOW GAMES

*M*r. *Darkness likes to play wicked games, and, within his brilliant symphony of the macabre, he toys with his prey. Teasing, tempting, savoring the interlude he gives you to think you're finally free from his grasp. He watches. He waits. And when the crescendo of your bliss for life is at its absolute highest, he calls your number.*

No pomp and circumstance.

No curtain call.

Your show is now over.

So funny really, his ultimate deception is not that he'll eventually claim you; it's that the dangerous games he crafts are addictive, sensual, and far too tempting to ever stop playing.

So, let the games begin.

THE VAMPIRE SOCIETY from all over filled the Grand Hall. Old World vampires from other monarchies that normally would never bother to cross the waters were in attendance to pay honor and respect to Javen's consort, Ivana of Bainsborough.

Aisles of royal blue and black fabric lined the hall, along with miles of fresh cut lilies that took the after-hours work of a dozen florists to construct. The gaslights shined down on the hordes of vampires entering the hall, many in black clothing, but also in red, which was considered a more traditional color of mourning in the vampire culture.

Dashiell and the members of the Royal Guard stood at attention, watching in silence and without their commander. The dais held the thrones of The Three, where Valette and Kostya sat quietly looking out to the crowd.

Valette stared out, almost devoid of emotion, and smoothed out her crimson, satin gown. Her Elizabethan collar gave her a regal but chilly aura which was apropos to her current attitude. She cast her eyes to Kostya who, dressed in his black suit, resembled a robin with a red vest.

The air held a dark charge of anger, mysticism, and fear. An atmosphere ripe for The Three to plant the seeds of what they referred to in secret as the reaping.

Javen walked out from the royal blue curtains to the cheers and applause from the congregation of vampires in attendance. He swaggered to the podium like a confident politician, giving a stern but warm expression as he silenced the crowd.

"Power should always be tied to action, not rhetoric," he began, staring into the sea of vampires. "That is what my dark flower, Ivana, said often. She believed that we as vampires, as a people of fierce strength and superiority, owed it to ourselves to attempt building peace with the other Supes. This fighting was slowly weighing on our people. We've lost so many of our own. Ivana had sought for this peace with our full support. She'd convinced us, even me, that this was best for our race."

Javen took a breath and his head dipped down. The crowd stood attentively as he finally sighed and brought his crestfallen eyes back to the crowd.

"It is with deep sadness that I tell you all that Ivana was

brutally slain by the very Supes with whom she tried to make peace."

The congregation erupted with hisses, yells, and dissonance.

Javen raised his hand. "While en route to engage in talks with the Green Girls and Were-shifters, her motorcade was attacked. She was captured and staked in what appeared to be a sacrificial ritual."

The crowd exploded with hateful slurs.

"Wicked bitches!" screamed out a female vampire, her eyes blazing red.

"Fucking dark-hearted, backstabbing green bitches!" a male vampire near Dashiell belted out in anger.

Kostya shook his head. "I wish we had better news, but this is dismal and quite unexpected."

Valette frowned. "Indeed. We've wanted so much to make peace with the witches as well as the Were-shifters. It doesn't look optimistic over the circumstances."

Javen leaned against the podium. "We're still investigating, but the cleaning crew reported bodies of both Were-shifters and witches at the scene. They were in tactical clothing and engaged in the attack.

"Nothing has come from either Remelia's or Otto's defense, and that leaves us with nothing but the facts that their people were involved with the killing of one of our own. Our Ivana. Our dark Lily was stolen from us when all she wanted was peace. They spat on that budding truce by betraying her, ultimately betraying us!"

Javen turned to witness Valette and Kostya nodding in approval. The vampires shouted in agreement.

"Now, I know Ivana wanted peace. But it's that same peace that the Green Girls chose to stab our beloved ambassador in the back with. The same peace that the Were-shifters used to attack her! I want everyone to be on their guard until this is sorted out. Stay alert, vigilant. Tomorrow night, we will hold the funeral pyre for Ivana, a ceremony she herself designed to remember our fallen." He peered up towards the sky. "Tomorrow night, we will remember you."

Javen turned to the restless and upset crowd of vampires. Their hisses and calls grew the tension of the solemn address to a fever pitch. The seed had been planted, and now it was time to let it grow.

"We are bold and dominant creatures. Tomorrow night, we will also remember who *we* are."

As Javen and The Three exited the hall, Javen eyed Dashiell and stopped. "I want Christophe found, and where the hell is your Commander Castillion?"

Dashiell shook his head. "I don't know. It's not like him to not be here. But then again, last I heard, you and he had a disagreement, didn't you? He was pretty broken up last time I saw him. And hell-bent on finding out what happened to Ivana."

Javen frowned. "Tristan has some mistaken thoughts about the events leading to Ivana's death. Thoughts that are both harmful to our race and treasonous in nature." A muscle ticked angrily at his jaw as he stared at Dashiell. "And I wouldn't go delving into messy little rumors if I were you, Dashiell. If you want to continue being of some use to the cause, you should inform us as soon as you locate him."

Dashiell folded his arms, popping his gum. "Is that an order, *sir*?"

Javen nodded. "Now that Tristan Castillion is released from duty, I have great concern that his loose cannon attitude will continue to add fuel to this rather raging fire between the Supes. His emotions can make him reckless, and we, The Three, find him dangerous. Until Christophe is found, he is considered a concern as well. I'm leaving nothing to chance."

He patted a tense Dashiell on the shoulder. "So, congratulations, *Commander* Gray. You've just been promoted." He then leaned in, glaring at him in warning. "Now go hunting."

TRISTAN PUSHED *through the heavy wooden doors, his armor and fatigues weighing him down. He could see the trail of blood form a unique pattern on the church marble. The rich crimson liquid dripped from her gown as she laid there.*

She laid peaceful while the war raged outside the holy doors. His sword and shield dropped from his hands. This wasn't supposed to happen. He was supposed to be here to protect them.

Never again would he hear her voice, listen to her sing, or admire the beauty of her face. She was so enchanting, so vibrant, but now everything on God's green earth was void without her.

Tristan dropped to his knees as he stood vigil over the blood covered mother of his son.

"Katya..."

Even as she cradled his lifeless body in her arms, she remained to the very end a wonderful, protective mother. She gripped their young, precocious son tight, as if still trying to shield him from the horrors they faced in the end.

"William," she whispered.

Tristan slammed his hands down on the marble floor, breaking his fingers. The pain of it was quickly absorbed into the mental anguish he felt at the loss of his family. Opening his hands delicately, he saw his them covered in not only his blood, but the blood of his wife and son that spilled on the floor.

He had promised Katya on the eve of battle he would come for them. But he had failed. In the end, they all were betrayed. He balled his hands again and wept.

Hatred threatened to turn his tears to rage, wanting swift retribution. A penance was needed for those who sinned against him and his beautiful wife and son. It would be paid in blood.

A deep voice in the darkness broke the silence with a tempting question.

"What would you be willing to give if I could grant you the vengeance you desire?"

Tristan's eyes flew open with a gasp as he snapped out of his dream that was more of a near forgotten memory than a mix of random imagery. Too bad, he simply wasn't that lucky. If he closed his eyes right then, he would still see Katya and William's faces as clear as if they were standing right in front of him.

His eyes focused on the old, wooden boards above him. The slivers of artificial light creeping through along with the sifts of dirt falling on his face told him where he was. He smelled the mildew and musty odor of his old, abandoned hiding place.

Tristan couldn't remember the last time he had technically went to ground down there. Part of him was tempted that if he ever made it a habit, he would convince himself to finally go under. The way things were shaping up lately, it didn't seem like a bad idea.

He sat up, attempting to orient himself. The Black Blood Demon wasn't in there with him. He groaned and patted down his body.

And neither were his weapons.

Shit!

Like lightning, Tristan leapt up and ran up the ladder, punching through the trap door until he found himself staring down not one but two-gun barrels. The clicking sound of his Desert Eagle pistols locked and loaded in his face made him halt dead in his tracks.

As he focused, Tristan saw the stark, green eyes of Zoë the Black Blood Demon and a very arrogant smirk on her ethereal face.

"Good evening, sleeping beauty. I trust you rested well."

Tristan slowly put his hands up and away from his body, not taking his eyes off her. He could've kicked himself for allowing this to happen. No one ever got the better of him this way because he never allowed himself to be vulnerable.

This was why he should've put a bullet in her as soon as he saw those wings on her back.

I just got what I deserved for being an asshole.

"Do whatever you have to do, demon. I haven't got all night."

Zoë sat cross-legged on the floor with both guns trained on Tristan. She arched an eyebrow at his ballsy, but expected response.

"No, you don't, do you? In fact, it's why I've been waiting here patiently for you to finally heal and wake up." She stood up and backed away, her heels clicking against the hardwood floor. "You can come out of there...slowly, please."

Tristan stepped out of the hole with deliberate, controlled movements and stood to his feet. He stood silent and dared not move. He had no idea how long he'd slept, but by looking at her, it was long enough for her to get cleaned up and find some clothes.

He barely recognized his black shirt covering her ample curves. It took him a moment longer to break focus on the third dress button that struggled against the tension of being fastened against her cleavage.

"Made yourself at home, I take it?"

"I did, thank you. I will say that I was surprised not to find any corpses of women you've lured here and eaten. I could've acquired some more fitting clothes. Was I fortunate enough to be tied to the only grotesque blood-sucker that lost the gall to kill innocent humans?"

Tristan grew a soft, devious smile. "Apparently, you didn't check the wine cellar in the back. Besides, I don't know which is more disturbing: believing that I keep corpses in my home or you wishing I did so you could take their clothes."

Zoë ground her teeth. "I know very well what you creatures are capable of."

"No matter. Didn't take you too long to go rummaging through my stuff, I see."

Zoë would've preferred a pair of pants that fit, but at least the shirt was long enough. This was New Orleans, after all. She shrugged. "A girl does what she can. I couldn't very well go around in my skivvies trying to get to the bottom of this. Who would take me seriously?"

"If you think my dress shirt is going to do that for you, then you're dumber than I thought."

Zoë's smirk deepened. "Someone's a little grouchy when they first wake up."

"Only when I'm greeted with a Black Blood Demon aiming my own weapons in my face. Otherwise, I'm a fucking peach."

Tristan shook his head. He stared deep into her eyes, ready to accept the eternal sleep he had denied himself for so long.

Life's a bitch when surviving is down to muscle memory. Tristan could remember several times he had been ready to die, ready to meet Mr. Darkness, and had been denied either by providence or his horrible habit of surviving.

"So, if you're going to shoot me, then shoot me."

Zoë sighed at his puzzled stare as she lowered one of the guns. "If I wanted to kill you, trust me, I had plenty of time to do it. Staying up to guard over me took quite a toll on you. I know you hate the sound of this, but I saved you today. You would've been roast if I hadn't intervened."

Tristan sneered. His broken memory did manage to hold the image of her face—light above her, but all around them was darkness. That angelic face of hers had held a confusing expression that he could remember. That look... he couldn't read if she had wanted to fight him or fuck him. With such a fine line, he didn't know if he was truly fortunate or not that she chose neither at his weakest.

"Then why didn't you?"

"Ah, the smartest question yet, vampire." Zoë circled him slowly, akin to a panther stalking. She had more questions than answers herself as she toiled while he slept.

She'd hoped her memory would come back to piece together what had happened before she was taken. She hoped someone would miss her and look for her. Tanzi, Margo, and the others surely would've realized she was gone and not on some mission.

Or, was this *the mission?*

IT COULDN'T BE. Why would they send her down on a silver platter to an enemy? Shut out from getting back? At a time where nothing made any sense, everything was a possibility.

She watched the vampire in her sights, who could very well be her demise or salvation.

"There you were in my arms and barely conscious. Already bleeding. I could've twisted that handsome head off your body and drained you dry before a fairy could bat its wings. I would've been freed from this bond and off to figure out who put me here in the first place."

She stopped moving but kept her gun aimed at him. "But like I told you. I need your help. Whether you believe me or not depends on what happens next, but it's clear neither of us expected to be here. Someone *put* us here. Now, we can either be puppets and do what I *think* they want us to do, or we can be smart and work together."

Zoë must've thought about what to say to him a hundred times while she was upstairs. She could see the turmoil in his eyes. He was smart to be cautious. They were, by nature, enemies. Would a rabbit trust a wolf? But he had to be wondering why she kept him alive—at least, she hoped so. She needed him to think about things as she did.

Her mind had trailed to the possibility of killing him more times than she could count while she showered. It was just easier. Even now, staring at him, she wanted to taste him again. Her body craved to claim him. But to heal her mind, she needed his help and his trust. It was a tall order that probably neither of them was ready to fill, but she had to take a chance.

I am more than just what I was built to do. Hopefully so is he, or else I'm dead.

Zoë walked up to him and lowered the gun. She flipped the other pistol that was in her other hand and presented it to him, handle first.

"There's a reason we haven't killed each other. I take that as a sign."

Tristan noticed the gun in her hands, and then at her. There was no arrogance, no fear. Just her searching him for the right response. He scoffed. She was either stupid or confident he wasn't going to light her up with an opportunity like that staring him in the face.

He had no doubt she was right in that she could've ended him. He wouldn't have known what hit him. Instead, she not only spared his life but allowed him to fully heal and strengthen.

He didn't pretend to know everything there was to understand about the dangerous Black Bloods, but he was a warfare expert. A Supe would never take that sort of risk to spare the enemy...unless they weren't an enemy.

"How do you know I won't plug a bullet in the back of that head, princess, as soon as I get the chance?"

She gave a small but alluring smile. "The same way that you know I wouldn't have bothered leaving your pretty little head intact if I haven't even considered that a possibility. We're both taking risks, vampire." Zoë nodded and glanced at the gun she offered him. "Now, what's your choice?"

Tristan swallowed. The answers to what really happened to Ivana were somewhere out there. Christophe was probably still missing, and he needed to find him. The Three were up to something, and it fell to him to figure it out before it was too late.

"What would you be willing to give if I could grant you the vengeance you desire?"

If this was the only way to get those answers, so be it.

He took the gun from her hand, popped out the clip to see it was full, and loaded it back. Tristan looked up at her and sighed while putting the pistol in his holster.

"All right, demon. I'll bite, no pun intended. We're partners on this, for now. But if I get one inkling—*shred* of an inkling—something's screwed, and you plan to fuck me over, I can't guarantee I won't ruin that face of yours. Do we understand each other?"

Her green eyes sparkled beneath the overhead lights. "Perfectly. Though I could do without the warning. I know I'm the stuff of nightmares to pretty little vampires such as yourself." Zoë put her hand out to shake. "Do you have a name, vampire?"

He glowered at her hand as if it were a foreign object. Then he cut his eyes back at her. "Let's not get too comfortable, princess. We're business partners at best, and I don't plan on being tethered to you for too long."

Zoë quickly retracted her hand and rested it on her hip. Fuming, she chewed her lip to bite back the frustration. "Fine. We need to leave and head to a church to get my memory back. One with a fountain or baptistry."

Tristan grabbed his coat from the floor and shook the dust off it before slipping it on. He rolled his neck, stretching his body for the hunt.

"There's a church four blocks away. If that doesn't have what you need, we'll just have to keep walking. We're in the bible belt, after all."

He watched as Zoë took the belt holster from the rack and fashioned it around her. She lifted the shirt, so it rested against her hip. The movement gave him an unabashed view of her thighs up to those lacy panties he couldn't forget if he tried. She pulled the black shirt down and broke the spell.

Zoë felt his eyes on her, sensing his brief thrill of arousal. It was then she realized what easy prey he really could be if he let his guard down. But as she transferred her gaze to him, meeting his now steely eyes, she also knew that this vampire would never let his guard down with her ever again.

And here I thought I had every vamper pegged, she thought to herself.

She flung her tawny hair and let it cascade down her back as she put on Tristan's leather jacket.

"Good. The sooner you take me to church, vampire, the sooner we get a piece of the puzzle."

TAKE ME TO CHURCH

*T*he night called to them both as Zoë and Tristan made their way toward the neighborhood Catholic church several blocks away. The chilly air was a bit uncharacteristic of the typical, humid nights Tristan was used to, but there were a lot of things odd about tonight.

His eyes glanced to the fiery-haired demon at his side. She walked with purpose and it seemed her heels clicked louder than anyone else's as they shared the sidewalk with people embracing the November night.

It was hard to ignore the determined sway of her hips as she moved through the crowd. Hard to ignore the heads of wishful, aroused men that nearly turned—Exorcist-style—to get another glimpse of her, as if checking that she wasn't a figment of their dark, sordid imaginations.

Tristan tried to forget the taste of her when they'd kissed the previous night. He remembered the dark, heady flavor of ecstasy that seemed to be bathed on her smooth skin. He wanted another taste of her, as if his body wouldn't let him forget how she felt against him.

Tristan continued to watch the pedestrian men stare and

noticed that, though they gawked, even the human men had the sense not to approach her. Pretty smart.

They would do well to push her out of their minds—just like I've been trying to do for the past half-hour.

As they kept to the shadows, they stopped at the large brick church. The weathered structure had the old, red bricks of a younger New Orleans. There wasn't a soul around except for the passers-by on the sidewalk.

Tristan looked up at the sign of St. Benedict's Church and shrugged. "I've never been in this one, but it's the closest."

Zoë started to walk up the steps. "This will do."

Suddenly, she halted as her eyes caught a small structure about two blocks away.

"Wait!"

Tristan quickly surveyed the area. "What is it?"

Zoë kept staring at the quaint and almost picturesque church a bit further away. Complete with a steeple and vented belfry, to her, it was awfully hard to ignore.

"There's something about that one." She motioned to the little white church and Tristan reviewed the building.

"Well, it's Protestant and probably likely to have water," he added.

They both raced down the steps and onto the sidewalk as they headed to the location. Tristan moved through the small packs of clueless people walking, talking, and snapping photos with their phones. As he moved through with Zoë not too far from his side, he watched as humans and creatures of the night roamed the city together.

He slid to the side as an inebriated blonde woman stumbled past them with her hipster vampire companion corralling her through the crowd. Tristan shook his head with a smirk, but as his eyes followed them he met the furious eyes of Zoë, who obviously saw the vampire with his future prey.

Stopping in her tracks, she turned to follow until she felt the tight grip on her arm as Tristan gave her a chiding stare. "Let it alone," he warned with his velvet-edged voice.

Zoë stiffened against him, pulling against his grip. "This is bullshit."

"We have work to do, and you can't save everyone." Tristan tightened his grasp around her bicep.

Zoë's hardened face conveyed the fury in her as she stared Tristan down. The packs of people moved passed them as Zoë yanked her arm free. Had this been any other night, she'd be hunting. Then she'd be on that predator vampire like stink on shit, ready to let him meet the edge of her sword.

With eyes still locked, she exhaled a hard breath through her flared nostrils. Then she walked on towards the church because this wasn't one of those nights. She kept her eyes focused on the little, white church, all the while afraid she would see more tragedies waiting to unfold at the hands of vampires, demons, and other nasty Supes who couldn't keep their filthy hands to themselves. Her focus was so steadfast, she ran into pedestrians often.

The church seemed a bit bigger when they walked in through the old wooden doors. The gentle hum of the air conditioning units in the windows was all she heard besides the clunking of their feet onto the creaking floor of the chapel. The glossy, oak pews appeared to be the only new item in the dated building.

Tristan followed in behind her as Zoë let her fingertips brush against the smooth, warm finish of the wood as she continued toward the shimmering pool of water near the pulpit. The lights under the pool illuminated the area and gave it an otherworldly glow, reminding Zoë of the portal to her home.

Zoë stepped up to the baptistry and nodded. "This feels...familiar."

Tristan watched her as the reflection of the water danced on her face. "You've been here before?"

She scanned the church, looking for anything to trigger a memory. "I don't know. It's possible."

Though the church was in his neighborhood, there wasn't much research he'd done on it. His eyes scanned around, ready for anything to give way to surprise. After all, she was still his enemy, and for all he knew could have some scheme up her sleeve.

He walked closer to the baptistry and frowned. "So why are we here? Why do you need water?"

Zoë shook her head. "It only seems to work in water. Blessed water is best." Her hand dipped in the clear, cool liquid. "Holy water triggers the healing, like rebooting a computer. It's been a very long time since I've done this, but, from what I remember, it could piece together the missing memories I have."

"And this works like a charm? You take a baptism and you're square?"

"No, it doesn't work that way. It's difficult to explain, but, at the end of the day, I'm a demon—I'm not going to want to stay in there. It's gonna be painful as shit, and without force, I won't stay in long enough to get some memories back. This is where you come in, vampire." Her green eyes cut upward to him. "You're going to drown me."

"What? You can't drown."

"Well, not in regular, run of the mill water. I am a demon, after all, and thereby still shunned from His light. I'm not an angel. I'm of the Fallen. I won't die, but I'll be incapacitated and vulnerable. I can't just do this anywhere."

Tristan folded his arms. "And you're trusting me?"

She sighed. "It would appear I don't have much of a choice. Bully for you."

Tristan shook his head in disbelief. They used to be angels. How could holy things hurt them? "I don't understand. Didn't you all *choose* to fall? To protect humanity from us?"

Zoë, with a stoic face, nodded. "Yes."

His expression stilled and grew serious. "So, wouldn't that somehow absolve you from being victim to those rules of being a demon?"

Zoë rolled up her sleeves and looked up to the majestic crucifix in front of her. Many times that question had been asked, and every Black Blood Demon was ashamed of the answer. The curse about legends is that the horrid pieces are always omitted out to make a better story. It was that omission throughout the centuries of existence that almost tricked her into believing the same half-truth as well. All her brethren were fools to think they were anything more than the demons they'd become.

"I wish that were true." She cut her eyes to him. "Gimme your blade."

"For what?"

Zoë sighed. "This would go a lot faster if you didn't ask so many questions. This should be fun for you." She leaned in and smiled. "You get to see me suffer and nearly kill me. I imagine that would give you quite a thrill, as it would any vampire."

Tristan reached in his boot, pulled out his knife, and handed it to her handle first. "I'm not a sadist, and I don't get off on others suffering."

She scoffed. "That's rich, coming from a creature who feeds and slowly drains the life force out of their victims. You mean to tell me that wouldn't have been you luring that poor, drunken woman to her death?"

"She's a big girl. You take a stranger home, you pay the price," Tristan replied sharply. He had no time to mourn human folly. Everyone lived and died by their mistakes. He was no different.

His cold response filled her with disgust. It never ceased to amaze her how calloused vampires could be. Appearing to look human was the closest to actual humanity the blood-suckers would ever get again. Perhaps the old scripts were right; they were beyond redemption.

Zoë cleared her throat, realizing an argument could abruptly end their shaky partnership.

"In any event, this needs to be done, and, unfortunately, I cannot do it without your help. I'm not able to do this willingly." She unhooked the belt holster and handed it to him.

Tristan hoisted the belt over his shoulder, watching her with scrutiny. "So, you want me to hold you down and drown you in holy water?" He searched her eyes and saw no insincerity. The flood lights in the baptistry sent a moving reflection of waves over her delicate skin. His eyes moved to the water. Ah, the myth of holy water. Tristan wasn't sure how the myth got associated with vampires, but it couldn't be further from the truth. Vampires were never shunned from holiness. However, apparently, some creatures were. So close, and yet so far away was their curse, as the legends said. Her presence made him feel a mortality he hadn't experienced in ages. A danger to him in every sense of the word. Finally, he nodded. "You're right. Sounds fun. Let's get to it."

"Wait, there's something else." Zoë glared at him. "This is when things get a bit messy, blood sucker. I need to provide a small sacrifice...your blood."

Tristan drew his gun, his eyes flared bright as she stepped back. "I don't think so, princess."

"Don't be such a baby. I only need a few drops. It's just how it works, but, usually, the vampire is dead. You living proves for more complications."

He scoffed. This demon was a piece of work, in more ways than one. "Sorry to disappoint you, bleeding heart."

She kicked off her heels, twirling Tristan's curved dagger in her hand, cavalier as if she were born to handle it. "I'm serious. Vampires and Black Bloods are drawn to each other's blood. It makes us want to kill you, and we're designed to do just that."

"You'll try to lure me again, won't you?" He thought about his options, and there weren't really any except for the obvious. It didn't matter. The outcome would be the same. They would try to kill each other.

And one would succeed.

If he failed, that would be that for him. If she failed, he would have to live with failing. Of letting Ivana's killer walk without punishment. Of hell continuing to break loose among the shadow world. Mr. Darkness did love his games.

Fuck it. Tristan stood next to Zoë as they both looked into the pool. Slowly, Tristan held out his hand where Zoë held it over the pool. "Okay. Do it."

She sat on the edge of the baptistry. Discomfort already showed on her face. "If I shed your blood, I'll want to enthrall you again, so you have to be quick to keep me in the water."

Zoë held the blade over his palm, almost hovering as she gazed into him. "I'm going to be really strong at first. If you can hold on, my strength will eventually subside." Her other hand gripped under his palm. He found concerned but firm violet eyes. "But if you can't, it will be hard not to try and kill you. And I will come for you."

Tristan opened his coat to reveal his gun, showing no signs of relenting. "I know."

Zoë nodded as they both understood each other. She quickly slid the knife across his palm as Tristan hissed. As the deep red blood spilled into the water, Zoë followed the flow as it ran down his finger. A moan escaped her lips as she grabbed his hand.

Tristan tensed as the slick texture of her tongue ran across the pad of his fingertip, tasting his blood. The warm, wet sensation of such a seductive gesture made his groin tighten. When she closed her soft mouth around his finger, sucking, he grew even harder. That dark look in her vixen eyes was somewhat familiar as she slightly parted her legs wider in an open invitation.

Groaning, he felt the pull of his body closer to her. Clawing within him, he ached to tear the clothes from her and take her on the altar. An encounter with her would be the ultimate sacrifice.

Shit. Shock forced him to snap out of the budding trance. "What are you doing?"

Tristan reached for his gun when Zoë quickly put her hand over his to stop him. Her eyes were bright violet as she stayed trained on him like the most delicious prey. Her fangs were drawn, and his blood smudged on her full lips. Her dark laugh echoed through the little, white church as she replied with a sinister, disembodied voice.

"Just savoring the flavor, cowboy." She stretched her arms out and fell backward into the baptism pool.

With no time to waste, Tristan jumped in after her. As she tried to rise up from the water, he quickly grabbed her by his shirt. Smoke and mist rose from the surface, and the pool that once was cold began to escalate in temperature.

Her arms reached upwards as her talon-like nails lashed out to his face. Tristan growled at the intensity of his flesh being torn across his cheek. Zoë started to thrash about, flinging the water across the church. Her deep, demonic voice yelled and screamed in agony as Tristan wrestled her down, holding her with every bit of strength he had. She clawed and pushed him, but Tristan didn't let go, despite the pool beginning to bloody with his injuries.

Tristan gritted his teeth as he watched her. His mind contemplated what logic had been trying to scream at him since the moment he realized what she was.

When she weakens, all I have to do is put two in her chest, and this will be over. Why am I keeping a deadly Black Blood alive?

He growled as he shook the thoughts away, but they kept coming back. The only sliver of salvation he had was the fact that, so far, she'd put herself in just as much risk as he had.

As her shirt began to rip against the struggle, he quickly wrapped his hands around her delicate throat and clenched, pushing her down further into the water until they were both submerged.

He watched her as the bubbles from her mouth violently

escaped to the surface, and her eyes shot open with deep sadness in her eyes. The expression was so haunting, he nearly froze. In those eyes laid a window to pain. His pain. An image of Katya pleading with him to stay flashed in his mind, before it followed with him cradling her body in his arms.

Ivana visited him next as she smiled from the corner of her lips, only to later lie bloody and motionless on the altar.

Zoë clutched her hands around his arms, digging into his skin as Tristan held fast. He shut his eyes, looking away until her thrashing finally subsided. Tristan slowly opened his eyes as he felt her locking grip on his arms loosen and slide off him.

He gently loosened his grip around her neck and quietly backed off as everything went silent. Not even the hum of the window units was heard as Tristan stared at her curving, regal body suspended, motionless in front of him. Her long, auburn hair swayed in the water like dancing flames. She was an ethereal but dark angelic force that Tristan couldn't take his eyes from.

Still standing in the baptistry, he cautiously backed up, drew his gun, and aimed it at her, ready for the unexpected.

Zoë laid still in the smoky, hot water, her mind becoming a deprivation chamber. Closed off from stimuli, a wave of serenity washed over her, and darkness became a sought haven as glimpses of memories and voices that hid in that void suddenly came to light.

Remelia.

"I was supposed to protect her."

The red grimoire.

"We can't let anyone get their hands on this book."

Her insubordination.

"This isn't your fight."

"You will pay the price for your disobedience!"

The Three.

"The vampires want an uprising. And I'm going to stop it."

With the images and memories came the flood of emotions.

Anger. Fear. Hate. Like the Furies themselves tormented her, she was compelled to wring every drop of emotion from her heart. She was right; something dark was brewing with the vampires and other Supes. She stood in the center of the storm.

And now it was time to go to work.

Still suspended in the pool, Zoë's eyes shot open and the lights and candles in the quaint little church blew out, putting a soaking wet Tristan on alert. Standing vigilant, Tristan stepped back as the foundation of the baptistry cracked beneath his feet. Not taking his aim off Zoë, he stepped over the edge of the pool and hopped out.

Water flew up to the ceiling as Zoë suddenly sat up from the pool, screaming. The edges of the baptistry shattered and cracked, releasing the water in a flood against the oak pews and pulpit. Tristan braced his footing as the wave rushed and crashed against his boots.

Looking around with new eyes, she realized now why she was drawn to the church. She had been there many times before. It was a checkpoint where Black Bloods would meet an ally—a human who assisted them on the mortal plane.

Other memories started to come to vision as Zoë slowly rose to her feet, steam rising off her drenched, half-naked body. Her hair, now dark from saturation, fell like curtains around her oval face, but her violet eyes were clearly visible and trained on Tristan.

"I know who Remelia is."

"That makes six of us!" A loud, but slightly muffled female voice called their attention to the front of the church. Tristan and Zoë turned to see four women standing at the doors. Two of them held silver chains with little barbs between the links in their hands. Vampire shackles. It was hard to tell which spoke because all of them wore half face masks with the likeness of a grim reaper, but Tristan saw the green pentagrams on the arms of their jackets and it was clear who they were.

"Green Girls!" he snarled, feeling his fangs extend. His aim immediately shifted to them, but Zoë put her hand on top of the gun to stop him.

"Don't!" she commanded.

Tristan cut his eyes to her. "Have you lost your fucking mind?" At the same time, two Green Girls stepped forward with silver orbs in their hands, and Tristan froze.

"Nuh- uh," the woman in the middle warned. "Make another move and we'll light your ass up, vamper."

Zoë shook her head in defiance. "They are human," she whispered. "I can't harm them, and neither will you." She countered his icy gaze with one of her own. "I will *not* allow it." She turned to face the four witches, her face softening as not to scare them. "We mean no harm, so just take it easy."

One witch stepped forward, her gun complete with a suppressor in her hand. Her blonde ponytail was pulled high atop her head and her black-clad body moved deliberately slow. Her combat boots clomped gently on the wet, hardwood floor as she got a bit closer then stopped just shy of Tristan and Zoë. The witch's coffee eyes darted between them both and seemed to detect no trust among them.

"We've been looking for the vampire Tristan. Word has it that you have insight to our Supreme's whereabouts. Now, where is she?"

"Not a fucking clue, but if I was a betting man I would say to start with who gave you that bad information. I had nothing to do with her disappearance."

The witch shook her head in disbelief. "You and the redhead were just mentioning her name, vamper. Do I look like a fool? She went missing, and so did her grimoire. I know you blood sucking shits have drooled over getting your sticky hands on either one of them, so I ask you again. Where is Remelia?"

Zoë stepped forward. "Look, I don't know what happened to her, but I know I was supposed to protect her. Let me help you."

As she tried to step forward, the witch cocked her gun and shifted the aim toward Zoë. Holding her hands up, she paused with brewing anger on her face. She was growing tired of having guns in her face. She wished she was immune to blessed rounds, but being technically a demon was a bitch.

"Don't get cute. You can help by staying out of my way, Fallen. This shit doesn't concern you, and, frankly, I'm a bit confused and disgusted I'd find you with this parasitic sack of shit. In any case, between the white light and these blessed bullets, I will put you in your place." She turned to meet Tristan's reflective eyes and scoffed. "And you, handsome devil, are coming with us."

Tristan slowly shook his head. If he went with them, he'd never come back. He could tell in their mannerisms they had their minds made up.

With a confident smirk on his face, he replied. "There's no way in hell. Back off. You're being played, and I'm being set up. Who told you I had Remelia? The Three? I didn't touch your Supreme. Now let us go."

The witch pulled down her face mask to reveal a sullen but furious face. "You will tell us what you know, vamper. Or we have ways of getting you to talk."

"You'll have to catch me first, Green Girl," he responded sharply, the challenge deep in his tone.

The sound of a pump action weapon suddenly cocked behind Tristan and made everyone tense immediately. Apparently, someone else had decided to join the party.

"What the hell is going on in my house of the Lord? " A young, tall man in a bleached white dress shirt stood a few feet from them. Near the pulpit, his short barreled shotgun aimed at all of them with equal discrimination. That is, until he and Zoë locked eyes.

The preacher's deep, hazel eyes briefly softened before his face twisted into a firm scowl seeing Tristan and the witches.

What the hell did Zoë get herself into now?

"I said, what in the world is going on here? What are you all doin' in my church? Somebody better start talking."

The head witch still had her weapon drawn but backed up slowly. "Put the gun down, preacher. Don't do anything stupid. We only came for them, and this isn't your business."

The preacher rolled his tongue across his teeth, then shook his head at her command. His eyes caught the pentagrams on their sleeves and he swore under his breath. "You're in my house of worship uninvited. This is my business. Now I need all of you out of my church or—"

The witch scoffed. "Or what, preacher man? Gonna shoot us, your holiness? Gonna sic the fire and brimstone on us as well?" The other witches joined in her laughter. "I'm gonna tell you what you're gonna do, preacher man. You're gonna drop the gun and back away while we take these two with us. Don't make us hurt an innocent. Cause we will."

The preacher sighed and cut his eyes to Zoë, the vampire, and the witches. He stifled a chuckle. It sounded like a bad joke. *A Black Blood Demon, a vampire, and four witches walk into a church...*

"Welp. I was hoping it wouldn't come to that type of thing. I have no idea what's going on, but in any event, I only really give a shit about one of you." A wicked smile grew on his face. "Which one, now, is for me to know." He glanced up at the two inconspicuous red boxes attached to the ceiling. Everyone in his congregation thought they were fire alarms. Guess in a way, they were. "You see, I'm not much of an innocent, darlin'. And I don't like fuckin evil witches in my house!"

With a swiftness, the preacher aimed and blasted one of the boxes, releasing a thick smoke into the church. Coughing, the witches backed up but started firing their weapons through the haze of tear gas. The preacher grabbed Zoë's arm and pulled her. "Let's get the hell outta here!"

Tristan didn't hesitate as he saw an orb fly through the sky towards him. Turning on his heel, he leaped over the pulpit and shielded himself against the blast of light as the silver orb ignited, sending shrapnel across the pulpit.

As the witches gagged and fired blindly through the church, he seized the opportunity to push himself away from behind the podium and follow the preacher and Zoë out the back door, when a flash of light hit the side of his body. Tristan hissed at the searing of his exposed skin but continued out the back exit and to the parking lot.

Zoë and the preacher ran to a black, extended cab truck and beeped the alarm to unlock it. He jumped in the driver's seat as she circled around to the passenger's side.

"Dammit, Z, what the hell have you done where even the witches hate you now?" He kicked on the engine as he saw Tristan run towards them. Zoë clenched his arm. "Wait! He has to come with us."

He gave her a WTF look, his eyes blinking in confusion. "Fuck that. You know I don't deal with vampires. Last time I checked, neither did you!"

Seeing the witches on his tail, Zoë pulled the preacher closer with clenched teeth. "We're bound together, Jay. He has to come with us. He has to, so let him in. Now!"

Jay slammed his door as Tristan jumped into the back seat, just before pinning the pedal. The grinding sound of gravel popped against the tires as they burned through the street and into the night.

SPELLBOUND

Zoë and Tristan violently shifted against the truck door as Jay skidded around the corner and took a left through a red light. A cacophony of blaring horns and blazing headlights surrounded them for a moment until Jay managed to cross onto the other side of the street.

"This is bullshit!" he shouted as he turned another corner. "I don't hear from you in days, then all of a sudden you show up wrecking my church with this asshole. Then, you got witches coming around all pissed off on top of that. What the hell is going on?"

Zoë clenched the grip assist handle. "Jay, slow down before we're pulled over." She turned back to Tristan, who had half of his face scorched by white light. His hand rested on his injured skin, covering his right eye as the healing took place very slowly near his lips.

"Are you all right?"

His bright eye blazing, he nodded. "I'll live." Casting his one eye to the only human in the truck, his scowl deepened. "Who the hell is this guy?"

Jay scoffed, darting his eyes to the ungrateful vampire in his rearview. "Who the hell am I? I'm the reverend saving your unholy ass, blood boy." He looked at Zoë. "And you. You've got some explaining to do! Where the hell have you been, and why are we saving a fucking vampire?"

Annoyance continued to grow on one half of Tristan's face. First Black Blood demons, then witches, now humans. Where did it end?

"I'm right here, asshole, if you have something to say to me."

"Hey man, fuck you *and* the dark horse you rode in on, all right? You pissed off those witches. Do you have any idea what they're probably doing to my church right now? I'll be lucky if the sumbitch's still standing, thanks to you two." He whipped the truck in a hard turn that ended in some violent curbing and the barely avoiding of frightened pedestrians. He shook his head as he narrowly missed the red light. "I should've let them finish frying your ass."

Tristan sat up and moved up in his seat towards Jay with a growl in his throat.

Zoë pushed him back down. "Back off!" She turned and pointed at Jay. "And you. Don't provoke. Just get us to the safe room and I promise I'll tell you more, okay Jay? There's an explanation for all of this."

Tristan glared at the back of her head. He didn't have too much patience for those with means to kill him, which was why he didn't understand Zoë's need to preserve the lives of those Green Girls.

"Are you sure? Because I don't understand why you allowed them to attack us." Tristan frowned, still holding one side of his face. The stinging of the burns and his irritation of being in such close quarters to a preacher and a fallen wanted to culminate into one big explosion. "Whose side are you on?"

She didn't turn to face him. "The human side."

"They could've killed all of us."

Zoë whipped her head back around to face him. "But they

didn't. Despite what you may think or feel, witches are human, and I'm here to protect human souls. Not yours." Her violet eyes met him in earnest. "Besides, they wanted to know where their leader was; they didn't come for blood."

Tristan scoffed at her comment. Either she was naive or delusional. It couldn't be both. "Like hell they didn't. I don't know if you've been schooled on the history between Green Girls and vampires, but it's not paved in flowers and fucking puppies, Black Blood. They hate and fear us. Someone knew what they were doing when they sicced them on me. This was a setup. I've got to find out who's giving misinformation. Those were not your average Green Girls."

"Oh yes they were," Jay interjected as he pulled into a driveway. "Those bitches are on the level now. They see everything. Got tired of having vampire and Were soldiers coming to kill them and started having soldiers of their own. They hunt and they hex—I put nothing past them."

Tristan uncovered his eye and checked his weapon as the stinging slowly subsided. "Great, so why are we coming here?"

"Because this place is protected. Even from them. This place is even safer than my church."

Jay pressed a garage door button near his dome light and waited for the garage door to open. Pulling in over a massive paint drawn seal in the concrete, Jay finally turned off the engine and closed the garage door behind them.

"Home sweet home."

He hopped out the truck and moved to the front of it, where he opened a steel door cut out of the concrete. "Follow me down here so we can talk," Jay commanded as he proceeded to descend the nimble staircase into the darkness.

Zoë followed behind him quietly, then paused to notice Tristan eyeing her with caution. She rolled her eyes.

"If he wanted to kill you, he would've just left you behind for the witches. Trust me. I've known Jay for a long time. He's trust-worthy, despite his valid hatred for vampires."

She continued down the trapdoor while Tristan sighed and made his way, following behind her.

Down the stairs, they followed Jay till they hit an old wooden door. "This used to be a tunnel that went from this house to the other across the block. This spot used to be where a plantation stood, till it was torn down." He opened the door with a creak and walked through. "Now, it's where I keep all the crap for demons."

Zoë walked through, the area now familiar to her. The shelves were lined with books from all over the place and the smell of frankincense and myrrh filled the room. Oh, how she loved that smell.

She sifted around at the myriad of apothecary jars of powders, liquids, and metal pellets Jay used to make defense weapons and other items for the Black Bloods and himself. Every ally had their own way of serving the Black Bloods, and she had considered herself lucky when she converted Jay.

The tough preacher knew a lot about the occult and religion alike. Of course, he wrestled with his own share of demons that only strengthened his resolve and swearing vocabulary.

Tristan scanned the large, smoky room, careful not to touch anything. The place seemed rife with silver as his eyes caught it immediately—knives, coins, and even medieval torture devices coated in the anti-vamp metal. It'd been a long time since he'd seen items of the grotesque designed for vampires, and never in human possession.

His eyes cut to Zoë and her human ally. Someone had been busy. Humans didn't tend to live long in the shadow world, yet the Black Bloods seemed to find use for them. No sooner than it crossed his mind, he hissed as his hand brushed against a medal-lion hanging off the table.

"Who are you? How do you know about all of this? "

Jay set his phone down on his work table and pulled his shirt up, revealing scars of vicious claw marks and fang marks on his upper shoulder

"Several years ago, a vampire came knocking at the church. I didn't know what he was there for or what he wanted. Guess in the end, it didn't matter. He killed my other pastor right in front of me. Bit and tore into him, laughing as I watched. And then was going to kill me. Asked me to pray to the Creator to come save me."

He lowered his shirt to conceal his past wounds. His hazel eyes were dark as he retold the grim memory that taught him that more than humans and animals roamed the earth. "Those last few seconds. You know, those seconds where you know you're going to die? I could've prayed. That's probably what I was supposed to do, but I didn't. I wanted him to pay for what he did. I wanted to make sure he didn't get a chance to do that to anyone ever again. I was fighting him with everything I had when Zoë showed up. One moment he was on me, and the next, parts of him were all over the place."

Tristan looked up to find Zoë on the other end of the room, preoccupied with looking into chests. To ignorant eyes, she seemed like a normal, lithe woman. Apparently, looks were terribly deceiving as he thought of her ripping a vampire apart.

The two visions didn't seem to fit, but Tristan knew better. It was why his eyes never seemed to leave her. Whether it was caution, desire, or both, he wasn't sure.

His attention finally circled back to Jay as he continued to talk.

"I opened my eyes to find her helping me up, blood all over her like she bathed in it. I didn't know if I should thank her or run for my life. She told me she heard me calling, and she was there to protect us from those like you. Those who fed off us. Who terrorized and took. She asked if I was ready to help, and I said yes. I wasn't gonna let another bastard like that hurt

someone else. Years later, here I am, still fighting. Still preaching."
He rubbed the Saint Jude medallion around his neck before
shifting his eyes back to Tristan. "Now, I've seen some pretty
fucked up shit, but I still got my faith."

Tristan saw the angst in the reverend's eyes before looking
over him to Zoë again, who sifted through some jars. "Where did
she come from?"

Jay shrugged as he grabbed a set of keys off the wall nearest
him. He started to sift through them. There was no way in hell he
was going to share that information with a vampire. If Zoë
wanted to divulge those details, then that was up to her, but Jay
didn't owe that vampire shit, let alone the true origins of his
rescuer.

"I don't know. All I know is that she's pest control for a higher
power. Her kind aren't in any books or bible I ever read. To tell
you the truth, I really don't care. Just like I don't really care where
you come from. I'm just glad she's around." Jay gave Tristan a
snide smirk. "I take it that's bad news for you."

Tristan moved past him. "Well, I'm not here to win any popularity contests."

"That's good. Cause you won't. Allies like me believe the only
good vampire is a dead one."

Tristan grunted at the all too familiar saying that rode on the
lips of witches and Were-shifters everywhere. Guess he shouldn't
be surprised any privy humans would feel the same way.
Vampires were bastards; it was true. Finding an enemy was easy,
and, thanks to that, he was sure the Black Bloods found it easy to
recruit.

He wasn't a fan of human attacks, but he never really gave a
shit if others participated in such activity, as long as it wasn't
recklessly exposing their kind.

"Have the same sentiment for the Green Girls and Were-
shifters?"

Jay slipped a key off the keychain and looked at Tristan in

earnest. "Witches are complicated. They piss me off and cause a world of trouble, but, to me, they are simply humans that lost their way. Usually they stay away from me, and I them. And the jury's still out for me on the Were-shifters. That's not to say they don't piss me off too, but at least they haven't tried to kill me."

He whistled at Zoë before tossing the key across the room to her. Not looking up, she caught the key, then finally turned her attention to him. "Your stuff's in the red chest over there."

"Thanks." Zoë walked over to the red chest. Kneeling down, she popped the latches open. Raising the top, she sighed with relief as she lifted her sword and scabbard out of the long chest. She examined the handle with Aramaic symbols etched in black on the silver and wood handle. Gently pulling it out, she felt the reflection of the sword's light on her face. The clove scent from the oil filled her nose as she smiled at her pristine weapon.

Good thing she made a habit of leaving it with Jay. This last time returning home did not pan out well for her, and she was certain her superior would've stripped it from her.

Just like they stripped me of everything else.

"I cleaned it up for you." Jay interrupted her thoughts. "I wanted to wrap the handle, but I know how you feel about seeing the words on it."

He cleared his throat as he noticed Tristan staring at the half-naked Black Blood. Jay wasn't sure if the vampire was even aware he was sucked into her vision. He had to admit, her design was quite effective. It distracted him, too, as the torn shirt didn't cover much. "There's some, um, changes of clothes in there for you too, Z."

"Thanks Jay." She slipped the blade back into the scabbard and laid it on the floor next to her. She reached in the chest to pull out some of her clothing.

"You owe me some answers, Z. You go on a mission and then you don't rendezvous as we discussed. I was left with my ass hanging out and wondering what the hell happened."

She scooped the bundle up and sighed at them both. "My memory got zapped, which was why I healed in the church. Before that, I found myself chained up in his place."

She began to unbutton the shirt, when Jay quickly pulled the curtain in front of her with a sigh.

"We'll meet you in the other room and you can tell us more." He turned, annoyed, passed Tristan and unlocked another wooden door. He tapped Tristan, watching him finally focus.

"Hey Romeo, follow me unless you want her to enthrall and eat you in here." He clicked his teeth. "Just so you know, I don't like you enough yet to try and stop her, so it's best you get some distance."

He walked through the door as Tristan quickly followed. "She said you two were bound—when did that happen?" He turned on the lights, and the room went completely washed in a red hue.

"Yesterday. I come back from a mission gone bad and found her chained half-naked to my bed." Tristan examined the room as his eyes immediately adjusted. There was another symbol on the floor that didn't look like anything he'd ever seen. In the red light, the symbol appeared orange as it glowed softly on the floor. "What is this place?"

Jay struck a match and slowly moved around the room, lighting candles. "This is where Zoë invokes her portal when she needs to enter or exit this plane. That symbol there is the mark of the Fallen."

He lit one last candle, then cut his eyes to Tristan as he went back to the previous subject. "You're lucky you aren't dead. I've seen her make easy work out of vamps with less. Must've taken some restraint from Z." He extinguished the match he held in his hand and laughed. "The fact you're still alive now is just as baffling."

Tristan walked around the symbol on the floor. In truth, it partly baffled him too, but they had an agreement that, so far, both had been sticking to. That wasn't to say he completely trusted her, but he was having trouble maintaining his initial desire to kill her.

Seeing that she was probably having the same inclinations but had yet to act on them, Tristan could only keep his suspicions of Z at bay. At least for a while longer.

"We have an agreement until we figure this shit out. There's something going on bigger than this, and it just couldn't be coincidence I found myself with a Black Blood delivered to my house after the assassination of a prominent vampire."

"He's right, Jay," Zoë suddenly replied behind them. She watched their eyes fix on her as she walked into the room. She was dressed in black with a white shirt with her sword strapped behind her back.

It was good to be armed with her weapon of choice again. She felt the pull of the symbol on the floor, but it didn't hold a candle to the gravity of the vampire in the room. The heady scent of his blood moved through the small space that was supposed to be her sanctuary, and when his eyes caught hers, she had to divert her gaze before she found herself luring him again.

A deep pang hit her beneath her ribs, and she sucked in a breath. Being well-behaved hurt like a bitch, and if they didn't get freed soon, she didn't know how long their so-called truce would last. She nicked her tongue on her sharp canine and tried to calm her urge.

"There's a connection here on what happened to us. What have you heard on the street?"

Jay crossed his arms and started to pace. "There's been a budding of vampire activity everywhere, and with the witches on high alert for their missing Supreme, it's getting pretty hairy out there. If the myth was true, the night sky would be littered with broom-flying spell-twisters. Word has it they are looking for the vampire responsible for the disappearance of their Supreme witch."

"Remelia." Zoë's voice lowered as she leaned against the wall.

The vision of her face got clearer as she focused. The last image she remembered was the fearful expression the witch held before everything went black before finding herself back home. But the homecoming this time wasn't pleasant. Then again, they rarely were anymore.

Now, a witch's life—a human life—was unaccounted for. Her voice softened, feeling shame for her missing on her watch. If she was down here, maybe things would've been different.

"I was supposed to protect her. Now I don't know if she's dead or alive. Something went really wrong." She inclined her head over to Jay. "When was she declared missing?"

Jay shrugged. "Had to have been at least two days ago. Not too long after you disappeared on me. Could've been longer; I don't think the witches would be too quick to let on they were leaderless."

"Yeah, not with the Were-shifters and vamps waiting to take a bite outta them." Zoë felt another pang and leaned forward, more noticeable than before.

Tristan noticed the uncomfortable look on her face and paused. "What's wrong with you?"

She straightened her body, but still relied on the sturdiness of the wall. She needed to kill something. Soon. Food. Fucking. Fury —it all was feeling the same for her right now. Her body wanted her to feed and if she didn't soon, the painful side effects would make her wish she was dead.

You've got a strong vampire over there with fire in his blood. Take him and end this madness.

Zoë shook her poisonous yet logical inner thoughts away. Her eyes didn't meet his gaze out of concern he would read them. "Nothing," she dismissed. "So, we've got a dead vampire and missing Supreme witch. Who was the vampire that was assassinated? One of The Three?"

Tristan sighed. If only things were more just, perhaps. But life didn't work that way, whether you were living or undead. The

Three used her for something they were up to, there was no more doubt in his mind, but he had no proof.

"No. Her name was Ivana of Bainesborough. Javen's companion. She was in talks with the Green Girls and the Were-shifters when she was attacked."

"When was this?" Jay asked.

Tristan turned to him. "Just the other night. I was on her security detail when the motorcade got ambushed. She didn't make it."

He felt Zoë's eyes on him as he tried not to remember his failure to protect her.

Jay leaned against the desk, and rubbed his temple. "This is getting interesting. Like a really shitstorm from heaven kinda interesting." He turned to see the approving nod of Zoe before he continued. "Who was it? The witches or the Were-shifters?"

"Neither." Tristan shook his head. "I killed some of those assassins, and the ones I unmasked were vampire."

"What?" Jay's eyes widened in alert.

"I know what I saw and who I attacked. I believe someone made her murder to look like witches did it, but vampires were definitely involved." He raked his fingers through his hair. "When I addressed it to The Three, they dismissed it as if I saw some fucking illusion." He took a few steps toward Zoë. "There were Were-shifters and witches at our morgue, but I don't believe they were actually there at the attack."

Zoë grimaced. "Why not?"

"One of the bodies there was a Green Girl I met the night before. Now, she managed to kill my vampire partner, but, trust me, she wasn't an assassin. It just didn't fit."

Zoë crossed her arms over her stomach as the details Tristan shared sank in. "The Green Girl," she added, "...did you kill her?"

Tristan turned to her, feeling a pull to be closer to where she stood. Her guarded stance loomed in the darkest part of the red room, only a gentle glow on her profile, but he could hear the concern in her voice over the human life.

Cognizant of the pull of her presence, he grabbed the edge of the desk next to Jay and leaned against it. "No. I spared her so she could live another day. Unfortunately, that's only how much longer she lived."

Zoë quietly nodded, finding herself both relieved and surprised at the vampire's answer. She was almost sure he, like the others, would have simply killed because they could.

"I see."

"But there's more," Tristan continued. "Only a handful of contacts knew the route we were taking. Me and two other guards were on her detail. Before the fray, I lost contact with one. No one's seen him since."

"Perhaps that's the vampire the witches are looking for?" Jay asked.

Tristan shook his head. "I don't know, but I have to find him. It didn't make sense, but when I addressed it to The Three, they dismissed it as if I saw some fucking mirage."

"That doesn't make any sense. Why would the vampires kill one of their own? I hear you guys have a strict rule about that," Jay asked.

"That's what I've been trying to figure out. Ivana wasn't trying to start any shit. She believed she could come to terms with the other Supes and bring them together. She foolishly, but genuinely believed in peace," Tristan said.

Jay scoffed. "Guess we see where that lands you if you're a tree-hugging vamper."

Tristan turned to Jay, his eyes dark and fangs bared. "Tread carefully, Preacher," he snarled. "I don't like you much either."

"Both of you calm down. Shut up before I eat you both," Zoë droned as she attempted to move toward the symbol, now that Tristan had moved farther away. "Ivana's name sounds familiar to me. I think I remember Remelia mentioning her once or twice in our conversations."

Remelia had wanted peace as well, but her suspicions of the vampires hadn't gone away. It was why she'd asked Zoë to protect her. It all made sense to her with the vampire's details added.

"Doesn't anyone find it odd that we have two important people from opposite factions either dead or missing at the height of negotiations? Ivana may have wanted peace, but someone close to her apparently didn't. Remelia wanted the same thing; she often talked of peace, but then she disappeared," Zoë supplied.

Tristan nodded. "Vampires involved in a vampire assassination. I bet my life that Javen has told the vampires that witches and the Were-shifters were involved in Ivana's death, but we know that's bullshit."

Jay scratched his head. "So, this may be a dense question, but who stands to gain the most out of a missing or dead Supreme and a dead vampire leader made to look like witches and Were-shifters did it?"

Zoë and Tristan pretty much responded in unison, mirroring angered scowls. "The Three."

WITCHING HOUR

*I*t made sense to Tristan. He knew that The Three were up to something, he just had no idea they were up to something so heinous.

Ivana's death was a set-up, and he wasn't crazy. The vampires wanted the blame for her death to fall on the other Supes for her assassination. If that wasn't enough, there still was a missing Supreme witch out somewhere with an anxious group of Green Girls itching for retaliation. Chaos was growing, and all things pointed to the The Three being at the center of it.

"We have to find Remelia, or this will continue to swell, and The Three will continue to manipulate the masses into an all-out war." Tristan pulled out his phone.

"Who are you calling?" Jay asked.

Tristan began sifting through his contacts. "I need to reach out to Dashiell about all this. He's one of the few people I trust."

Jay shook his head. "Well, you can trust him outside of my humble abode. If he's a fellow neck-biter, forget it!" He looked over to Zoë, then back to Tristan. "I'm not entertaining any other vampires here. You should be lucky I tolerated you."

Tristan frowned. "Relax, I'm not bringing him here, but I do need to talk to him." Jay took a couple steps to him. "Trying to stop me would be unwise."

Jay stepped closer to Tristan. He was growing tired of turning the other cheek. "Are you threatening me, blood boy? "

Their pissing contest reaching a zenith, Zoë yelled. "Enough!"

She didn't realize her voice had dramatically changed until she noticed both Jay and Tristan frozen, staring at her. She stopped moving, nearly clutching her chest. Biting the dark pieces of her nature down, she tried to move past their reaction. "We'll leave after the vampire makes his call, all right?"

Jay took a step back as her symptoms were growing more apparent. "Uh oh. Someone's getting hangry."

Tristan also stepped back, his eyes locked on Zoë as she stood in the shadows. She possessed the same, dark tone in her voice that she had at the church. His hand on his pistol, Jay stood in front of him to block.

"Don't you ever draw on her in my presence, you understand? You want to live, then let *me* handle this!"

He turned back to Zoë, moving towards her with urgency. This was lunacy. He didn't know why it was so important to keep the vampire alive, especially seeing as it tortured the Black Blood to fight it.

"Z, it's just gonna get worse as you stay near him. If you don't feed, you'll kill him, and even if I wanted to stop you, I wouldn't be able to. We need to break this bond between you two. Can't you call the portal open?"

She shook her head. "No. It doesn't work. Probably because I'm bound to him." Another pang hit her, and she cried out. "Don't let me kill him, all right?" she whispered to him. "It's important he remains alive so we can get to the bottom of this."

"Z, listen—"

"Promise me, Jay."

Jay swallowed and rolled his eyes. "I promise, Z."

She nodded as she cut her eyes to Tristan, then to Jay. "Good. Get the bag, Jay. Now." She slinked to the floor as Jay ran out into the other room.

Instinct urged Tristan to move towards her, but after taking two steps, she hissed at him, holding her hand up.

"Stay away from me!" Her voice deepened again to a demonic resonance as she clutched her stomach. "I need to feed, and if you don't want it to be you, stay the hell away from me."

Tristan stood quiet, but she could feel herself slipping. She waited far too long, and now with food and relief so close to her, resolve was being thrown out the window.

A shiver running through her body, she backed up against the wall as Jay slid down to the floor. He held a foggy, plastic bag filled with red fluid in his hand before putting it to Zoë's mouth.

Nearly growling, she snatched the bag and ripped into it with her fangs, moaning as the thick, red fluid gushed into her mouth.

Tristan watched the Black Blood Demon suck in the blood as Jay stood vigil. "You keep vampire blood?"

Jay didn't look at him, worry in his eyes. "Yeah. For her." Instead, he watched Zoë drink nearly every drop of chilled vampire blood from the bag and gently close her eyes as her body relaxed. "It's usually what happens to the vampires we interrogate. It helps when she's worn down or been on this plane for a long time."

Tristan's eyes caught something familiar and shiny in his field of view wrapped around Jay's wrist. "Is that a...sully chain?"

Jay followed Tristan's eyes to his wrist and frowned. "Yeah. I didn't know if I'd have to restrain her, and this is the only thing I can think of that could do that. I figured if it got bad, she would've asked me to...for you."

He eyed Tristan with conviction. "For some weird reason, she's trying like hell to keep you alive, so I guess it's my job too."

His eyes went back to the resting but blood-stained Zoë and smoothed her hair back. "Looks like she's calming down. Somewhat."

He studied the chain, then turned to Tristan. "The Black Bloods use these to subdue other Black Bloods. They are created specifically for the offender and are unbreakable to them. I, on the other hand, just need some bolt cutters." Jay sneered at him suspiciously. "How the hell you know about sully chains?"

"Those same type of chains were on her when I found her half-naked in my bed."

Jay scoffed. "Well, sadly, I'm not surprised. Zoë has had some run-ins with her superiors in the past."

He walked over and pulled open a cabinet in the far corner and took out a vial of black liquid. "She doesn't get along with them too well, you see. She's a crusader, and you know what happens to crusaders."

Tristan instantly thought of Ivana, her bloody body lifeless. "Yeah, I know exactly what happens."

"Anyway, last time she came through the portal here, only her hands were shackled, not her feet, like they were in the middle of it or something when she got zapped here."

Tristan thought about that for a minute. Something didn't make sense. "Wait, what's the purpose of chaining her for punishment, when she can just escape to this plane?"

Jay shook his head. "She didn't escape. She couldn't when she's chained. Z said she had help."

"Who?"

"A witch," Zoë replied in her normal voice, forcing them to turn to see her standing against the wall. Her statuesque frame stood confident, healthy, as she started to walk toward Jay.

Her vibrant eyes flashed like amethysts. "A very, very strong witch brought me here." Slowly, she walked further in, calculating her moves around the vampire whose blood made her crave the hunt with unfathomable need. "I can't think of many times I've been amazed at the power of some humans, but when Remelia opened the portal to bring me back here, I was truly lost for words. No one should be able to do that."

Tristan followed her movements until she settled before him. "Remelia, the Supreme witch, has the power to pull you out of your plane down here?"

Zoë nodded, her memories working to paint the past images and conversations she had with Remelia.

"She said she called me down to protect the grimoire, the book that was the source of her powers and gifts." Zoë looked off into the symbol on the floor. The witches had thrown in all their hopes on a Black Blood Demon who couldn't fulfill her promise. "Of course, I was taken back by my people before I could guard it from thieves." She turned to Jay. "That's why I never returned. I was pulled back home for punishment."

No wonder the witches hated her too. She hung them out to dry. If it was in her control, it never would've happened, but it wasn't.

Her superiors wanted her to stay out of it, and she didn't listen. Now, a witch—a human—could be dead because she failed to keep her promise.

"But Remelia is the answer of how I got here. It has to be. But this time, I don't know why unless it was a last ditch effort to save her." Running her fingers through her hair, she sighed, looking into Tristan's eyes. "And it still doesn't explain why I was delivered and bound to you of all things."

Tristan shifted his gaze and walked away from her. The grimoire being taken was his doing. The Three wanted it, which made it even more damning that they had something to do with Remelia's disappearance.

Without Remelia and the grimoire, the witches had no real protection. They were as good as dead since the vampires would claim them coven by coven.

His eyes followed Zoë. If she found out he was involved with the grimoire being taken, their truce would certainly be over. He needed someone else he could trust to back him before all of this got too volatile to handle. Tristan picked up his phone and walked out of Zoë's sanctuary.

DASHIELL WALKED down the corridor past the morgue when his phone rang. A swear escaped his lips until he saw whose name popped up. He quickly accepted the call.

"Tristan? Where the fuck have you been, man?" He leaned against the glass that separated the dead from the undead. "Half the damn world is out looking for you!"

Tristan, back at Jay's safe house, nodded as his friend chided him. "Yeah, I sorta figured as much."

"Why weren't you at Ivana's memorial? The Three were livid."

Tristan scoffed. "You mean The Three's *address*?"

"Whatever. I had to cover for you, and I don't even know what the hell for, man! What's going on? Where are you?"

He turned toward Zoë's room to find her bracing herself against the frame, watching him. The curves of her hips were prominent from the black jeans that hugged her.

Ignoring her, or at least trying to, Tristan turned his back to her. "It's a long story. Listen, I need tell you some things but not over the phone. We need to meet somewhere. I'm in a pretty sensitive situation, and I've got witches gunning for me."

Dashiell frowned. "They are gunning for anything that moves. Especially vampires. Those bitches are getting violent. First the attack, now this. Look, why don't we meet at Patsey's off Decatur? It's vamp only, so at least you can lay low until we straighten some shit out."

Tristan nodded. "Sounds good. We'll meet you there in twenty."

Dashiell frowned at the phone. "Huh? Who's we?" he asked. But all that answered was silence. Tristan had already hung up.

∼

SLIDING his phone back into his pocket, Dashiell continued on down the corridor until he reached another set of doors with a keypad. Humming a tune to kill the silence, he punched in his code and waited for the door to slide open to reveal an elevator that only went up.

The Three put precautions in, but Dashiell couldn't help but wonder if it was enough. *Guess we'll find out.*

As the elevator dinged, Dashiell whistled as he turned the corner to the giant circle in the floor. "Ah, there you are."

He walked closer. There was a woman in the giant circle of salt, yet all Dashiell could see was her head. Her hair was pulled back into a tight, black bun. Her tired, angry face was surrounded by a pond of white salt.

He inched in, sensing she was rousing. Her jade eyes were a soft contrast to the gaunt cheekbones and thin lips. Pity, her skin used to be so pretty, like porcelain. The witch's cell didn't seem to do her any favors. The suspension in that much salt without food and water had to be suffering close to biblical proportions.

She's a lot stronger than she looks. But wonder if she's smarter, too?

Dashiell leaned against the rail in front of the salt tank and began to rap against it with his nails. "Wake up."

The witch slowly lifted her head, finally meeting his eyes as he stood across from her. Above her. Like a superior.

The gag in her mouth was tight. Too tight. She felt it cutting into her mouth, leaving the other side numb. The vampires were smart to gag her, otherwise she would have showed them the true meaning of pain. All of them, including the smug bastard standing before her like he'd won.

A muffled grunt was all she could offer with her controlled

breaths. The salt not only prevented her from casting, but the weight of it constricted her abdomen, making it hard to breathe. Sleeping helped, but her slumber filled with nightmares. Dreams of fallen witches, vampires, and even Were-shifters terrified her. Warned her. This was only the beginning.

Dashiell smiled. "Well, the legend finally awakens. I'm honored." His fingers tapped the metal rails in rhythm to the tune in his head. "You know, I must say, I didn't expect you to be so easily captured. I mean, you knew that you were in danger, right? When are you not?"

He began to pace. "And yet, you got lured out and snatched up. Your witches are not very resourceful after all. Losing you means they are leaderless. Lost."

He picked up her dress that draped over the rail. The same dress she wore when he found her waiting for Ivana, who would never show. "Now, I know by now you've must've learned that your friend, Ivana, met her untimely death at the hands your witches."

"Lies!" she muffled out.

Dashiell shrugged. "Well, they may as well have. You and the Were-shifters can't seem to play nice with anyone anyway. Besides, if it walks like a duck, talks like a duck, chances are it's a witch planning an assassination."

He walked around the tank, his feet stepping into the salt, packed so tight it was like a floor. "Let's face it. If there was a totem pole for supernatural beings, Green Girls would be pretty fucking close to the bottom. Your girls can barely get out of their own way."

That's why they needed Remelia. She was not only their leader, but their source of power. Without her or the grimoire, they were dog food. It was above his pay grade why The Three chose to keep her alive, but he personally found it foolish. If the Green Girls knew she was dead, it would break them all.

Easily.

Instead, they were all riled up and looking to slaughter a vampire. Tristan was gonna give them good exercise at least. He walked back around to face the sullen Supreme witch. "I was told that witches had a sixth sense about bad omens. If that's true, then you must have a plan B somewhere. Am I right?"

Dashiell walked over to a lever and as soon as he grabbed it, the witch yelled through her gag. He froze. "Does that mean you're going to tell me your plan?"

A muffled "Fuck you" belted out through her gag.

Dashiell shrugged. "Guess that's a no."

He pulled the lever and salt poured down into the tank. He watched as the salt mounted up higher and higher past her chin, then to her mouth. Her muffled screams were drowned out as the salt covered her face and most of her head. She shook off what she could, only to find more piling over her, smothering her.

Finally, he turned the lever back and waited as the terrified but muffled cries continued. Coughing and gagging prompted him to walk over to the tank and push away the salt from her nose so she could breathe. He lifted up her chin, forcing her to look at him. Her nose was bloody from the inhaled salt, and her jade eyes were red.

"I wish I could do this all night until you finally break, but I have another engagement."

He turned to see Takeshi and Valette enter the room. Dashiell stood up and faced them, noticing a funnel and tube in Takeshi's hands along with a jug of some fluid he was afraid to ask about. Clearly, the Supreme had it lucky with him. He shuddered to think what Valette was enlisting her cleaner to do for her to make the witch talk.

Valette cut her eyes to the near buried Supreme witch. "Did she tell you anything? Did she agree to submit?"

Dashiell shook his head. "No. Actually, I just got started, but she's resistant. I've made contact with Tristan. He called me not too long ago to meet, so I'm heading there now."

Valette nodded, finally looking at him. Her chin ever so slightly lifted. "Good. Then you know what to do, Commander. We'll take care of the witch, won't we, Takeshi?"

"Hai," he replied, eyeing the witch where he stood.

"Let me, Javen, and Kostya know when it is done." Valette walked past him, holding her dress as she settled in front of the witch. "And find Christophe! I can't believe there are so many loose ends to all of this!"

"I'm fairly certain he's dead."

"No body, no death," Takeshi replied softly.

Dashiell popped a stick of gum in his mouth and cocked his head. Seriously? "You know that theory doesn't really work for vampires, right? Sometimes we're fucking ash, like Gregory." He glared at the creepy vampire with annoyance. "I took care of him."

Valette crossed her arms. "Well, just make sure."

With a sigh, Dashiell walked out, hearing the muffled yells behind him as he left them to their horrid devices.

Valette smiled, revealing her pearly white fangs. "Remelia and I will continue to prime her for a decent, civilized chat. Won't we, Rem? Or Takeshi will show you how Sangri-la was attempted in the old days."

Remelia closed her eyes, readying herself for another round of pain. She was ready to die, but she needed to stay strong for her coven. They were out there fighting for her. Looking.

Her heart ached for Ivana since Remelia refused to believe that she had nothing but the best intentions. They were both naive, and now everything was falling down.

As she watched Takeshi connect his funnel and tube, she clung to one hope. The vampire Dashiell was right about one thing. She did have a plan B. It was reckless and haphazard, given the information she had, but nonetheless she prayed it would turn things around. She knew the incantation by heart and bled for it before they came to take her. Though her body ached and bled, the thought of the reckoning she'd called made her feel safe, if only for a second. Her one last weapon to use in this battle.

I do have a backup plan, you three bastards of hell. And she *will destroy all of you.*

RESISTANCE

$\mathcal{W}$atching Tristan hang up, Zoë turned her attention to the symbol on the floor. "The vampires are trying to cave the other Supes for dominance. Setting up the other Supes is a good way to eliminate your enemies."

"I'll say," Jay replied. "Ever since last night, there's been skirmishes everywhere. Witches versus Were-shifters, Were-shifters versus vampires. Before, there was some control, but now?"

"It's chaos," Tristan added. "That's just the way The Three like it. While they are out playing victim, they can manipulate the masses to attack aimlessly. It's only a matter of time before the others fight back." He took a step towards Jay. "Have you heard anything about Otto? Is he all right."

Jay frowned, thinking about the Lord of the Were-shifters. Otto 'The Lycan' Krause happily made his home in Louisiana after falling in love with the hunter's paradise. Him and his not-so-merry pack of wolves lurked in both the city and the boonies. The beasts with a human heart hunted the vampires, for which Jay was grateful.

"Who? Otto? That dude gives me the creeps. There's no news

on the street about him. Far as I know, he's alive and well, and he's pissed that some of his Were-shifters turned up dead."

Zoë put her hands on her hips. "Lemme guess. He's looking for a vampire responsible?"

Tristan felt her eyes on him and faced her. "Knowing Otto, he's going after everyone he thinks is even *remotely* responsible. Green Girls, vampires…he'll just consider it open season. All the more reason we need to get moving to sort this out. Or things are going to get bloody."

"Give me a moment to grab something, and we can leave," Zoë said before stepping out of the sanctuary. She closed her chest after slipping her dagger into her hip sheath.

Finally, the sting of the cravings subsided long enough for her to bring real thought to the situation. She was there for the witches, to protect them. Somehow, Remelia, with baffling skill, had reached out and pulled her from one dimension to this one to help. She had to make good on her vow where she had failed before. Reaching to zip up her jacket, her eyes lingered over to Tristan, whose back was to her as he spoke to Jay.

I'm here for the witches. The vampires are the ones who will feel my wrath.

But all vampires? Now that she knew the truth, a question clawed at Zoë. Did she truly need the vampire anymore? Her fist tightened as she stared at him. He'd kept his word, which couldn't have been easy considering every ten minutes she looked at him like dinner. But he was the enemy. All vampires protect their kind. Yes, he wanted vengeance, but that was different than allowing a Black Blood Demon to start slashing through his friends. Would he allow her to seek justice even if it meant destroying the people he'd known?

Her eyes watched him intently. His scent was still alluring and powerful. The vampire probably had no idea how close he had come to being hers just a short while ago. The pain of resisting kept getting worse with every abstinent episode. How long could she keep that up before the hunger took over? Jay was right. If they couldn't break the bond soon, her vampire would be as good as dead.

Kill him. Make it quick. Easy. He deserves that much.

The internal suggestion jarred her as she noticed Tristan turning around.

He doesn't deserve to die. He's fighting for someone too. Just a little more time to get to the witches...

But time was not on her side. The other Black Bloods would soon notice she was gone and come looking for her and put her back in chains. They'd warned her before to stay out of the fray of witches and biters, but when a human called for help, who was she to turn a blind eye? Were they not handed down the decree to protect the human souls from the supernaturals that coveted hem?

The war was becoming too much. Soon, the world of witches, Were-shifters, and vampires would be unveiled to the world of man, and once that happened, life on earth would never be the same. But instead of pride, she was stripped and chained for her disobedience.

Blinking away the thoughts, she finished zipping up her jacket as Tristan and Jay walked up to her.

Jay handed her a keychain. "You can't take my Beast, but there's another truck in the alleyway that runs pretty good. I know you won't bring it back, just like the last car I loaned you, so that's the best you're gonna get."

Zoë accepted the keys and kissed his cheek. "Thank you, Jay. I'll be back to help you rebuild the church."

Jay laughed. Wouldn't that be a sight? Some hot ass demon up on a roof hammering away. The old ladies of his congregation would have a fit. "Uh, don't worry about it. I have a good contractor."

Zoë eyed him suspiciously. "Really?"

Jay shrugged. "Wouldn't I have to for dealing with this stupid ass shadow world of yours?" Not to mention, he knew all the contractor's nasty little womanizing secrets. Secrets he wouldn't want to get out to his pretty little pious wife and mother of three. Sometimes absolution came with a price.

"You guys better head out. I'll have my cell if you need me. All hell is breaking loose out there. You better watch your ass."

Zoë nodded and walked ahead to climb up the stairs to the garage. Tristan watched her exquisite form glide up the steps before he turned to Jay and extended his hand to shake. Jay frowned at it as if it was road kill, and then surprised Tristan by returning the gesture, gripping his hand tightly.

"Saying it was a pleasure would be a lie."

"Agreed."

"But let's just leave it at the fact we didn't kill each other. So that's a good sign."

Tristan nodded. "Fair enough." As Tristan was about to head upstairs, Jay stopped him.

"Speaking of not killing each other..." Jay reached into his pocket. He couldn't believe he was doing this, but Z made him promise. He never planned on breaking a promise to her. Not ever. He pulled out the bundle of chain and placed it in Tristan's hand.

Tristan frowned in disbelief that the preacher had given him some of Zoë's sully chain.

"Zoë's struggle with enthrallment is no picnic, and it has a breaking point. Do not underestimate her power or her hunger. That blood earlier was just a temporary fix. She will need to kill and feed or it will just get worse." He sighed. "She's designed to hunt, so if she's denied too much, then she will rampage."

Tristan didn't like the sound of that.

Jay continued. "I've never seen her do that, but allies have told me of other Black Bloods who have, and it isn't pretty. It's like fishing with dynamite. She'll enthrall large numbers of the soulless to come to her. And then she'll kill them all. Every single one."

Tristan scowled at the mental picture of what that would look like. Terrifying. He clutched the chains in his hands and jammed them in his coat pocket. This was a way to subdue her if it got to be too much.

"Thanks."

"Don't thank me just yet." Jay glanced upward to the stairs, then back to Tristan. "I've seen the way you look at her, Romeo. Just know that Zoë cannot love. She's a Fallen One. A demon. She fights. She kills. She... fucks." He cleared his throat. "But then she just kills what she fucks. What you feel is the pull of her enthrallment, and if you give in she'll kill you just like any other vampire. Remember that."

Tristan nodded as he went up the stairs to meet Zoë. Walking along the side, he met her violet eyes near the entrance of the garage.

"Are we leaving or what? " she asked. "What did Jay want?"

Tristan walked past her, barely looking at her. "To reaffirm his hatred of me."

Knowing Jay and finding that totally plausible, Zoë shrugged and followed him to the truck. "This bar...it's not a vampire bar, is it?" she asked. Alarm rattled within her at the thought of finding herself among a buffet of vampires to seduce, enthrall, and kill.

Tristan shook his head. "No, mostly humans. Think of it as a vampire's meat market. But we won't blend in long if you try to make a scene in there."

"Why should I trust one of your vampire buddies? And considering what we know now, why should you?"

"I don't trust anyone, Black Blood, but everybody needs friends. I've known Dashiell for a long time. He's not that big a fan of The Three, but he does his job. Besides, I trusted one of yours, you can stand to trust one of mine. Just don't eat him."

Her eyes narrowed to thin slits. She didn't know why his refusal to call her by her given name irked her, but it felt like a kick in the teeth when he did it in that arrogant tone of his. "I have a name. My name's Zoë."

Tristan continued walking ahead. "So you've said. Still couldn't care less."

Ugh, why am I sparing him again?

He really shouldn't tempt her. That old vampire's blood was just an appetizer, and her craving now was for more than just the kill. A body like his would be a waste if she didn't get some fun out of it first. A strange mixture of lust and sarcasm forced her to reply with more truth than she wanted. "And don't worry. If there's anyone ranking at the top of my menu, it's you, vampire."

Amusement curled Tristan's lips at her haughty retort. "Thanks, I'd hate to think I'm second place, considering all that we've been through."

Zoë followed through the field. The idea of going to the vampire's hunting grounds was less appealing than walking into a buffet of them. Watching them prey upon the humans was not something she was willing to just let happen.

Not while I still have a means to stop it.

"Why are we going there when we should find the witches? We still have a bond to break, and maybe we can team with them to find Remelia."

Tristan laughed. "Yeah, that's a plan," he added with sarcasm dripping from every word. "Did you forget they want to hook, drain, and interrogate me for their missing Supreme?"

Zoë frowned. She wouldn't have let them take him. Didn't he know that?

"We know that The Three have Remelia."

"Wrong. We know The Three have something to do with her disappearance. We've yet to actually prove any of it." He wasn't going to deal with Green Girls right now, especially knowing that he was tethered to a creature who cared more for their well-being than his own. "For all they know, they think we were just trying to save our own skin pointing them back to The Three."

"But she was the one to call me down. She sent for me. Maybe if the witches knew this they would calm down and listen—"

Tristan whipped his head around. "What makes you think they would even listen to you? Hmm? Did they even *want* your help when they saw you in that church?"

He walked up to her, his eyes locking into hers, watching the realization darken her eyes. "Let me answer that for you. The answer was no. You know why? Because they don't trust you any more than they trust me. That's why. *You failed them.* I know it sucks, but to them, you're not one of the good guys right now." With that, he snatched the keys out of her hand and continued walking to the truck to unlock it.

She braced her hands on the passenger door, glaring at him. "You think I don't know that I fucked up? That I left Remelia unprotected?"

Tristan looked off to the field and raked fingers through his hair. "No, I'm saying you think nothing's changed *despite* you fucking up." He turned and stared at her. "But it did. Trusts were broken. Perceptions were twisted. People were hurt. Shit keeps happening, Ivana."

Zoë froze at his words. It only took him a second to realize he'd called her the wrong name, too.

Clearing his throat, he got in and started the truck. "Let's go get some proof, and maybe we'll have a leg to stand on to convince the Green Girls to stand down."

Driving down the highway, Zoë kept her eyes on the road as Tristan drove. His bright, reflective eyes flashed against traffic headlights. They drove in silence for a bit, but in that quiet, a small tension was brewing between them.

She had not addressed his outburst of calling her the name of the assassinated vampire. He had seemed very protective of her at Jay's, and there was a level of fascination that a vampire could love or care about another. Were they lovers? They had to be for him to care so deeply, but if so, why did he call her that name?

"Were you in love with her?"

Tristan glanced over, knowing exactly who she was referring to.

"Who?" he asked flatly.

Zoë peered over to him. "The assassinated vampire who you were charged to protect. Ivana."

Tristan sighed. "Why do you care?"

Zoë shifted in her seat. *I don't know.* "She's the reason why you got involved in all of this. I thought—"

"I never touched her," Tristan said quietly. "She was Javen's consort, and I respected that."

He had to admit, there were times he'd wanted to break that rule, and even more times he wondered if he loved Ivana as well. She was brave, kind, and a stubborn crusader. She made him want to believe in a better world, and that sort of influence was bewitching.

His wife, Katya had that same effect on him, but in the end, he always came to the same conclusion. "And the answer is no. I didn't love her. But I loved the idea of her. Of what she stood for. All she wanted was peace, and she died because of it."

"Do I remind you of her?"

Tristan shook his head, trying to knock both of their faces out of his mind. "Perhaps. At that moment, you did. Just not for the reasons you may think."

Zoë didn't press further, but saw the struggle in his eyes. His sincerity intrigued her just as much as the idea of him avenging a consort that wasn't even his.

He turned down the road to pull into a parking garage. Pulling into a spot, they quickly stepped out when Zoë caught him glaring at her.

"What?"

"I know this is New Orleans and all, but can't you do something about your sword? We're going amongst humans, and the word of the day is inconspicuous."

Zoë straightened up, crossing her arms. "I'm not going anywhere without it. End of story."

He gave her the evil eye.

And she gave one back. "Relax. They won't see it."

Tristan stared at the handle of the blade behind her as he slammed the truck door. She seemed confident, and he wasn't in the mood to fight.

"Fine. Just make sure they don't. Not much we can solve if we're running from the cops."

The streets of the Quarter were packed as usual. Tons of faceless, nameless patrons occupied the sidewalks and streets. Now, they were among them, blending into the sea of human and unsuspecting others that hunted tonight.

Side by side, Tristan and Zoë walked to the bar to meet Dashiell. Both of their cautious eyes looked around them, anticipating anything to come at them. Tristan was a target now, and it was only a matter of time before a supernatural saw him and either snitched his whereabouts or engaged them.

Zoë tightened her grip on the dagger riding on her hip as she thought of someone daring to approach them.

Just let them try.

Tristan slipped past a crowd of festive people. The scent of food and alcohol was strong on them. And blood. Another vampire slipped past them, following the human herd instead of either of them. Tristan cut his eyes to Zoë.

"Can you pass for vampire?"

Zoë smiled, her fangs receding. "And human, apparently. Isn't that what you thought I was at first?" She cut her violet eyes to him that slowly turned hazel. "A blood-bag stripper, was it?"

The corners of Tristan's mouth threatened to curve, but not

quite. "More or less. The jury's still out on that if I'm being totally honest."

"I wouldn't be much use to the cause if I couldn't blend in or infiltrate my prey, now could I?" She walked ahead of him, ignoring blatant cat calls from a few men on the sidewalk. She was anxious to hunt, but not the human flavor. Yes, she was thinking something more of the soulless kind.

Tristan crossed the pedestrian-filled street, watching her follow him, then finally catching up. There was far too little he knew about Black Blood Slayers. They were part myth, part horror story to vampires. However, he didn't doubt her for a second. There was a reason whole breeds disappeared without a trace, or other demons that managed to break free onto this plane, only to suddenly vanish.

It was common to blame the humans or other supernaturals to have been responsible, but, in reality, the older vampires knew better. The Divine's breed of Fallen were pest control, and supernaturals were the pests.

"So what kind of powers does a Black Blood Slayer possess besides seducing and killing vampires?" Tristan asked, watching the determination in her steps and the men who couldn't take their eyes off her.

So much for inconspicuous.

Zoë suddenly possessed a confident smirk. "A Fallen never tells. Besides, most of my other powers are triggered by fight or flight, unless..."

"Unless what?"

She clenched her dagger tighter. "I lose control of my beast." It was a long time since that had been a risk, but the predicament she found herself in now made it as big a possibility as ever. The beast within her would want blood. Lots of it. The darkness within her would call for it, and no soulless would be able to resist her. Not even her brave, brooding vampire beside her. "If that happens...let's just say, you shouldn't be near me."

She continued walking, and Tristan nodded.

Meaning I would have to put a bullet in her. Or sixty.

"Duly noted. Listen, Dashiell has no idea you are part of the package, so I need you to be whatever he thinks you are. He'll most likely think you're a vampire, so go with it."

"I don't get it. I thought this was someone you trust?"

"Trust is overrated. I need to find out what he knows first. Besides, no one should know what you really are in that bar. You'll spread panic. Maybe even to Dashiell, and he's the only ally I have right now."

Zoë rolled her eyes. A brooding, friendless, warrior vampire. Just perfect. "Lucky me, I get bound to a vampire who doesn't have any fucking friends. Guess that charm of yours isn't as alluring as you think."

Tristan scoffed at her sarcasm. "I wouldn't say that. It apparently got you chained half-naked to my bed ready to fuck my brains out."

She sneered at his accusation. Sure, it was true. She *did* want to fuck his brains out. From the moment she had first locked eyes with him, that's what her body had wanted. That's how it always started. Then, like a venomous black widow, she would've drained him dry. *If* he was lucky.

"That only would've been a short...very short interlude to the main event. *Trust me.*"

As they approached the entrance of Patsey's, Zoë frowned as the bouncer held his hand to block her from entering as she attempted to pass. Tristan stood behind her, watching the tall, tattooed male shake his head at Zoë. He had a grim reaper image crowning his clean-shaven head. His bright eyes shone through his contacts.

"Hey, you can't enter with—"

He stopped in mid-sentence as he stared into Zoë's eyes which held her natural violet hue. The air around them seemed to hum and snap with energy and the vampire bouncer suddenly couldn't remember his last thought. He blinked and finally waved her in.

Zoë turned around and inclined her head, signaling Tristan to follow her in. A bit dumbfounded, he walked in, eyeing the bouncer suspiciously. However, he just looked annoyed as he had before they approached him.

The music inside blared with many humans drinking, smoking, and having fun along with the vampires who watched them like lions ready to pick off a zebra from the herd. He pulled up a seat at a table and kicked one out for Zoë.

But she didn't sit. Instead, she stood there staring, watching the meat market display. These humans were here to have a good time. They didn't expect to be some vampire's dinner. Or plaything. A low growl rumbled in her throat.

Tristan shook his head at her. "Sit down. This is not what we're here for."

She turned her head briefly at his command. "Fuck you, vampire. This is what I was *created* for."

Tristan rubbed his neck. The protector was in her bones. There was no stopping it, and trying to tame her was a fool's challenge, but she couldn't start a killing scene in here. Not without alerting everyone what she was and putting all the patrons in a panic. They'd come too far.

"Do you want to find Remelia or not?" he simply asked. "Do you?"

At the mention of the Supreme's name, Zoë shifted her focus away from the unsuspecting vampires. She felt her resolve soften as she thought about his question. "I do."

"Good. Well, don't piss it all away to start any shit in here. We're here to stop something bigger. Don't forget that."

Her teeth clenched to the point of aching thinking of another life taken by some smug fucking parasite. Anger in her muscles, she finally sat and pulled her chair close to the table so he could hear her. "This isn't right. You can't expect to just sit here and—"

"I don't." Tristan stared into her hazel eyes that were a lie. He found himself preferring her purple gems. Even when they glared at him with conviction. "Just long enough for us to talk with Dashiell and get some information." Tristan propped his feet on the table. "Then you can do what you wish to them."

Zoë's eyes widened in surprise at his remark. She didn't expect such a thing to ever come from a vampire's lips. "You aren't going to stop me?"

Tristan shrugged. Mr. Darkness must make a visit every night. Perhaps he was truly waiting on Ms. Darkness to bring the death. "If things get too bloody, I might. But a charmer like you probably wouldn't need to make things bloody, I imagine. One battle at a time. I know it's in your nature to hunt my kind. I understand it. But just like everything else, there must be rules." He crossed his arms. "Though, I will say, you're a bit of a hypocrite."

She grimaced. "Why am I a hypocrite?"

"I've seen you battle sickness and pain to fight your nature since you've met me. Must be torture. I bet all you want is to let go and do what you were, as you stated earlier, 'created to do.'"

Tristan looked around, and then focused on her. "I'm proving to be tolerant of your nature to hunt vampires, yet clearly you share no tolerance for us giving in to our nature. To hunt, to feed."

Zoë sat back with a smirk. "What? I'm supposed to just let vamps eat every human they can get their grubby little hands on to be tolerant of your need to kill, hunt, and feed? I couldn't care less that feeding from humans is in your nature. That's the difference between predator..." she pointed at herself then to him "...and prey. As a predator, I don't have to allow you to do *anything*." She leaned forward. "I can just *take* what I want."

Tristan smiled, realizing she just validated his sentiment as a vampire. "Exactly."

Zoë's smirk dissolved as it clicked to her, but the thought was short-lived as a tall, dark-haired vampire in all black came up behind Tristan and placed a hand on his shoulder. His eyes lingered over her for a moment.

"What the hell? You're entertaining company at a time like this?" Dashiell asked in a piss-poor whisper.

NATURE OF THE BEAST

*T*ristan caught the hand by reflex and turned to see Dashiell standing there. "Glad to see you could make it. I don't understand how you're always late for everything."

Dashiell popped his gum. "It takes practice, Tristan. Practice. At least I'm not the one on the most wanted list. Besides, I had to deal with some Green Girls prowling around like renegades. Apparently, some have it in for some poor vamp bastard. I'm thinking you."

Tristan grumbled. "Who knew I'd ever become so fucking popular."

" I certainly didn't." As Dashiell pulled up a chair on the edge between Tristan and Zoë, he looked at her as if she were on the menu in this very low-key meat market. "And who's this?"

Tristan frowned, waving dismissively. "She's a friend."

"Actually, I was just leaving." Zoë offered a smile that had Dashiell returning a heated gaze. She caught herself before she rolled her eyes at his ogling. Sometimes she wished she could turn it off. Especially when it came to situations like this.

Both of them there within her grasp was far too tempting, along with the other vampires there hunting for food. She greatly misjudged her ability for restraint, and if she didn't get away, that control she talked about earlier would finally snap.

Ugh. Fuck my life.

She had no intentions of attracting or eating his friend. Not unless he deserved it. The scent from this one's blood was lighter, his essence weaker, like a passing fancy. *Like chocolate—probably dark and sweet for only a moment, then gone forever.*

Dashiell must've been a much younger vampire. Not weathered and seasoned like...

"Tristan."

She finally said his name, letting it linger on her mouth as she began to stand up while Tristan and Dashiell watched her. The name suited him, and she liked it.

Leaning over the table, her eyes locked on Tristan in a way that made him hungry for her. Her look felt like the kiss they shared when he first saw her in chains, dark, demanding, and seductive.

Zoë stared at his lips, inches away. "I'm going...*hunting.* I'll leave you two to talk." Straightening her body, she turned and walked towards the back exit. Watching her walk way, alarm tensed Tristan's body, but she couldn't leave, and she couldn't go far. At least, not without him.

Dashiell leaned back in his chair. "Whoa. She's interesting. You say she's a friend?"

Tristan didn't respond yet. He just watched Zoë whisper into the ear of another, unsuspecting male vampire who, within seconds, followed behind her like a lost puppy. Then Z urged a young female vampire to join him. Z's purple hair and plaid skirt both swayed in the wind as they quietly walked out the back exit.

Hunting, indeed. She was the pied piper of vampires, leading them off to their death with a nice ass and a come-hither look. At least she wasn't tearing up the place, but it proved a point her ally made to him in that basement.

Jay had been right. There was nothing emotional about her

whatsoever. She was a machine designed to do one thing: thin the herd of vampires.

Tristan cleared his throat, still eyeing the door. "Yeah. Something like that." He finally turned to Dashiell. "Look, the witches think I had something to do with their Supreme's disappearance. They came after me earlier. What the fuck is going on?"

"It's fucking bedlam out here, Tris, that's what's going on. The attack has gotten all the vampires in a fucking tizzy, and everyone's ready to fight. Javen told everyone what happened, and all bets are off, man. Now I'm out looking everywhere for Christophe, and no one's seen him." His face went stoic. "Suspicions are everywhere now. Especially on Christophe."

"He's been MIA since the attack. You think the Green Girls are looking for him too?" Tristan asked.

Dashiell scoffed. "Who the hell knows? Those bitches are looking for any lead that will take them to their Supreme. They couldn't care less. For all we know, they killed Christophe and have their eyes set on you now."

"Somehow I doubt that. They would've said they had another vampire in their grasp. If anything they could use it to work me into a rage."

No, the witches had their sight on him specifically. They were hunting him, not picking random vampires off the street.

Dashiell crossed his arms, surprise evident in his bright eyes. "They *spoke* to you? What did they say?"

"That they wanted to know the whereabouts of Remelia. And that someone told them I had something to do with it." He looked into Dashiell's eyes. "Has anyone seen her that you know of?"

Dashiell spat out his gum across the room, admiring the arc before the white clump hit the floor. "Yeah, right. No one's seen their Queen Bitch. And we have our own drama to deal with. Who cares if the Green Girls lost their leader?"

"Don't you find it odd that Remelia disappeared roughly around the same time as Ivana's attack? That couldn't be coincidence, Dashiell. We know that The Three sent me and Greg after the grimoire around that time as well. You're telling me that Remelia turning up missing just in time for me to cop the witch's book, then find myself in an ambush where Green Girls were responsible is just a fucking fluke?"

"I didn't say that."

"Good. You're not a total asshole."

Kicking Zoë's former chair, Dashiell shot up, glaring at Tristan. "Instead of insulting me, dickhead, why don't you just say the lunacy you're thinking out loud! Just fucking say it."

A petite waitress approached them with her tray tucked under her arm. Her worried eyes darted between both men as if anticipating a punch to whip out from either of them. "Is everything okay, guys? Drinks?"

Dashiell took a breath, then briefly looked at the waitress. "No, we're good. My friend was just about to tell me a joke."

With a nervous laugh, the poor waitress backed away, "Okay. Just let me know if you need anything." Quickly, she made her way over to another table, which seemed to have more cordial people there.

Tristan stood up and met his eyes squarely. Without the whereabouts nor confirmation on Christophe's allegiance, Dashiell was his only ally in this major shitstorm. He needed Dashiell to believe him.

"Fine. The Three are in on *all* of this, Dashiell. I know they are."

Dashiell shook his head and sighed. "Tristan..."

"No, I asked you to come here because I need you to listen to me about this. You need to hear it. Ivana's death was a setup. It was designed for The Three to point fingers at their enemies. Think about it. No one knew about our whereabouts except us and The Three, yet we get ambushed. Christophe disappears, then Green Girls and Were-shifters get blamed for Ivana's death?

You can't stand here and tell me something doesn't stink, Dashiell. I trained you too well."

Dashiell slowly sat back down and waited for Tristan to sit back down next to him. A beat or two passed. Then finally, "Okay, I'm listening."

"Takeshi had a body of a witch and a wolf shifter, but that wasn't them shooting at us, Dashiell. It was our own. Vampires killed Ivana and made it look like the Green Girls and the Were-shifters were responsible for her death."

"Why would they kill Ivana? She had no power like The Three."

"They needed a martyr, and she was a threat."

"What do you mean?"

"When I talked to Ivana, she told me that she was in talks with making peaceful negotiations with Remelia when she disappeared. Remelia wanted peace, too. The reason The Three were brought to power was because of the wars. What would become of them if the wars stopped? If the Were-shifters, witches, and vamps made peace? Where would they be in this new world? They couldn't just tell the vampires to attack. They needed something caustic to make the vamps get behind them. Everyone loved Ivana. She was the vampires' poster girl for peace."

"How else to light a fuse for war other than kill a symbol for peace?" Dashiell replied, staring at the table. With a deep sigh, he looked up at Tristan. "This is insane, Tristan. You know that, right?" He leaned in closer and lowered his voice. "You're saying that Javen had his own companion murdered. That he and the others *allowed* it to happen. And not only that, but they framed the Green Girls and biters?"

Tristan nodded.

Dashiell exhaled slowly and popped a new piece of gum in his mouth. "This is some hairy shit. Do we have any proof?"

"Takeshi likely destroyed the bodies of the vampires I killed during the attack; that was my concrete evidence."

"You think Christophe was in on it?"

"It's possible. Like you said, he's been gone and no one's seen him. If we find him, he may know something. Someone there killed Ivana. Found her and brutally killed her. I aim to find who did it and make them pay."

"I don't want to think of Christophe killing Ivana. That's too dark. Even for me, Tristan."

Tristan ran his fingers through his hair. He tried not to consider the possibility either. Christophe had his own rules, but he proved to be trusting. But he was the only one who no one knew where he'd gone.

Was he in on it? Or did he know who was? Either way, Tristan needed to find the Templar vampire before The Three did. If the vamp was still alive, that was.

"We need to find him before The Three find him. He may be the evidence we need," Tristan said.

"Ivana's funeral is tomorrow night."

"I know."

"Guess I also don't need to tell you that The Three don't trust you now any more than you trust them."

"Glad we're mutual on something."

"I'm serious, Tristan. Don't attend. I believe you, okay? I can help you track down Christophe when I can, but as your friend, stay away."

"That's real sweet, Dashiell, but I'm not under The Three's thumbs anymore. No offense. I do what I damn well please. If they want to accuse me of something, they can have it. Cause so will I."

Dashiell put his hand up to block Tristan. His hazel eyes glared in warning. "Fine. Then as *Commander*, I'll warn you again. If you approach The Three tomorrow, you'll put me in a position to put you down. Don't force me into that position, Tris."

Their staring showdown suddenly paused as Tristan watched Dashiell's eyes shift past him to the bar's entrance.

Tristan only had a second before he ducked as the spraying sound of bullets fired through the bar.

ZOË STILL HELD the vampire's hand as they made out against the wall. The female's lips were sweet, but she was a bit too slender for Zoë's personal taste.

The tall, blond biker vampire leaned back against the dumpster and watched them. His eyes were black, but held every possible twinkle of lust in them. He was consumed by it. Consumed by her.

She wanted him to watch, and when they were this enthralled, all they could do was what they were told. The blonde was straining against his jeans, eagerly watching as the petite, purple-haired vampire slid her tongue into Zoë's mouth with a moan, and when Zoë took a hand and lifted her little plaid skirt to show the biker his little cupcake was commando, Zoë swore she heard the guy whimper.

She sighed. It was pathetic how oblivious they were sometimes. Did many of them think they were the supreme rulers of the night? Seriously?

The vampires recruited on a lie. Be superhuman, hunt the weak, kill your enemies, and never grow old. The dominant paranormal race, yada yada yada.

What they failed to mention was that another beast lurked in the night, and it also hunted the weak. Speaking of weak, Zoë couldn't even taste the years on this one. Far too young a vampire. Zoë wouldn't have been surprised if she was turned within the year.

She could've had another life—a better one. Yet here she was in an alley, tasting death.

Moving to the female's throat, she felt her fangs descend further as well as her bottom canines. The slow fire that burned within her was desperate to be sated. With a breath, she sank her teeth into the female's throat and she responded with a hiss.

With her free hands, the young vampire caressed the back of Zoë's head tenderly as she reveled in the dark kiss.

Zoë growled at the first real taste of vampire blood from a hunt in who knew how long. The thick elixir was chilled refreshment on a busy night, and as she drank, her eyes captured the biker, using her free hand to crook a finger, calling him over.

Eagerly, he trudged forward to them until he pressed behind the little cupcake vampire with feverish desire. His fangs extended and he kissed one side of her neck as Zoë drank from the other.

Finding it was now time to bid them goodnight, Zoë slipped around to behind the biker, making him the meat in this blood-sucking sandwich. Her hands roamed his muscled torso, up to his neck. She grabbed a handful of his hair and yanked him back.

The biker released the cupcake with a sensual hiss as Zoë whispered into his ear, "My turn."

No longer holding back the facade, she sank her teeth into his throat as he growled through gritted teeth. Now, this one was more like it. He had a bit more age on him, perhaps a century, maybe more. Unable to hold back, she pulled in greedily, not even hearing the cupcake scream as blood oozed from his ripped, open jugular as he dropped to his knees.

As the cupcake vampire backed away, Zoë wiped her bloody mouth with the back of her hand. In fact, as Zoë closed in on her, it was another sound that caught her attention. Several, actually...

Gunshots. A *lot* of them.

Both Zoë and the vampire froze and turned to the exit door.

Shit. What the hell was Tristan up to now?

Witches? She smelled the air and sighed. Nope, far worse. "Were-shifters!"

She quickly unsheathed her sword, and as her eyes changed

back to violet, she glared at the fearful cupcake vampire. She got to live another night.

Zoë raised her sword to her in warning, the tip pointing to the bite marks on her neck. "Pray you never lay eyes on me again, vampire. I'll be the last thing you see. Ever."

Turning towards the sounds of gunfire in the bar, Zoë quickly beheaded the nearly drained biker on his knees and was through the door before his body dropped onto the concrete.

TRISTAN FLEW over the table as the Were-shifter assaulted the bar with rapid fire rounds, and he wasn't alone. Three more walked in seconds before the gunfire started.

The area filled with screams, broken glass, and falling bodies as the clash of Were-shifters, vampires, and humans erupted into pure chaos. Trying to quickly get his bearings, Tristan pulled his body tight against the back of the table and pulled his gun. These shifters weren't looking to chat. They were on a search and destroy mission, and it didn't take a rocket scientist to figure out who they were searching for.

Looking around, he barely saw Dashiell in the swarm of people running around in a frantic spell, but just like that, he was a ghost.

Tristan looked down and sighed. He missed his other gun. Were-shifters needed high caliber rounds, and lots of them if you didn't get them in the head. Then again, poor shots didn't last long. And if they bit a vampire, the toxins in their saliva would make the vamp wish they were dead. It caused insanity and the bleeds. Not the way Tristan was planning to go.

Cocking his gun, he leaned down, pressing his belly to the floor. He popped a few shots at the Were-shifter's feet closest to him, taking one down. The blonde shifter growled and yelled, dropping to the floor.

"You blood-sucking piece of shit!" he yelled.

It was all he said after Tristan stood up and locked a headshot on him. He pulled the trigger; suddenly, the Were-shifter on the floor didn't have much of a face.

Aiming at another, he fired, but not until he felt the piercing pain from three bullets. The close quarters of the inside of the bar combined with the sounds of chaos about him had hindered his ability to avert any wayward shots, and he was feeling the pain. The third shifter had slipped past his field of view, enough to clip him in the shoulder and his stomach.

The silver set fire to his veins.

Yelling through clenched teeth, Tristan fired at the sneaky shifter but missed, only grazing her face. In a couple of bounds, the shifter ran on all fours and leapt onto him as he ran out of ammo.

Anticipating her attack, Tristan pulled a chair and knocked her across the room with it. Trying to load his weapon, he under-estimated her rebound time. Tristan yelled as the Were-bitch suddenly bit into his arm before Tristan kicked her away.

Aiming his gun, a flash of light quickly moved past him and the Were-bitch's head fell from her body. His eyes adjusted to Zoë shaking the blood off her blade.

With escalated anger, the leader shifter continued to shoot into the bar, though now most were gone or dead. With a growl, he aimed fire at Zoë, who kicked a five-foot long table at them, knocking them back.

She sheathed her sword. With determined steps, Tristan watched her face turn completely black, her violet eyes glaring at them. The haunting image was the last thing he saw before he collapsed.

Before the leader shifter could move, she was on him. Her hands wrapped around his throat, lifting the Were nearly a foot off the ground. The other shifters tried to aim their guns, but a wave of energy washed against them, and they stood quietly, staring at their leader who struggled against her hold. Enthrall-ment kept them from running, and they lowered their weapons.

"So obedient," Zoë voiced with a dark, demonic tone. "I can appreciate that in your species, Shifter." Her eyes narrowed. "I take it you're the smart one and thereby know what I am, yes?"

Everett stared into her devilish, purple eyes and nodded. He clawed at her hand as she tsked him. "Wait!" he choked out with his Balkan accent. "We aren't here for any humans!"

"I don't give a shit," she replied, shaking him. Were-shifters were always more balls than brains in her experience. Otto let his people run around like lost mongrels half the time until, of course, a chunk of them wound up dead. They had a lot to learn about hunting in the human world.

"You must have gone rabid, coming in here where there are humans present and fostering an attack on the vampires. Who are you looking for? " Zoë's face slowly turned to her normal complexion. She wanted to know the truth. "Who?"

Everett shook his head. "No one! We deserve retribution over our fallen people at the hands of vampers! That's all. We only wanted to chase out the vampires. Otto demanded it."

"Where's Otto now?"

Everett was silent.

Zoë brought him closer to her. A low growl in her throat. "The human authorities will be here soon, but that will not stop me from turning you and the others into unrecognizable pieces of meat. Do you understand? Now, where is he?"

"He's in Metairie planning a strike. 5905 Pike Drive. Please!"

Zoë's thinking was caught off guard hearing Tristan groan behind the table. She returned to Everett and the sound of sirens. Time wasn't on their side. "Take us there. Now."

With a quick nod, Everett agreed as she lowered him. "Okay." He pointed to the back exit. "This way!"

Zoë relaxed her body enough to ease the hold of her enthrall-ment over the others. "You assholes cover us," she demanded, eyeing them both. They nodded and picked up their guns, and Zoë moved over to Tristan. She froze for a second, not realizing the trouble he was in.

She lowered herself to examine him, but it was hard to see through the blood. "Tristan..." she called to him, as his eyes were barely open. Cradling his head, she called again, moving the bloody hair from his face. "Tristan?"

He had lost so much blood. Where was it all coming from? The faint scent of burning flesh wafted into her nose as the silver ate into his body. She didn't have time to dig them all out. They had to move fast.

"Katya," Tristan answered. "You shouldn't be here. I told you, it's too dangerous." He coughed and retched, spitting out more blood.

"Shit." Zoë steadied him long enough to see the large bite mark on his forearm with scarlet streaks. He was infected.

Shifter bites were nasty infections to vampires, causing madness and sickness. It wouldn't be long until he succumbed to it. Then, he would have to be put down.

"Come on vamper. You're not dead yet."

Zoë lifted his arm behind her neck, despite his growl of pain. She helped him up and quickly moved to the exit with him in tow.

TEMPTING DARKNESS

The voices called to him through the shadows, first soft, then loud and distorted. Master Darkness was coming for him. He could feel it this time. The desperation. The pain. It wouldn't be long now.

High-tailing out of the realm of humans and cops, Everett drove on as Zoë cradled Tristan's head in her lap. She watched him shiver, shake, and bleed.

As if it were even possible, his head was warm. Brain fever was going to set in soon, and then it would be too late.

She looked up at the Were-shifters in front yelling at each other in what sounded like Albanian. "You need to hurry up, or he's not going to make it."

"Not our problem. The fever's got him now. He's lucky he didn't get eaten. Lousy blood-sucker. " His words paused as he felt the cold metal of a gun barrel press against the back of his head. The others watched with wide eyes. Their teeth bared in a growl, she cocked the gun and they went silent.

"It is your problem if he dies. He can help Otto destroy The Three. Step on it."

Everett pinned the pedal and began to dodge traffic to keep up.

Tristan opened his eyes to view the night in a red hue. The voices were distorted, but soft, as if they were whispering in his ear. But as he saw the distressed face of Zoë, he realized she wasn't whispering. She was shouting. Her mouth was wide and angry, but no sound of her voice. No. The distorted whisper came from someone else…

Listen.

Closer.

Tristan shivered as Katya looked down at him with ruby red eyes. Someone had walked over his grave. Then the voice in his ear finally became crystal clear.

"What would you be willing to give if I could grant you the vengeance you desire?"

No!

Zoë looked down at Tristan struggling, writhing as his eyes stared up at her, looking at her as if she was death.

"Tristan! Can you hear me?" She gently shook him again, then looked at the silver and orange horizon in the east. Dawn was approaching.

Swearing under her breath, she clenched the Were-shifter's shirt. "How far to Otto's, wolf? Tell me how far!"

"Another twenty minutes, give or take!"

He wasn't going to make it. "Change of plans, we need a den. What's nearby? Quick!"

Tyler looked it up on his phone the location of the nearest flagged den. "There's one five miles up the road!"

Zoë laid Tristan down and looked around in the back. It would be remiss if Were-shifters didn't have at least one black body bag or trash bag. Anything to hide body parts on the fly. Of course, she'd managed to ride with the most incompetent Were kill squad ever.

"I need something to shield him till I get him inside."

They looked at her as if she were insane.

She pulled the coat off Tristan and threw it over his face as he mumbled incoherently. She looked at the burley shifter in the other seat. "You! Take off that jacket!"

He quickly took it off and she snatched it. She laid it on his lower half. The sun was rising with each passing minute and in his state, significant exposure would kill him.

As they approached a dirt driveway leading to a secluded two-story wood home, Zoë got ready to act fast.

"Get us as close to the front door as you can." Slamming the brakes, Everett stopped just short of the steps. Zoë hopped out and grabbed Tristan under the shoulders, dragging him out. "Help me get his feet."

Rafe shook his head. "No. He killed Bronwyn. I will not help my enemy."

Zoë glared at him, but he stayed put.

"You can kill me if you want, Black Blood, but I will not lift a finger to save him. Vampires are the violators here, yet you're helping them?"

She was getting tired of having to explain their arrangement to the likes of other supernaturals. "You will not sit there smugly while the humans are back there cleaning up your mess! An aimless killing spree that did more harm than good, and for what?"

Oh, they'd better believe Otto was going to pay for such sloppiness and hubris. But first thing first: save the vampire.

Everett and the other shifter remained quiet while Rafe got down as the sun peeked through the trees. He grabbed Tristan's legs and helped her carry him inside. As soon as they were inside, Rafe quickly released him with disgust and turned to leave.

Zoë stood up, eyeing him with daggers. "Tell Otto that I expect him here. Tonight. No tricks. We have information and need to speak about The Three."

"I'm sure he'll have some questions for both you and the

blood-sucker. Granted he even makes it through." He walked out as Zoë kicked the door shut.

Without another moment to waste, Zoë ran and pulled all the shutters and blackout curtains closed and ran back to the mumbling Tristan lying on the hardwood floor. He was a bloody mess. His hair was glossy with the thick crimson, and she barely recognized his face. His blood ran like tears from his eyes and mouth, and it was too hard for Zoë to ignore.

Tristan looked to his right, away from her. "I'm in hell, my love."

Zoë shook her head. "That's just the fever."

"Hell is when you must relive your mistakes day after day, forever. As if forever was something one could escape." He coughed up blood. "Death eludes the proud on purpose. Instead, you took Ivana. You took my Katya. You took my asshole partner, Greg."

Standing over him, she realized he wasn't talking or looking at her. Tristan was speaking to someone else in the corner. He was already hallucinating.

She ran to the kitchen and pulled at all the drawers until she found a towel. Running it under the faucet, she saturated the towel and ran back to him. She didn't know if it was his vulnerability or what, but he smelled delicious. It made her think of all the ways he could sate her. It made it even that much harder to do what she had to do.

And keep her shit together while doing it.

Removing some of the temptation would be a start.

At the same time, a million different reasons flew into her mind about how everything would be so much easier with him gone, and the fact that everything that could've gone wrong tonight had didn't help.

Especially with his precious blood all over the place. Her stomach growled and cramped. 'Challenge' wasn't a strong enough word for this, and it was like that biker vampire was just an appetizer in comparison. Why did she crave him so badly?

She began to wipe his face and mouth, finding herself staring at it. "Tristan. Do you enjoy killing?"

He closed his eyes. He needed a break from the beast staring at him, the dark shadow that seduced him into this curse so long ago. It watched and taunted him for being a fool. It knew his secrets. It fed on his misery.

On that night four hundred years ago, he traded his chance to be joined with his wife and child to avenge their deaths. He could still feel the blood of their killers on his face, on his tongue. But the beast who bargained with him never told him the high from such vengeance was only a moment, nowhere near enough to fill the hole of his loss.

He sighed. "No. Who does? I kill out of necessity. Always have."

Even then, he was haunted by the memories of the battlefield. His own wisdom tormented him. *A victory today is funeral pyres for the enemy tomorrow.*

"And everyone's needs are different." None of it mattered. His arm throbbed, and the heat radiated through his body. Growling, he shifted. "Why are you tormenting me over a stupid question?"

Straddling him, she pulled off her jacket and threw it to the side, then peeled off her tee, revealing her bare torso with the gentle bounce of her breasts. She pulled his head toward her, trying to get him to focus.

The blur in his eyes registered only a silhouette of her soft, nude breasts. He squinted them shut, mixing the image of her and the beast. "What is happening to me?"

"Tristan, listen to me. You have to feed from me or the infection is going to drive you mad. This is the only way I know how to draw out the toxins. My blood is immune. You'll need to feed."

Tristan stared at Greg who stared back at him behind Zoë. He looked angry. The ghosts in his mind wanted to play. Perhaps it was time to let them run free.

"Master Darkness is calling my name, vampire killer... he calls...he waits..."

She shook him gently, making him focus again on her. When he finally locked his gaze with hers, she held on and didn't let go. There was something beautiful and broken in his hazel eyes. Vulnerable.

Weakness never turned her on, but this was different. It was as if there were a glimpse of a soul there. Dark and painful, but every bit as strong. Vampires didn't have that kind of humanity within them. They were cold as death and impulsively violent. This was strangely new and arousing. A throb between her legs began to ache as desire grew within her at an alarming pace.

"He doesn't want you, vampire," she purred. She wiped the blood from his eyes, while pulling her thumb into her mouth. The contact of his blood to her tongue felt like licking a battery. "But *I* do." Her enthrallment clawed deep inside him, enough to calm him towards her throat. She dragged her nails along the line of her neck, and Tristan gasped at the dark, thick, black blood trail down in delightful temptation.

Her scent enticed him. Even as the dead haunted him behind her eyes, the pull to her was sobering. Attraction was magnetic. He would've embraced death more fondly if he'd known earlier that Master Darkness had a mistress. An untamed beauty of frightening proportions.

Tristan's eyes followed the line of blood as it trailed down the valley of her perfect breasts, gently flowing along the honeyed curve, forcing his cock to harden as his eyes watched the smooth skin of her areola pucker around her erect nipple. It begged to be tasted.

Claimed.

His hand reached out and held her face as he pulled her closer with a force and quickness that surprised her. She hissed as he ran his tongue over her flesh to catch the tempting trail of black blood. Slowly, his tongue licked up between her valley, across her sensitive nipple and up the hollow of her throat.

A foreign shiver ran through her at the sensation of his touch on her skin. It flowed directly to her core that already ached for him. Her resistance already ran her hot like an engine. Then, finally, she closed her eyes as he sank his teeth into her throat.

She had a pulse like a human, and the hypnotic rhythm drove him even further from sanity. Her warm blood flowed into his mouth and began to beat away the agony of the shifter bite.

"More," she whispered as he drank.

His lips were soft against her flesh as he sucked. He was lost to the bliss of such fire in his veins, and his other hand curved around her waist, pulling her closer against him. Her breasts flush to his chest as she sat almost grinding against his already steel erection straining in his pants was too much to bear. He crushed her against him and he swore he heard her moan.

Her fingers raked up from the nape of his neck and through his hair. Her touch was dangerous, urging. Mistress Darkness wanted to claim someone tonight, but he wanted to claim her first.

Her fangs extended in the promise of his blood, and her body begged for a taste of him. *Just a little,* she soothed to herself. *Enough to take the edge off while he fed.*

Tristan pushed himself away, panting. He ran his tongue across his lips, tasting the last of her precious blood. Watching the puncture wounds close and heal, hunger still lingered in his eyes. As he leaned toward her, Zoë backed away, trying to put some distance.

"Don't," she warned. "Your blood calls to me like the hounds of hell, vampire."

She trailed a finger down his throat, down his torso where his blood-stained shirt clung to his chest.

"Tristan..." She was now horny as hell, and he'd become her

favorite torment. He was both the carrot and the stick. "In fact, if I wasn't so hell-bent on proving that I had some self-control, you'd be either in unfathomable pain or abysmal pleasure. I haven't decided yet."

He didn't remember how she'd finally learned it, but he loved the way his name sounded in her mouth. Her sultry voice captured it, toying with the syllables against her full lips. The tone chased away the distorted voices that taunted him.

There was nothing safe about being in the arms of a Black Blood Slayer. Not for a vampire, and, yet, with his sanity and resolve being stacked from one risk to another, dying either beneath or on top of her seemed to make all the sense in the world if Master Darkness wanted him tonight. If a shifter bite wasn't going to take him, surely Zoë would.

"I think you'd already made that decision when you brought me here, Zoë. Why are you so determined to save me? You have no idea what I've done."

"I don't know. Perhaps I want you all to myself. Maybe I want to choose how you die, vampire."

Tristan leaned closer, looking her over. "I make no fantasies about what it is you really want from me. I'm barely coherent enough to stand, but if I'm dying, then here's what I want from you." He gripped her wrist and jerked her toward him.

Zoë grabbed his shirt, leaned in and kissed him. Her mouth passionately ravished his, letting a soft moan escape as she felt his tongue stroke against her fang as she nicked him.

Just a little taste...To calm me.

Oh, her body roared at the heady taste of him. This was much more potent than mere chocolate. Far more than a passing fancy. With the way it heated her bones and rocked her core, she felt his blood could sate the appetite of a hundred Fallen.

She was a liar. Zoë wanted much more than a taste.

"More." She ripped at his shirt, ignoring the buttons that flew off as she stripped him of anything barring her gaze of his flesh. Their lips barely broke union as she helped him pull off his shirt.

Tossing it aside, his hand cupped her breast, teasing it with his thumb as she moaned into his mouth. She leaned forward to unbuckle his pants when he rolled her over onto her back.

After she kicked off her boots, Zoe felt him grip the edges of her jeans and tugged them as she slightly lifted her hips to the sky. All that was left was thin, lacy panties that reminded him of the pair he'd first seen her in. The tension between them turned into a dark lust that would damn them both, but neither of them cared.

Tristan kneeled between her silken thighs, ready to worship her, but first, he needed to see the altar.

"Take them off for me," he commanded in his deep, husky tone. His gaze was forceful, ready, and his bold command made her wet and anxious.

Slipping her thumbs inside the hems of her thong, she gently and slowly slid them until they were past her ankles. Bending her knees, she parted her legs in invitation, all the while eyeing Tristan. Even as her hand lowered to stroke her drenched folds, Zoë crooked another finger as he positioned himself between those thighs and reclaimed her lips.

Within seconds, she unbuckled and pushed his pants down, finally freeing him. Almost purring, she wrapped her fingers around him and gently stroked.

He hissed at the seductive feel of her hands on him. He pulled back. Nudging her legs further apart, he lifted her hips onto his lap, and with full force, Tristan slid into her—deep.

Her tight walls contracted, gripping him even as he pinned her hands over her head. He wanted to claim death's dark mistress with everything he had. Her beauty, her danger; he wanted all of it.

Zoë gasped as he thrusted into her, his thickness building her pleasure with each stroke. She locked her ankles around his waist, eager for more. He leaned against her clit, and her hands balled into fists as he took her with primal need.

She wanted to sink her teeth into him, taste that old fighter's blood that lured and tempted her, to feel that sweet pain and pleasure all wrapped up in a delectable wrapper.

Picking her up, he shifted her onto his lap and she rode him hard, crooning at the position change that she loved so much. Face to face, she found herself staring into his lust filled eyes and realized the position offered much more intimacy than she preferred with her prey.

But he isn't prey.

Oh, yes he is. He just doesn't know it yet.

Her internal thoughts were desperate to be appeased, but she wasn't ready yet. The thoughts were blown away when he leaned down and took one of her breasts into his mouth. He alternated between light tongue flicks to hard sucks, grazing her nipple with his teeth, exploring her body in a fashion that most failed to bother.

Her body shuddered with his intense thrusts and the sensations of his hands and mouth. She gripped him in an embrace, her arms around his neck as each stroke kept her climbing higher and higher towards a zenith.

Tristan didn't know how much longer he could keep from coming. As bizarre as it seemed, he craved to stay inside her forever, like he belonged there.

But it was daytime. Though her blood was a sweet elixir to nasty shifter bites, he needed to rest or else he wouldn't be much good to the fight. He still needed to heal.

Fuck it. She felt like a goddess wrapped around him, moaning her pleasure against his ear as she rode his cock deep and steady. Then, when he felt her fangs brush against his throat, he tilted his head away for wider access.

"If that's what you want, take it."

Zoë, torn between pleasure and hunger, violently shook her head. "No. I don't trust myself."

Taking a page from her twisted book, he dragged his finger-nail across the flesh right below his ear, opening his skin to shed a bit of his blood.

She breathed it in and clutched him tighter. "Damn you," she breathed. He wasn't playing fair. Her fingers raked through his hair, and her tongue sought out the trail of blood until she gave in to the thrill and her fangs bit into his neck as her orgasm erupted, sending shockwaves between her legs.

Tristan sucked in a breath as her nails dug into his flesh. He reveled in her muffled moans as she drank from him. He held on tight as he felt her come, close on the heels of his own. Her sheath tightened and, combined with her thirst, Tristan roared out as he found his release.

Shifting onto his back, Tristan felt Zoë continuing to drink. His body grew weak, and he clenched her shoulder. She was a succubus of sorts, siphoning everything from him until she had her fill. It was a dangerous foreplay for a vampire in his state to have initiated.

"Zoë..."

Just a bit more...

Zoë clung to him, reveling in the taste, until the sound of the back door breaking finally broke the trance.

With a growl, she looked up to see several Were-shifters run in, including a grey-eyed one towering nearly six and a half feet tall. His pure blonde hair fell around his shoulders as he crossed his muscular arms.

Otto looked at the display and said something in Albanian to the shifters behind him.

"Hmm. I thought you said she was protecting the vampire?" He tilted his head at the Black Blood Slayer, nude and wrapped around the equally naked and possibly late great Tristan Castillion of The Three's Royal Guard.

I always knew the vampire loved to play with matches. Seems like this time he fucked with a blowtorch.

"Doesn't look like that to me."

Zoë looked down, shocked to find a half-drained Tristan unconscious on the floor.

"Shit!"

HOWLING FOR YOU

ristan woke up with a start, greeted with total darkness surrounding him. As his eyes adjusted, he shifted on the soft platform of the bed and ripped the covers from his naked body.

He scanned the room, but there was no sign of anyone in there. The thick curtains were tightly drawn, but the heavy scent of wet dog told him this wasn't a vampire's sleeping quarters.

He looked at his arm, which was completely healed. Zoë. She hadn't killed him. In fact, he felt a lot like his old self. Maybe even more than his old self. His internal clock told him it was two hours past sundown and gave him plenty of time to recuperate from...

Where the hell was she?

The soft sounds of talking were coming from below him but were too low to recognize. Tristan quietly slid off the bed and sifted through his clothing piled in a chair for anything to be used for a weapon. To his surprise, his gun was on the floor behind the chair.

Stooping down on his haunches, he checked the clip to find only a couple rounds left. *Well, this time I will not miss.*

Tristan tugged on his pants and boots, staying quiet until it was time for his exit. He guessed maybe three or four Were-shifters were downstairs

They were probably thinking he was not quite ready for questioning; however, his thoughts couldn't go forward without the concern for Zoë. She'd made light work of the Were-shifters before, so what did they do to her? Her soft, powdery scent was all over his skin, a stark reminder of how close he'd come to death. Or life.

Hearing voices move up the stairs, Tristan moved swiftly to the other side of the door, his gun cocked and ready against his shoulder. The male voice lowered and went back downstairs. He used the opportunity to slowly, very slowly, open the door just a crack.

Peeking through the sliver of light, he saw the steps cleared as a large shifter walked past his view at the base of the stairs. Opening the door wider, he cringed as the hinges made more sound than he anticipated.

A low-pitched creak droned for a split second until he caught the door. The talking continued downstairs without hesitation, apparently unaware of the noise. Tristan began to step out when he heard a toilet flush to his right.

Waiting back, he watched a male walk out. Before he made it down the stairs, Tristan quickly stepped out for a hostage.

The shifter froze as Tristan's arm caught him around the neck, pressing the gun against his temple.

"Make one sound and your pack will be eating your remains in remembrance by daybreak," Tristan whispered to the subdued Were-shifter.

His only response was a curt nod and slightly raising his hands in surrender.

Good. He had his attention.

"Now, how many are down there?"

The Were-shifter hesitated, then finally bent his pinkie and ring finger on one hand, leaving eight. Damn. He was gonna need more bullets.

Pack sizes varied, but eight was nearly half a pack of wolves. He was outgunned, but that wasn't nearly as alarming as the fact they were down there just hanging out while he slumbered.

Something didn't feel right. He needed to find Zoë and get the hell outta dodge before they even knew they were gone. He wasn't trying to get bitten again.

"Okay, where's the woman? Hmm? The Black Blood Slayer? Is she alive?

Another quick nod.

"Good boy. You're going to take me to her. Nice and quiet. If you do anything to warn your brothers, I will end you. Do you understand?"

Another quick nod.

The Were-shifter proceeded to move down the stairs quietly with Tristan following close behind as they walked. The shifters sounded like they were in the kitchen area, speaking in maybe Albanian, which was where the alpha spawns originated from.

Thirty-one alpha male shifters of different species were born in the Balkan Mountains, and when the time came, all of them spread across the globe, building packs and societies. Otto, of course, was the ancient wolf alpha, and he now called the Americas his home.

Walking down to the base of the stairs, the wolf turned to the other side of the staircase toward the library room. Pushing the Were inside, he looked through the darkness to see Zoë against the wall with her hands pulled above her head in restraint.

Walking closer, he saw she was chained up. They'd used the bit of sully chain Jay had given him. She dangled quietly. Unresponsive. Growling low in his throat, Tristan felt the anger rise within him.

"What did you do to her? Tell me."

The Were-shifter shook his head. "Nothing! She's fine," he whispered.

"Oh yeah? She's fine, eh?" Tristan pushed him towards her. "You have five seconds to untie her." He frowned in disgust. "Five..." His counting paused as the Were-shifter quickly turned to challenge him.

"Eat shit, vamper!"

A gunshot would have all of them aware, so Tristan used the shifter's momentum to flip him onto his back. Greeting him with the gun to his forehead, he refrained from rising.

Instead he growled. "You fire that shot and every one of them out there will be on your ass!"

"Perhaps," Tristan sighed. "Wanna call my bluff?"

"I'm going to rip your limbs off and eat them for Bronwyn, vamper!"

Tristan heard one of them coming towards the room. Grabbing Rafe, Tristan backed towards Zoë's body, his gun aimed as another ran into the room.

"What the hell is going on here?" the shifter asked. "Rafe!"

Tristan's eyes reflected as he zeroed in at the growing threat. "I will put a bullet in your brother before another shifter comes closer. I'm not fucking around. I'm just here for her. Let me take her and we're square."

"Ah, he's alive," a smooth Balkan accent rumbled as a tall, familiar shifter walked in behind them, making his way to the front. His bright grey eyes were eerie through the darkness of the room.

Otto never seemed to rush for anything. Unless it was time to kill. Then all you saw was death and only heard silence.

"For a moment there, we thought you were not going to make it. I'm sure Rafe there was hoping a bit more than the others. Speaking of which, why don't you lower your weapon and let him go?"

"Fuck you, Otto. At least I didn't tie him up like an animal like you did to her." He pushed the gun harder against Rafe's temple. "So, this fuckhead is going to untie her before I really get pissed off."

Otto shook his head. "She asked us to do that, Tristan."

He frowned. "I don't give a shit. She can't speak for herself right now. What did you do to her?"

Otto cut his eyes to her, then to Tristan. These last several hours had been quite interesting. First, starting with an emergency call from Rafe and the others about the mission having gone bad and a Black Blood Slayer who had forced them to take her and a vampire to one of his dens. And if that hadn't been enough, he'd gotten to see the Black Blood in flagrante before she had to work a miracle to revive him. All of this on a Monday night.

"You did that to her," Otto stated.

Tristan scowled. "What?"

"You don't remember much, do you? I don't think I'd ever forget. I caught you two banging away like dogs in heat, and she was feasting on your blood like it was the last call at a local vamp bar. If we didn't barge in, you'd probably be dead. If she didn't break her trance and give you her blood, you'd be dead." He crossed his arms. "Don't believe me? Talk to someone you would." He turned and said something in Albanian and one of the wolves left.

"I want his blood, Otto!" Rafe hissed with a sneer.

"Hesht, budalla!" Otto replied, seething to the Were held captive. "Your defense is for shit, Rafe."

Another familiar face was pushed to the forefront by the shifter who ran out to fetch someone.

"Jay?"

His face was less than pleased, but nonetheless clean and void of bruises, blood, or black eyes. The shifters hadn't touched him.

"She's okay, Tristan," he said in a flat tone. "She needs to rest so she can recoup what strength she lost. We had to tie her up, but she also asked us to do it so she wouldn't try to go back for seconds."

Tristan glanced over to her dangling in silence. He didn't like seeing her so vulnerable, but with Jay there, the story checked out. He looked back to Jay, then Otto, pushed Rafe over towards them and lowered his gun.

Otto sighed. "Good. Now, we talk." He turned and walked out, and the other shifters followed behind him.

Tristan watched them until Jay walked up and punched him in the face. Hard. Tristan felt the silver from his ring gash his cheek, but other than that, it was the extent of the damage.

"Are you done?"

"You're an asshole." Jay stood facing him with daggers in his eyes. "I got alerted with a text message with the address of this shitty place in the middle of the boonies to help save your stupid ass after rolling around with Z. Not to mention having to deal with fucking Otto and his flea-bitten crew watching every move I make!"

"Otto allowed you to save me?"

"He had no choice with Zoë telling him that is what she had to do! She couldn't get you to drink, so I had to put a line in you."

Jay walked over to Zoë and checked her pulse against his watch.

"Is she going to be all right?"

"What the hell do you care?" Jay turned to him. "You wanna know something about her kind? You wanted to know what you were dealing with? Well, let me tell you something. Zoë is different. Black Bloods have the same DNA as an angel. They do as they're told and always follow the rules. The others do just that. Had you met any other of her people, you'd been dead the second after you laid eyes on them. No remorse. No afterthought. But Zoë likes to bend the rules, because she can. Always has. And she takes a punishment for that. She's made sacrifices. Even now, I've seen her suffer just to keep you alive. All of this drains her strength and makes her vulnerable. She's closed off from the portal and tied to Black Blood bait. It's only a matter of time the others will come searching for her, and the Fallen only protect the weak. They don't allow them in their ranks. And we need her strong to fight whatever bullshit The Three are up to right now."

Tristan stood quiet. The preacher was right. Zoë was a formidable ally in all of this. Her enthrallment alone could probably bring The Three to their knees, but he didn't expect Zoë to work so hard to save him.

He examined her tired face. He didn't get it. Someone obviously had a penchant for saving lost causes. Like someone else he once knew.

Jay raked his hair and sighed. "I warned you about her. If you let your emotions and miniature Tristan get in the way, you'll die."

"What the hell are you two going on about? Can't you two stop attacking for two fucking seconds?" A dreary voiced Zoë broke the tension.

Both Jay and Tristan stopped talking to focus on her slowly coming to. Jay breathed a sigh of relief.

"Shit, you scared the ever-loving crap outta me. That was far too much blood to give at once, are you crazy?"

"Not quite, but I'm getting there." She slowly pulled to her feet, allowing her body to straighten. The ache in her bones was gone, and so was her thirst.

Looking at them both, her eyes naturally gravitated to Tristan. He didn't realize how close he had been to dying. Yet here he was, alive. The taste of him was still on her tongue, a souvenir of their dangerous encounter.

Even as she stood there, chained, she craved another encounter, regardless of how foolish and short sighted it was. It wasn't like the thirst pulled her anymore. It was something else.

"You look healthy," she said.

"You don't."

She shrugged. "I'm rested and not ready to drink myself silly. Everyone wins. Where's Otto?"

Tristan moved towards her. "He's here. He wants to talk." As he grabbed the chain, Zoë stepped back as he pulled the links apart. "Why did you let them chain you up like this?"

"You know why."

Tristan sighed. "You know, Jay's right. You're causing your own pain, Black Blood."

"Funny, I thought it was more along the lines of saving your pasty ass. If you had a brain lapse, I nearly drank you dry."

"I get that, but you are working too hard to save an enemy you don't even know. You're being naive and stupid."

"I don't understand what the hell your problem is."

"Do you even know who I am? Or what I'm capable of? Let's not complicate things, demon. You and I aren't the same. And you being merciful almost put everything at risk."

"What?"

"Don't you get it? You're the only one strong enough to end this shit with The Three. It's a fucking no-brainer. If you care so much about your precious humans and ending the war, you need to think about that. Me? I don't give a shit. I never have."

"You're lying."

"Who do you think stole Remelia's grimoire from the Green Girls? Hmm?"

Zoë's frown grew deep. "You stole it for The Three?"

He nodded. "That was going to be my final mission before Javen talked me into protecting Ivana. Ivana didn't even know, I suspect. Here she was trying to talk peace with the Supreme, and there I was snatching the grimoire behind Ivana's back."

"And Remelia?"

"Who the hell knows? She wasn't a part of my mission, but maybe she was a part of someone else's. Maybe Christophe. Dashiell is making me suspicious. It's all fucked."

"Don't you believe in anything? You don't give a shit about

any of this. You just follow orders and don't give a shit about the consequences, do you?"

"Don't you?"

Zoë began to pant as her anger began to thrive through her body. He was apathetic, just like all the rest. Jay stood between them.

"I hate to break up this lovers' spat, but can we go finish talking to Otto so I can get the hell outta here?"

Tristan and Zoë eyed each other until she finally turned to leave. "We aren't done yet."

They walked into the living room where they were surrounded by Were-shifters of every size and build leading into the kitchen. As they walked, Tristan had his guard up, never for a moment trusting a pack of shifters. They worked as a team, and when one got irate, they all seemed to get irate.

Many vampires, even The Three, felt they were hot-headed by nature, but obviously they didn't put Otto in that same bracket. Either the stereotype was just that, or Otto was quite the anomaly.

The blond-haired, ancient Were-shifter sat down on one of the folding steel chairs. He wore all black jeans with biker boots and a black tank. Otto's bright, honey-colored eyes reflected as his head shifted away from the kitchen lights.

Unlike the panting of his pack, the old wolf sat silent. Just standing before him was a deception. Tristan couldn't begin to count how many times his colleagues had wished they got to be this close to the leader of the Were-shifters. How the war could be chopped by a third if they could zero out Otto Hannibal Krause? Tristan nearly laughed at the thought. Those were words from baby vamps who didn't have the slightest inkling on how complicated the war really was, nor how powerful the ones at the top were. Many foolish renegade vampires met a very painful, untimely death trying to topple a regime as old and as strong as Otto's.

He extended his hand to the chairs next to him. "Please," he cooed. "Have a seat. We've much to discuss, I imagine."

Cautiously, Tristan moved past him to the chairs, but neither he nor Zoë sat.

They turned to see Jay quickly sitting down in the chair farthest from Otto. Tristan raised an eyebrow at the preacher, who looked around clueless as some of the shifters laughed.

"What?" Jay asked.

Otto stirred his tea, watching them. "So, we have two alphas and one..." He glared at Jay, who literally sat at the edge of his seat. "... scapegoat."

He took a sip of his black tea and eyed Tristan and Zoë. "Nothing, human. It wasn't a test, but it's always easy to tell, in any case. You, Tristan, should know that not everything I ask for is a challenge."

"There's no telling with you, Krause." Tristan stood attentive. "What are you doing here?"

"Why, the Black Blood sent for me. She strong armed Rafe and his team into taking you to me after they tore through Patsey's like a bunch of rabid *mutts*." He cut his eyes to Rafe.

Tristan turned to Zoë.

"Of course, with a fast infecting bite poisoning you and daylight approaching, she made a call to bring you here to recover." He cleared his throat. "If that's what they call it nowadays."

The wolves chortled, and Tristan took a step towards him, only for Zoë to block him.

"So, you wanted to talk. No games, right? So talk." He looked at his watch and tapped it. "You have ten minutes."

She growled. "You're overstepping, Otto..."

"And so are you, Black Blood. I'm sure your superiors, Suni and Constantine would be interested in the kind of company you're keeping."

"They are bound by witchcraft," Jay uttered boldly.

"Oh, excuse me. What I meant was, the kind of company you're *fucking*."

This time, it was Zoë who advanced. The sleek sound of the metal clink as she drew her sword hummed as the shifters started to growl. In her fluid move, her blade stopped at just an inch from Otto's throat.

Before watching a few strands of Otto's blonde hair fall from her blade, she cut her violet eyes to his pack. "You mongrels will be silent! Your alpha isn't an alpha of mine."

Zoë turned to the proud, ancient king of the Were-shifters. He always had a mouth on him. Always enjoyed provoking. "And you...the only reason you give a damn as to whom I'm fucking is because in all these long years of existence, it's never been you. And it'll never be you, unless I want fleas. Now, by the Order, I can't end you, but I can make things very unpleasant for your people. So how about we cut the insults, because I'm pretty sensitive."

"You and the others are playing into a setup designed by The Three," Tristan informed them. "You know your people aren't involved, but neither the Were-shifters nor the Green Girls were involved in the assassination of Ivana of Bainsborough,"

"The Were-shifters had nothing to do with that. But the vampires feel differently," Otto added. "And I cannot speak for the magical Green Girls. Who knows what they are up to? They'd do anything to get back at the top of the food chain again."

"They were set up as well. The Three used the Were-shifters and witches as a scapegoat for what really happened."

Otto scoffed. "The great Three on Sangrine Hill." With a laugh, he shifted in his seat. "Ancient leeches turned political. What was it that really happened?"

Tristan clenched his fists. "Ivana was murdered by The Three."

Otto stopped stirring his tea.

"Vampires were in the kill squad. I killed one personally."

Otto sat up. Javen and the others were not above the common pettiness of their human counterparts. It shouldn't have surprised Otto that Javen, Valette and Kostya would be so bold to stage such a thing.

"Ivana was a very kind soul. One that I regret had to share such a fate as being a vampire. An even greater regret of her untimely death. But I was never convinced that The Three wanted the war to end, no matter how much Ivana wanted to believe it. She was naive and in that, sealed her fate. Just look at the vampires. Their numbers have grown over the years. More vampires being made than before, to grow their army and presence."

Zoë nodded. "It's kept us busy to say the least."

"If The Three want to come at us full force, we're ready for them. We've always been ready for them."

"You need the witches on your side, Otto," Zoë encouraged. "They are being used, and we have a feeling that the reason I'm here has to do with Remelia's disappearance."

"We have no reason to make allies with those bitches of the cursed words," Rafe interjected. "They have attacked us on several occasions, chasing after someone to blame for the fact they couldn't even protect their own Supreme from harm. Speaks volumes that she couldn't even protect herself."

Otto sighed. "Rafe's got a point. The Green Girls are too volatile for our tastes. We'd rather kill them."

Rafe spat at the ground, then glared at Tristan. "And vampires."

Tristan scoffed, then turned to Otto. "What's his fucking problem?"

"He will not let it go until it is settled."

"What's settled?" Tristan asked.

"Bronwyn's death. His mate. They have been together forever. At least, to how a human would calculate. She was always hot-headed, following her equally hot-headed mate wherever he went. I've warned him time after time about hunting with her, but he'd never listen. Because of that, he is partly to blame for her untimely death. Nevertheless, she ultimately died by your hands, vampire," said Otto.

Zoë crossed her arms, eyeing Rafe then Otto. "Rafe perhaps failed to mention that he and his crew of pups went gung ho into a human bar and raked up casualties. For that alone, I could take all their lives for such a stupid, thoughtless act."

"This is true. I would not be able to stand in the way for your punishment for him and the others mindlessly taking human lives and endangering exposure. I've sent a cleaning crew to take care of it and any Were-shifters in the law enforcement have been made aware. But I cannot defend the cost of lives." Tristan looked to Rafe, who seemed a bit too quiet for normal. Perhaps the wolf realized he had bitten off more than he could chew. But Bronwyn was one of his own, and Rafe deserved the right to avenge his love. "May I make a suggestion?"

Tristan looked at him. "What?"

"Instead of making this situation so messy, let's settle this the old way."

Zoë pursed her lips and nodded. She looked over to Tristan with a raised eyebrow. "How about it, cowboy?"

"Which is?"

Otto smiled. "A challenge to the death. No guns. No knives." He clenched his massive fists. "Just your bare hands. Prowess of a true fighter."

"Still love to see a good blood match, eh Otto?" Tristan crossed his arms.

"This is different. Rafe will hunt you down until he avenges her death. It is the nature of our species. When we mate, we do so for life. When that is taken from us, we seek vengeance. Rafe will turn mad without this opportunity. So as Alpha, it is my duty to grant him this."

"You have to give me more than that, Otto. As a vampire, I

couldn't give a shit about your mating customs, or the lament of a dead lover."

Otto sighed. "If you should be the victor, Tristan, I will agree to parlay with the Green Girls. No problem. No promises. Just peaceful talk. I will hear what they have to say." He reached out his hand. "Do we have a deal?"

Zoë smiled as Tristan nodded and shook Otto's hand. "We have a deal."

A deadly grin grew on Otto's scruffy face. "I'd be lying if I didn't say this won't be a real treat for me and the boys. The Three's prized commander getting his ass handed to him by a Were-shifter? Hell, we may be able to end the war right here, yes?"

"Save the shit talking for the mutts, Otto."

Otto turned to the pack. "Rafe, do you challenge this man?"

Rafe with a dark grin, nodded. "You bet your ass I do."

Otto held up his hand. "Everyone outside to the back. A perlesh has been struck."

Jay rubbed his forehead in angst and slowly followed behind. "What the hell is going on, Z?"

"A perlesh."

"A what?"

Zoë folded her arms. "A *cock-fight*. And Rafe and Tristan are the two cocks."

Jay shrugged. "For once, you're not wrong about that description."

"Jay..."

He moved closer to her, trying to whisper. "What is going on with you? You've been reckless with this vampire. Didn't you tell me you were on thin ice with the others? You were stolen from your realm still in chains. Doesn't that bother you?"

"It does, but it's not like this vampire had anything to do with it. He also had nothing to do with what happened to you either, Jay."

"What happened to destroying the enemy?"

"Things got complicated when I've seen my enemy care more for human life than a Were-shifter or a witch."

"I don't trust him."

"You don't have to. Trust me."

They all gathered in a circle in the thicket clearing in the pitch-black woods. Some of the Were-shifters could barely contain themselves, some howling and some partially shifting under the cover of night.

Rafe walked into the circle and stripped off his shirt, revealing the marks of the Dan'ai—enchanted ancient symbols that appeared on the abdomen of every living Were-shifter past puberty.

Legend had it, the first witches who cursed the first Were-shifters used the marks to identify them for hunting, their lineage written within their flesh. Rafe had several lines of symbols scrawled on his bulked abs. He'd been around for some time.

Jay shook his head. "He's going to fight *that*?"

Zoë shrugged. "Yep. I've seen bigger."

She turned to Tristan, who stood next to her. He was already shirtless and his dark hair was pulled away from his face with a rubber band. Though he wasn't huge and bulky like his opponent, his body radiated just as much power. He was all sinew and agility. She experienced enough of him beneath her to know. "You sure you wanna do this, cowboy?"

Tristan met her gaze. "Otto's not going to risk a meeting with the Green Girls without some sacrificial blood on the line. That's just how he works. Just be glad the opportunity presented itself this way. We don't really have a choice if this is the route we want to take."

Zoë nodded. He didn't trust nor like the witches, but she was thankful he was open to protecting them all the same. Curiosity struck her. Was he agreeing to this for her?

But even with that, he'd barely survived a shifter bite just hours ago. Her strength was just now getting back to normal, but she couldn't risk another enthrallment or feed him.

"Tristan, you need to watch your ass. I'm not going to be able to help you if you get bitten again. I need my strength."

"As do I. I've been in bare knuckle fights before." He moved past her, so close she could feel his breath on her skin. Tristan turned around. "Thank you for..." He cleared his throat. "...uh, you know what I mean."

She grabbed his arm. "No, I don't. Is it 'Thank you for fucking you senseless' or is it 'Thank you for pumping you full of slayer blood so can live another night?'"

Hmm, she made a great point. Perhaps both energized him much more than he realized. She'd made him give a shit about something. Enough to make him hope to actually survive this so he could get another opportunity to have her naked and writhing beneath him.

That would've been the proper way to go. Tristan stepped up to her, grabbed a fist full of her hair and pulled her into a roguish kiss. Quickly, he pulled away, offering her a smirk.

"Both."

BLOOD MOON

Otto walked through the circle of shifters and stood between Tristan and Rafe.

"Quiet!"

The howling and growling suddenly stopped. "Rafe has lost his mate in a recent skirmish to this vampire. Bronwyn was one of our own. A strong and loyal shifter to the pack. Rafe has challenged Bronwyn's killer, and that challenge has been accepted.

"The perlesh ends when one of them is dead. If one should run and desert the fight, they will be hunted down by the pack and eaten. And I will feast on your heart. I have no tolerance for cowardice."

Otto turned to each with an intrigued smirk as he stepped to the side. "Begin!"

Tristan calculated his move, as Rafe's eyes turned yellow. Charging towards him, Tristan quickly grabbed him and used his momentum to toss him into the crowd. A quick kip-up to his feet, he watched a seething Rafe cut back through the crowd.

Tristan quickly went on the offensive and connected a few jabs as Rafe threw a few of his own. The wolf packed a wallop as Tristan's teeth rattled.

Rafe lashed out which such power that the air hummed as he missed, nearly taking his head off. Tristan countered with grappling him to the ground, as he knew it was more to his advantage to get a wolf shifter lower than his natural stance.

Trying to pin him, Rafe went limp and rolled away. Heaving breaths, Rafe's face was twisted in anger.

Good, Tristan thought. *Rage will make you stupid or burn you out. Either way, you'll make a mistake.*

"Had enough, Fido?"

Rafe shook his head. "You have no idea who you're fucking with, blood boy! None!" He dropped to his knees as his face distorted and elongated into a muzzle as he began to transform.

Jay stepped behind Zoë as he watched Rafe stand as a man one moment, then a beast the next. His thick chest was covered in fur, and the jeans he wore ripped at the thighs as they could no longer hold his mass.

Tristan braced himself as he watched Rafe's teeth grow and sharpen as he morphed into a werewolf. Charging for him, Tristan slid underneath him to grab a thick log of wood within the circle. He turned just in time to shove the piece of wood into Rafe's mouth as he loomed over to bite him.

Punch!

Tristan cracked his knuckles over Rafe's animal face before Rafe started to throw blow after blow on Tristan's face. On his back, he was forced to endure it, yet it was not as painful as he'd expected it to be.

Tristan pushed against his jaws with the wood, until he kicked Rafe in the groin and shoved him away. Rising to his feet with superspeed, Tristan kicked Rafe in the ribs repeatedly until Rafe threw a kick himself, sending Tristan flying backwards against a nearby tree. He landed with a thud. It knocked the wind out of him as the wolves cheered and howled at Rafe's prowess. Even Rafe himself roared as he closed in on Tristan like a rabbit caught in a snare.

Tristan pulled himself up, but not quick enough to escape Rafe's grasp. Grabbing his throat, the wolf shifter raised high against the pine trunk as Tristan struggled.

"I'm going to rip you apart piece by piece and feed you to my brothers!" Rafe leaned in and bit into his arm.

Excruciating pain sent shockwaves through him, and he yelled in agony as he tore through muscle.

"No!" Zoë yelled as her worst fear came true.

"You taste pretty good, vampire. Not like shit your kind usually gives off," Rafe taunted with a thick, dark voice.

Tristan felt his body heat and tingle as adrenaline pumped within him. With an angered yell, he gripped the wolf's forearms and broke them.

Yelling, Rafe backed away and turned as Tristan stalked after him. He watched his shifter bite bleed black then heal instantly. Losing his balance, Rafe dropped to his knees as he snapped his arm out to reset the bones.

Tristan speared him to the ground and began to wail on him with a series of brutal blows until Rafe's face was a bloody mess. Straddled over him, he sat back to catch his breath. Grabbing Rafe by the long, thick fur on his chest, he pulled him upwards.

"I don't want to kill you, Rafe. Let's not do this. What do you say?"

Rafe growled. One amber eye burned into him. Only hatred lived there, even in the face of imminent death. That was the pride of the Were-shifters in a nutshell, after all.

"I said to the death, blood boy. You stole the only thing from me that meant anything, and I want to see Bronwyn again. Or I'll kill—"

Tristan leaned in and tore into Rafe's jugular with his fangs to land the mortal blow. The shifter's blood gushed from his throat and onto Tristan's face and skin. With bright, fuming eyes, he released the near lifeless body of Rafe and stood up.

His body in the last, twitching throes of death, Tristan looked down and shook his head.

"So be it."

The Were-shifters howled at the loss of their brother and beat their chest. They looked over to Otto, who walked back into the circle. He held up his hand and the forest went dead silent.

"Rafe and the vampire Tristan fought bravely, and Tristan has risen as the champion. The perlesh has ended. From here on out, no strikes against the Green Girls until our parlay has ended. Is that understood?"

"Yes!" they said in unison.

"If I hear of any Were-shifters attacking Green Girls as a preemptive strike, I'll feast on your bones!" Otto looked down at Rafe's body. It was a true shame, really. Rafe wasn't his best fighter or anything, but he'd known the wolf since a pup and there was something surreal about seeing someone so young meet such an untimely end. At the hands of an enemy, no less.

"As for Rafe, take his body with us. Go."

Otto stared at Tristan's shoulder with scrutiny. Something wasn't right. Tristan looked far too healthy. His skin had already healed from the fight and it didn't even look like he had been bitten.

"Why aren't you sick?"

Tristan shook his head. "We had a deal, Otto."

Zoë came up behind him along with Jay.

Otto nodded. "That we did. As you can see, I plan to honor it." He looked at his watch, then the sky. "You have till 1 AM to convince the witches for a sit-down meeting. No silver. No spells. Get those hot-headed bitches to calm down, and I'll enter-tain a conversation for us to join forces against the fang boys. No offense."

"None taken." Tristan extended his hand. "Thank you."

Otto scoffed. "How did that feel in your mouth?"

"Molten silver would've been more palatable."

Otto grinned. "Do not thank me just yet. I have yet to see the light at the end of this tunnel. In either case, I've been entertained, even if at the expense of my people."

"I offered him an out."

He shook his head. "That only insulted him. Like I said, Rafe wanted a chance at vengeance and I wanted control. And you wanted neither. Now everyone's happy." He cut his eyes to Zoë and Jay. "A vampire, a Black Blood Slayer, and a human…" He sighed. "Sounds like a bad joke."

They all looked at each other. Yeah, a *really* bad joke. Otto pulled out his phone. "You are safe to stay in this den if you prefer. Call me when you're ready."

Tristan nodded as Otto walked away. The others growled low, passing them, but followed nonetheless. As he turned, Zoë examined him in awe. Her hand reached out to skim the arm where Rafe bit him. The skin was flawless.

Jay frowned. "Do we need to get the transfusion kit?"

Zoë gazed into Tristan's eyes with fascination as her fingers touched him. The transfusion had an effect she hadn't anticipated. "No. He's healed. The Were-shifter bite would've been still visible if he was infected." She anticipated her blood would give him strength, but not this level of power. He should've been dead, yet he was completely healed. "It would appear my blood had benefits we didn't expect."

Tristan wiped the wolf's blood from his mouth and looked at his arm. "Yeah, I don't feel anything. Not a mark on me." He stepped back from her touch, shifting focus. "We need to get a hold of the witches. Tonight."

"Yeah, you guys can count me out," Jay protested. "I had enough shit for one night, and my patience will wear thin with the witch that crosses me. I'm taking my ass home."

Jay walked between them. "If you need something *other* than a late-night emergency blood transfusion, you know where to find me."

Zoë turned to Tristan, who threw water over his body to wash the blood off him. His dark hair was soaked and dripping off his shoulders. She watched as water ran down the slopes of his abs down past his navel. "You smell like an animal."

Tristan scoffed. "I just got done killing one." He watched her raking him over with that sultry look that turned into curiosity. "What's the matter?"

"I don't think I've ever given someone so much of my blood before. It seems it makes you stronger." She pointed at his shoulder. "Heal faster."

"I take it you're more in the habit of taking blood, not giving it." He wiped his face. "Don't worry. I won't put you in that situation again, but I hope you understand, I don't regret you feeding me."

"I know," she said softly. "I get it."

"Good. We need to find the Green Girls and talk to them."

Zoë nodded. "The coven broke into regions, but I know one out in seventh ward. And let me do the talking."

"I'll leave it to you," Tristan conceded.

Zoë ran up to Jay as he kicked on the engine. "Jay!"

He stuck his head out the window. "Yeah?"

She leaned in and kissed his cheek. "Thank you for coming to help us. I'm sorry about this."

"I'm just worried about you, Z," he confessed. "This is getting pretty hairy, and if Suni or Constantine haven't started looking for you, they soon will. Then what the hell are we gonna do?"

"I don't know."

"This is getting over our heads, and I'm afraid for all of us."

"I won't let anything happen to you, Jay. You know that. As my ally, I'm sworn to protect you."

"And I want to protect you. Try at least, anyway." Jay reached into the back row of his truck and pulled out a small bag. "Anyway, I figure you'd need some clothes. You're so fucking messy the way you kill stuff. So here." He handed the little black plastic bag to her with a half-smile.

Zoë accepted the bag and smiled. "Thanks Jay."

"No problem. After this, you're shit outta luck. Don't plan on doing laundry this week. My church needs construction." Jay looked over to Tristan, who stood away, looking at the moon. He sighed. "Z…"

"Yeah?"

"Just be careful, all right?"

Zoë followed his eyes to Tristan and she shook her head. "Don't worry, I'm not going to kill him. My beast is in check."

"I'm not speaking about that. If you haven't noticed, there's something far scarier happening between the two of you. It's more than blood, and perhaps more than your nature."

Zoë shrugged. "What are you talking about?"

"Just…" His voice trailed off as he looked straight ahead. "Just either destroy it or embrace it, all right? Don't try to find a way in between. It'll just kill you both." Jay shifted the truck in reverse and pulled out onto the farm road.

Zoë watched his truck drive off and sighed a small sigh of relief. He would be much safer away from them. All the freaks seemed to be out tonight, and humans were the casualty when the supes came out to play. Jay was one of the few humans that was willing to lay down his life for the causes of Black Bloods and deserved her loyalty. She needed him to be away from this circus for a bit. Taking the stairs to the other bathroom, Zoë turned on the shower and tested the water as it rained on her fingertips. Stripping away every stitch of clothing, she breathed a comforting sigh at her freedom. Her body was sticky with blood and she just wanted to feel a bit less like a serial killer. Stepping in, she let the warm water drum over and down her body. The union of her skin and the soft water's temperature was blissful. It wasn't long before she felt a presence just outside the bathroom door.

"What are you doing?" Tristan leaned against the wall. Though the bathroom door was opened, he kept himself out, faintly feeling the steam as it flowed out to him. The mild but unmistakable scent of Zoë, blood, and citrus soap followed with it.

"I need to get your blood and everyone else's off me. I can't think, and I can't walk around in the world of man looking like I'm a murderer. Especially not if we plan to talk to the witches." Zoë ran the water over her face and pushed her hair back. She moved the curtain back a bit. "You can stand a shower yourself. You smell awful."

Tristan looked himself over and folded his arms. "I just fought a mangy Were-shifter; that's to be expected. Besides, I think the Green Girls wouldn't care less about my appearance, considering me just being there will be enough to offend them."

Zoë smiled. "They really aren't that bad," she shouted out. "I know you've been indoctrinated to hate them—"

"I don't hate them," Tristan interjected against the wall, but leaned towards the bathroom entrance. "I'm not some young, dumb vamp, willing to believe anything The Three put in front of me. I never was." He shifted, his left shoulder being the only thing anchoring him to stay out of the bathroom, but it was a losing fight. "Believe me, I've seen atrocities both done by and given to the Green Girls as with every other supposed oppressed groups of supernaturals. It's all the same shit, different toilet. I've seen it century after century."

Zoë let the water run over her body as she listened to him. "Is that why you don't seem to care about anything anymore? A cynical long-toothed vampire waiting to die?"

"I used to care."

She rubbed more soap casually over her breasts. "Right. When there was a Katya?"

Zoë jumped as Tristan ripped the shower curtain back,

exposing her to his frown. "How do you know her name? I never uttered her name to anyone." He grabbed her wrist.

"You called out to her when you were dying!" She jerked her arm free and glared at him. "You were delirious from the Were-shifter bite and talked to her as if she was standing right next to me. There was something dark and abysmal about your voice to her name. As if," she paused. "...you were still mourning her loss."

"You don't know anything about me, Zoë. I lost Katya because I had once believed the lie. The same lie Ivana believed—the same one you believe. I led battles across countries and believed I could change the world. That I could make things better for my family. For my wife. Katya was supportive and loyal to a fault. And it led her to her death as well as my son's. No one told me the world was full of undying darkness. Of monsters and soulless creatures. In the end, I let one seduce me into vengeance. Now, here I am. She and Kallax are dead in the wormy earth while I try to find some reason every day not to walk out into the sun one crisp autumn morning or lock myself away for the deep sleep. That's not mourning you heard in my voice. Just guilt."

"You feel guilty because you found a way to continue living. What have you done with that life? You can't bullshit me, Tristan, because you do believe you can change things still. Why else would you even bother to sort this out with The Three? Why bother to help me stop this?" The water cascaded over her body, but her nudity was the furthest from her mind.

His scowl wasn't as authentic as he wanted. "Pride."

Zoë sighed. "Why won't you be straight with me?"

"Because I don't owe you anything, Black Blood!"

She grabbed his shirt at the hem. "Yes, you do. You owe your life to me."

"Is that what you want?"

"No, what do *you* want, dammit?"

Tristan stepped forward and crashed his lips against hers, the warm water raining against their faces. He couldn't think anymore, as his id kicked into overdrive. His voice didn't have an answer for her, but his body did. Zoë kissed him back. Naked and wet, she rubbed against him, helping him peel the filthy shirt off him, and pants. He stepped inside and pushed her against the wall, their lips softly caressing each other. His hands explored her body as her soapy fingers kneaded his pale flesh. Panting, aroused and shaking, he reveled in her scorching touch. He wished he had more time to explore her. To take his time claiming what seemed to be the most enigmatic creature he'd encountered. "You complicate me, Black Blood. You complicate everything."

Zoë pulled back, gazing into his hooded but reflective bright eyes. His touch made her want something she couldn't name. His gaze allowed her to see past it and into a soul that shouldn't be there. Complicated. Yeah, that was the understatement of the century for both of them. There, as two natural enemies entangled in a wet, vulnerable embrace, defined their conundrum. Zoë's hand cupped his face with a tenderness never used before. "Likewise, vampire."

Likewise.

VIGIL

Zoë drove up to the house on the end of the street and parked. The minute she turned the engine off, an eerie vibe hit her. "Wait. Something's wrong."

"What do you mean?" Tristan asked.

She surveyed the front. "All the lights are out. Not even vigil candles outside. That never happens. Remelia's girls would have a vigil out for her." She slowly stepped out the truck, along with Tristan.

The moment he stepped outside and took a few steps forward, he turned to Zoë. "I smell blood."

Zoë's heart sank. "A lot of it. C'mon!" Drawing her sword, they both ran to the front door.

Tristan broke through the door that was barricaded from the inside. Zoë ran in and exhaled a shocked gasp as she surveyed the carnage. The floors that held various sacred circles and talismans were spilled with the blood of the Green Girls. She looked around to see broken bodies and bite marks across ethereal witches of all ages.

A faint movement came from behind the wall from another room. Running over, Tristan pulled a thick pane of glass off a younger witch. Her blonde hair was tied in a tight ponytail on top her head, and only Zoë recognized her as one of the witches who'd attacked in the church.

Coughing out blood, the witch groaned and shook her head.

Zoë supported her neck. "What happened?"

"It...happened so fast. I'm not sure who it was. They came in and tore the place apart. Said The Three send their regards for a safer world for vampires." She clenched her arm to her chest despite the puncture wounds on her wrist. "They fed off everyone."

Tears rolled off her blood-stained cheeks as her eyes shifted to the right. Tristan's eyes followed to the young girl's face down in the corner. She couldn't have been more than thirteen. Her cold, lifeless eyes stared out into nothingness... "even the little ones." The witch started to sob. "We fought with everything we had, but they were too many."

"Let's get you outta here."

"No, I'm not going anywhere." She removed her other hand from her side, revealing a large wound that freely flowed with blood as she released pressure. "They call me Echo."

"Was there a large vampire with them? German accent, goes by the name Christophe? He's been missing since Ivana's attack. Was he here?"

Echo shook her head. "I don't know."

"If he did this, we have to find him, Echo."

She extended her hand to Tristan. "I can help you. Give me your hand."

Hesitance forced Tristan to pause just a moment before finally putting his hand in hers. She closed around it tightly, the blood on her fingers staining his palm.

Putting pressure on Echo's wound, Zoë held her head in her lap as she panted her breaths, concentrating on looking through the haze of images, thoughts, and time. She thought of the name and the connection of that name to Tristan.

Grabbing her hand firm, Tristan felt the warm heat between them. Energy emitted from the witch.

"He's...alive...hiding." Echo gasped for breath as she closed her eyes. "In a sanctuary near Tulane."

"Why did he hurt you?"

Echo shook her head. "He didn't. I never met him. But he's waiting for you. I have to wait. But I need a chance to make this right. No peace. Pop. Pop," Echo started to ramble off in German till she shook herself awake. "Remelia is alive. Please..." She grabbed Zoë's jacket. "You have to save her. She's waiting for you. I'm so sorry that we didn't see this, I didn't see." She started to close her eyes when Zoë shook her awake.

"What didn't you see?"

"Give me your hand."

Zoë took her hand, feeling the chill of her grasp grow. Echo tightened her grip as she held both Tristan and Zoë's hand. The air around them began the hum and snap as energy surrounding them started to become visible. The glowing orange energy that looped around Zoë's waist stretched over to Tristan.

"Remelia had bound you together. She trusted you, Zoë, and Ivana trusted you, Tristan, to end this."

Zoë tried to calm her as she felt death take a tighter hold of the witch. Tears welled in her eyes as Echo shivered against her as the chill of death rattled her. "I'm so sorry I failed her and you."

Echo coughed out a laugh, more dark than weak. "We didn't give you a chance. We made a mistake, and this is bigger than us. The war will get worse and swallow us whole. We all wanted Remelia to save us, to send us some hope. She did that. Her last gift to her coven was you."

A wave of energy rippled from Echo's body and the orange energy tether disappeared, pushing Zoë and Tristan backwards. Gathering their bearings, they sat up to face a silent, lifeless body.

"Echo?"

Zoë shook her violently. "Echo?"

She stared at her eyes that gazed at the eternal heavens, no longer tied to the mortal coil where she and the others suffered. The harsh sting of tears gave way to a freefall over her cheeks as she released her body. Her body shaking, Zoë started to beat her fists against the cement floor. Tristan watched quietly before standing up. Zoë scanned the room again. So much blood. So much death. Lost souls, and for what? Lies? Greedy vampire lies?

Zoë's growl turned into a gut-wrenching roar as her skin turned all black for a split second. Her fangs drawn and her soul seething, she mourned their loss. Her superiors didn't understand it. They didn't care, but this was why she didn't want to turn a blind eye to the war. She didn't want to ignore Remelia's plea to help them.

Now they were gone. Her coven was butchered. Zoë shot up to her feet, ready to burn down Sanguine Hill and have The Three's heads on a spit.

"I'm going to fucking end this. I will watch them writhe in pain for what they've done!" Tristan grabbed her arm as she moved to the door.

"Wait a minute!"

Zoë jerked her hand away. "Don't touch me! This shit ends tonight!

Tristan grabbed her again. "Listen to me! Look, I understand that you want blood for this, but save it. We still need Otto, and we still need to find Christophe."

"No, *you* need to find him." She pointed a thumb at her chest. "*I'm* going for The Three. I'm through with games. We're no longer bound, so you do whatever the hell you need to do, all right?"

"We're beyond that now. Don't you get it?" Tristan pushed her as he walked past her to the door, when something caught his eye on the floor.

There were times in his life where it felt like the devil himself pulled a cloak over him, blinding him from the true nature of beasts and souls alike. The problem with the devil's cloak was not that you felt discomfort when you were under it. Oh no, you actually felt calm and content there.

Safe almost.

But it was once the veil was *stripped*, did you realize you had been blinded for so long.

Betrayal was a motherfucker. Tristan turned to Zoë, his eyes glowing with anger.

"What?"

"We have to find Christophe soon." He bent down and picked up the small white clump of gum sitting in the puddle of blood. Tristan knew someone with a nasty habit of spitting out gum. Someone who also worked for The Three, just like him.

Pop. Pop.

"Why?"

Tristan showed her the monumental evidence that could fit between his thumb and index finger. He should've fucking known. Ambition always got the best of his kind.

"Before The Three snuff out the only living link to Remelia."

THE NIGHT SEEMED COLDER NOW. More unforgiving. Perhaps it was more of a testament to Tristan's sentiments.

"Echo said he was in a sanctuary. I don't know of any near Tulane University."

Zoë walked ahead of him. "I know of one. But it's near a different Tulane." She got into the driver's side. "I'll take us there."

Zoë turned off the headlights as she turned down the alley of Tulane Ave. Maintaining stealth, she pulled to a stop roughly a quarter mile from an abandoned motel. There weren't any lights or people moving about, and the giant dumpster of junk made it more of a condemned building than anything else.

"Sanctuaries don't look like this. What is this place?"

Zoë continued to walk. "A sanctuary for those who abandoned more than just their freedom. No one manages this one, so it's truly a shithole—not just looks like one. Also, it's not really neutral, so be on your guard."

Tristan cocked his guns. "Agreed."

Entering the side door, Zoë walked in first, moving through the dark hall peppered with creatures keeping their distance. The stench of mildew, rotting flesh, and bleach filled their noses as they walked through.

"Christophe?" Tristan called out as Zoë searched ahead. Moving through, he continued until he felt the tip of a blade behind his neck.

"Make one more move and I'll take your head off where you stand," a German voice whispered behind him. "You understand?"

"Christophe, relax. It's me, Tristan."

He scoffed. "I don't give a rat's ass if you're Jesus Christ. I don't trust anyone anymore. The Three are lost, and so are you."

Christophe froze as he, too, felt the point of a blade at his back.

"You should lower that blade, Templar. We're here to help you."

"Bullshit!"

"Look, I know that the attack on us was a setup. Vampires were responsible for the attack on us and Ivana."

Tristan sighed as the pressure of the blade against his neck disappeared. He turned around to see Christophe in the same clothing he wore the night of Ivana's death, though barely recognizable from the layers of filth. He looked like he'd been living in a sewer for weeks, whereas in reality it was only a few nights since the attack. His blood-stained cheeks and hands signaled feeding, but his eyes were beaten and angry.

Zoë lowered her sword as Christophe and Tristan hugged briefly. "I'm sorry it's taken so long to find you."

"I did not know who to trust." He turned to notice Zoë standing quietly. His eyes widened as he drank in the vision of her. "Who are you?"

Zoë's violet eyes flashed as she sheathed her sword behind her back. "Vengeance," she replied.

"Shortly before we left The Three's mansion, I noticed something odd. Following the motorcade, I saw that Dashiell was no longer trailing on the ground. He was missing for a few minutes, so I went back to trail him. When I went back, I saw him talking to a vampire on a motorcycle. I watched the vampire pull a ski mask over his face before speeding off. Claude had no business there."

"What do you mean? You knew him?"

"Yeah, I made him. He'd been asking me about joining the guards, but he wasn't ready yet. I didn't understand their connection."

"What happened?"

"I approached Dashiell. At first, he shrugged it off and I wanted to believe there was nothing to it. That was a mistake. He blindsided me and we fought." His head lowered. "Son of a bitch got the upper hand and left me for dead. Before he left, he told me that night would mark the end of the piss poor truce, and that The Three had no room for saints.

"He mentioned that now The Three had collected the two prizes from the Green Girls, all bets were off." Christophe braced himself against the wall. "By the time I came to, it was all over."

Zoë tensed. "The two prizes?"

Tristan turned to her. "Remelia and the grimoire. With one, the witches had a chance to fight. But with both in The Three's possession, they had the upper hand. "I'm sorry, Tristan, but I couldn't trust anyone in the guards, and before I knew it, everyone was hunting me. This was the only place I could think of to hide until I could figure out how to find an ally to help."

Clenching his fists, anger tensed Christophe's muscles. "When

I got word that witches and Were-shifters attacked, I knew it had to be a lie. I could've followed The Three to the ends of the earth. But killing our own and using them for political gain disgusts me. My loyalty ends at the edge of this madness."

"Good. Because we need your help. Things have been escalating and we have a feeling a strike against the witches and the Were-shifters will happen at Ivana's funeral. We need to end this."

Christophe pushed himself off the wall and nodded. "I'm with you, Commander. Let's get out of here." He slid his blade into its sheath and checked his gun holstered on his thigh.

Running out of the side exit of the sanctuary, Tristan saw a red laser dot in the trees and immediately turned to Zoë.

"Gun!"

A bullet clipped him in the shoulder as he shielded her and closed the door. Christophe grabbed him under his shoulders to pull him up as the door became riddled with bullet holes.

"Move! Move!" Zoë pushed back as Tristan crawled to the other side of the wall. Christophe and the others scrambled at the gunshots as both exits were shot at. Finally, the shots stopped.

"This is the royal guard!" Dashiell casually announced as he and his crew of vampires came out of the darkness towards the sanctuary. Their guns were drawn as they quietly surrounded the building. "We're here to retrieve suspects from an assassination. We mean no harm to the rest of you. Crackheads, Were-shifters, or otherwise." He smiled. "Tristan? I know you're in there, man. And Christophe and that foxy, foxy little bangtail you showed off earlier. So why don't you come on out?"

"Then we can talk about how you turned your back on us? How you murdered Green Girls and Were-shifters alike?" Tristan yelled, leaning against the wall.

Dashiell shrugged. "You taught me to seize opportunities. The Three gave me a lot of perks to help them with this project. I suspect they knew you didn't have the heart to carry all this out. Considering Ivana was involved, I don't blame them."

"You can still walk away, Dash," Tristan warned. "The Three won't protect you."

"Oh, I don't need their protection, Tristan. I gotta admit, I didn't want to have to kill you. Besides, you taught me everything I know. But let's face it, you've wanted out of all this a long time ago. So now you'll get your chance."

"Come and get me, asshole."

"Hanging with a fugitive isn't a good look for the former Commander of the Royal Guard. Why don't you give us Christophe and make this even? It's either that, or we torch the place and force you out. Your choice!"

Tristan started to get up when Zoë pushed him down. She shook her head. It was time this ended.

"Wait here," she instructed.

"Come out slowly, now!" Dashiell demanded outside.

"What are you gonna do?" Tristan asked in a whisper.

Zoë stood up. "What I was made to do."

ENTHRALLED

Stepping over Christophe, she slowly made her way to the door. Turning to meet Tristan's gaze, her eyes flashed violet. "You'll be safe inside."

Christophe whispered. "From what?"

"From me." Zoë stepped out from the door with her hands up. "I'm coming out!" The semicircle of vampires and red lasers of their sights flashing across her eyes were the first things she saw.

Dashiell stood in the center dressed in black, his gun aimed at her. He scoffed. "Well, if it isn't the foxy bangtail. You mean, they pushed you out here instead of them? Pussies."

Quietly, she continued to walk further out toward Dashiell, toward his army of guns and madness. "Believe me. I'm more than enough."

With all her might, Zoë kicked the dumpster over against the door, blocking Tristan and Christophe and some others inside. Standing still, Zoë focused deep into her thoughts, pulling into the darkness where enthrallment dwelled, where the deadly recesses of her inner beast lived, waiting on bated breath to release. Summoning that power, her hands glowed amber, as did the rest of her body, as she used her power to pull them all to her.

It flowed from her in ripples disappearing into the air. It was like a whisper in the wind, telling them anything they wanted to hear, just as alluring as a siren's call and just as potent as a succubus' kiss. She watched their eyes hyper dilate and stay trained on her.

Dashiell felt the sensual caress of a touch that didn't exist on his body, and the scent of blood too sweet to ignore. It was coming from her. Who was she? He shook his head as if to remove a thought.

"What's going on?" He and the others began to pant, trying to steady their breaths as the enthrallment began to crank up. At the scale she was pulling, there was a risk of Tristan and Christophe being sucked in. All she could do was to keep them from getting to her before she had a chance to play.

They liked to toy with victims and slaughter them? Good. Cause so did she.

She walked up to Dashiell as he dropped his weapon. "You feel that fire in your veins, vampire? That needful hunger where you can think of nothing more than sinking your fangs into my flesh and sating your uncontrollable lust by driving yourself into me?

"That's me. I'm cold. I'm deadly. And absolutely not to be fucked with. I'm your wildest dream and your most terrifying nightmare. You may think you can control my seduction but sooner or later, you'll give in. *Every* vampire does."

She pulled her sword and placed it under his chin. "Now, kneel for me."

Slowly, Dashiell dropped to his knees on the pavement. He looked up at her like she was the Savior. But there would be no salvation for him nor the others. Atonement was upon them. His fangs drawn, he waited, pulling at his clothes. "Let me taste you. Just a drop."

"I'll kill you last so I can savor the taste of it. For now, you'll be my bitch until it's your turn."

Zoë walked past him, smiling. With a crooked finger, the

vampires began to lower their guard and approach her. Tristan peered out the window. Her blade ready, she slashed through the first wave with expert skill. Bodies and heads of vampires tumbled and dropped by the wrath of her sword. Bloodlust and thirsty, she felt like the kilns of Hades, fire in her blood. And she was just getting warmed up.

As she poised to land another devastating blow, her sword glowed red and flew from her hand. With a hiss, Zoë followed with her eyes as it landed in the hands of a familiar face. Her breath caught in her throat as she stared at the two Black Blood Slayers approaching her.

Shit. Not now. It can't be! "What are you doing here?"

Constantine examined the blade in his hand and eyed Zoë. "We're here to ask the same thing, Zoë. You shouldn't be here."

"I'm doing my job, and that is to kill vampires. Isn't that what you wanted?"

"We both know there's more to it than that. You were told to stay out of this pathetic skirmish between the supernaturals. It is not our fight."

"You must come back with us," Suni commanded.

"This is bullshit! They slaughtered a whole coven. That is reason enough for retribution."

Constantine frowned. He was in no mood to deal with her angst. "We are not in the business of policing all the supernaturals, Zoë. We can't choose sides, and we can't be involved like this. You must come now. Don't make us force you. You won't like how we do that."

Tristan and Christophe ran up with guns drawn.

Zoë rolled her eyes as Constantine and Suni looked at them like flies. "They're with me! Don't touch them."

"Oh, we have no intention to do so if you plan to come with us right now."

If she left them, they'd be as good as dead, but if she refused, they'd take her away—but not without torturing and killing Tristan and Christophe.

"You have to run, Tristan, or you both will be caught. You have to run now." Her warning carried a tone of urgent desperation.

Constantine and Suni both pulled out sully chains and quickly wrapped them around her wrists before all three of them flashed out of there. The pull of enthrallment instantly stopped and dissipated with Zoë gone, leaving Tristan and Christophe greatly outnumbered. Snapping out of the trance, Dashiell looked at the headless bodies with alarm. Drawing his gun, he and the others still alive rushed them.

Dashiell stood up to Tristan. "That's a neat little trick your bangtail could do, but didn't quite save you, did it?"

Tristan shrugged. "No but in all of two minutes, she managed to cut a swath through your shitty team and made you her bitch, kneeling for orders. I'll take it as a wash."

Dashiell hit him across the face with his gun. "We'll see who's a bitch after we're done with you." He motioned to two vampires wearing thick gloves. "Do it."

One of them reached into their bag and pulled out silver barbed chains and moved towards Christophe with a wicked grin.

Christophe attempted to dodge, but it was no use. He writhed as he saw the vampire chains coming towards him. "No! No!" He struggled as they began to wrap it around his torso. The sizzling sound as it hooked into his flesh accompanied his yells of agony.

Dashiell smiled. "A little souvenir I took from the Green Girls when we paid them a visit. Don't worry, Tris, there's one for you too."

"You dirty piece of shit! Let's end this right now! You and me! I want your head, you traitorous bastard!" Tristan growled behind the background noise of Christophe's groans and yells.

He was too weak to endure such torture. "Let him go! You know that it's me you and The Three want!"

Dashiell shook his head, cutting his eyes to Christophe. "Geez, what a fuckin' wailer. Would you shut him up? He's interrupting grown-up conversation."

Tristan bucked against the hold as he watched them proceed to wrap it around Christophe's face, gagging his mouth with the barbaric chain. His heart wrenched at the sight, and he pulled against the vampires holding him.

"I'm going slice that smile off your face, Dashiell."

"Save it. We gotta get back to The Three. They definitely want to see you before Ivana's funeral. You can save your tough talk for them. After delivering you, I've got a lot on my plate." He turned to another vampire. "Bag him, gag him, and you watch your ass with him. He's like a cockroach, so don't underestimate him."

The vampire nodded. "You got it."

Dashiell turned to Tristan as he unwrapped a piece of gum and popped it into his mouth. "See you in a bit, Tris. First, I gotta pay my respects to an old friend."

ZOË STOOD GROWLING, pulling at the sully chains that looped around her wrists and bolted to the floor of the hall. She couldn't explain it, but she could feel Tristan battling distress.

The feel of his blood in her veins continued to call to her, keeping her grounded as she found herself once again at the mercy of her superiors. If she didn't get back to earth soon, The Three would get away with all their treachery and launch a full-on attack on the Were-shifters and witches.

It wasn't right. She couldn't fail again. Not this time. It was too big. She yanked against the chains, letting the pain of it keep her lucid.

Suni walked into the hall. Seeing the display, she gave a disapproving shake. "I don't understand why you bother. You know those chains are made solely for you. There's no getting out of them on your own."

Zoë watched her with thin slits for eyes. "Just call it my nature not to turn my back on a mission."

"Oh, Zoë. There was no mission. That was just a childish attempt to make your own rules and fight a battle that can upset the Order."

Suni pulled up a chair and sat. "Humans and supernaturals alike. We do them no favors that do not help our cause. You know the Order is already complicated, and yet you make it even muddier by protecting witches who kill humans and supernaturals, by antagonizing the Were-shifters, and last, but certainly the most alarming..." She stood up and grabbed Zoë's face. "...a fraternizing partnership with a vampire."

Zoë pulled her face away. "Give me a break, Suni! You know I had no control over that. I was bound to him!"

Suni scoffed. "And yet he lives. You're made to seduce and kill. I've seen you in action, Zoë and what I saw was not normal." She frowned in disgust. "Do you have feelings for that creature?"

Her voice reeked of disdain and jealousy. Two things that Zoë just didn't have time for, but the question prompted her to think about her answer. *Do I?*

"It's complicated."

Suni grabbed her jaw again, pulling her close to her lips. "That is not the answer I was looking for!"

"I know the answer you're looking for, but if you're not here to talk about releasing me, then I've got nothing to say to you."

Suni exhaled a deep breath. She had no idea why Zoë felt the need to rebel against every damn thing she possibly could. As if she were better than the rest of them. As if she were more than a Black Blood Slayer. But she wasn't. Like the rest, Zoë was damned to protect the human souls if they wanted even a chance of being back in the Divine's light once again.

They were slaves for the crimes they did so long ago; the dust from those times was already half way away to the ends of the cosmos.

"You think you're special, don't you? That the same rules we all follow somehow don't apply to you?" Suni accused.

"No," Zoë replied, slightly raising her nose with confidence. "I just prefer to challenge them, that's all." She looked past Suni to see Constantine enter. "Now, if you're going to kiss me goodbye, now's the time. And know that I'll never kiss you again."

Suni's eyes turned cold staring into Zoë's stoic face, and she released her jaw with contempt.

"Goodbye, Zoë." With that, she turned and walked off, passing Constantine. "She's yours. Punishment and all." The door slammed shut, leaving Zoë and her other superior in the hall.

Constantine pushed his long, black braid away from his shoulder as he quietly walked to the dais where she was chained. His violet eyes were bright and expression visibly annoyed as he moved towards her.

Like all of them, he possessed almost immaculate features, from his chiseled chin and soft lips to his tall, masculine frame. The irony was that the use of those features was for anything but immaculate and innocent.

He stopped in front of her and put his hands behind his back. "Hello, Zoë."

"Constantine," she acknowledged. "I need to explain the situation."

He cocked his head to the side. "Do you, now? Perhaps I know all the dance steps to this one. It's not like we didn't have this conversation before, right?"

"This is different, Connie, and you know it. One side is getting too dominant and we have to intervene. The vampires are going to take the wars to another level. They have the numbers and have stolen the grimoire and Remelia. Forget what Suni—"

"Suni," Constantine interjected, "may have been forgiving and lenient the first time, but look at me."

Zoë met his eyes.

"I'm not Suni. And I know she has an unhealthy fixation on you. Please rest assured that I do not." He sat down. "Do you know why the Order is so complicated?"

Zoë nodded. "Because nothing in it is absolute. Everything is about balance."

He nodded in agreement. "Correct. We can't kill every vampire on the planet, just like we can't allow them to kill every human or Were. We just thin the herds so that humans have a better chance for dominance. But even then, we couldn't allow all the supernaturals to be slaughtered by humans, either. Balance."

"All the more reason we should've stepped in when the vampires were taking the witches' only protection. They are humans too, Constantine."

"True, but Were-shifters have a human soul too. Where were you eons ago? Where were you when the witches had the upper hand and nearly annihilated them?"

"That isn't fair," she said.

"No, it isn't. Like I said. Balance. We can't continue to nose into their wars, Zoë. Sometimes it can serve as a natural scale to reset the dominance between everyone. We're not gods. We just get the busy work. I know you think we're chickenshit and aren't willing to go the extra mile to help, but we're not angels."

"We just get their busy work," Zoë replied softly. "The Three will topple the scales in their favor. They are hungry and want to be the apex predator. If you keep me here and do nothing, count-less humans will be ripped away by them. It'll be like the Dark Ages again. Humans fighting for survival and fearing the night. Do we really want that?"

Constantine straightened his body and looked at her chains,

then at Zoë. He wished he could tell her that her brave tenacity would fade just like his did long ago, but why crush a spirit that reminded him so much of himself? He stood up. "No. We don't."

"I will face whatever punishment you have for my disobedience. I know how much you hate to set a bad precedent, but please. I will come back and face it all if you give me a chance to make this right. Send me back and let me replace the vampire leadership."

"Replace?"

"If we end The Three, the vampires will need time to regroup and build new leadership. Give the Were-shifters and witches time for peace. Maybe it can all end."

Constantine raised a curious eyebrow. "Peace?" Now he knew she was dreaming. "You're asking for a lot, Zoë."

"That wasn't a far cry before The Three tore it down. Ivana, Remelia and maybe even Otto were going down that road. It could happen again." She held up her bound wrists. "Please. Let me go to work."

Constantine deeply sighed. He reached over to grab her wrist. "Destroy the Order, and everything will crumble with you. Save it, and you save yourself."

With a clink, Constantine broke the chains and freed her. Zoë felt her energy pulse within her, eager to pull through the portal back to the mortal realm.

Coming back to this dimension did her some good, as her kind always gained more strength back on their plane. She looked him in the eyes and nodded. He turned and stared at the symbol on the floor glowing orange behind him. The black hole in the center began to grow, pulling against them.

"Now go, before I change my mind."

Zoë didn't hesitate. Running past Constantine, her body turned jet black as she dove into the portal.

~

JAVEN STOOD LEANING over the balcony, watching the droves of vampires making their way inside the hall. The scent of burning rosemary oil and fresh lilies filled the room and was a darker reminder of death than Ivana's coffin. Turning away, he heard the doors behind him open and Dashiell walked in.

"Are you here with good news?"

"I'm here with great news." He slowly moved next to Javen. "Found one of Remelia's covens and made an example. Also, we found Christophe."

Javen raised an eyebrow. "Really?"

"And Tristan."

Javen smiled, crossing his arms. "You've been busy."

"Damn right, I have. I'm doing the work of three guards, so remember that when you divide the assets acquired from the Were-shifters and Green Girls."

"Where are they?"

Dashiell looked to the crowd, admiring the view. "Takeshi has them. You wanna say goodbye?"

Javen nodded. "Yes, I do."

BLOOD-DIPPED WINGS

Tristan slowly came to as his eyes opened to darkness. The stench of old blood and burned flesh sobered him, only to realize the silver chains around his wrist and mouth were the culprit.

His arms pulled above his head; he didn't have strength to pull himself up. Moving his head, he groaned as the barbs hooked deeper into his flesh.

"Ah, you're awake," a male voice said across the darkness. "Good."

Suddenly, the darkness became intense light as someone pulled the hood off his face. His eyes adjusted to see Takeshi, Dashiell, and Javen standing in front of him. Javen wore scarlet funeral attire while Takeshi wore a butcher's apron over his suit. They were waiting for him.

Dashiell turned to Takeshi. "Take those off him; his burning flesh is turning my nose."

Takeshi moved toward him with rubber gloves and grabbed the bolt cutters. His eyes held a small delight as he put the cutter near his mouth and clipped the chain that wrapped around his face. There was a sigh of relief echoed as Tristan adjusted to his jaw being free to move. The silver wore him down, and, at that moment, he didn't know how much danger he was in. The pain in his mouth started to subside, but that was the extent of recovery. He looked around.

"Where's Christophe?"

Dashiell scoffed. "Don't worry about him. You have your own problems."

Indeed, he did. He'd never been in this room before, but he knew a torture chamber when he saw one. "Where's Remelia? I know you fuckers have her."

Javen stood there with his hands behind his back casually. "She's alive. For now."

Tristan gritted his teeth in disdain. "Javen, why am I not surprised?"

He shook his head. "I think you like to pride yourself in knowing everything about me and the others. After all, you've spent many years protecting us."

"And what a shit task that was." Tristan frowned. "Can't believe I wasted myself looking after a regime that finds it necessary to kill their own kind to bring everyone to the brink of chaos."

"I don't think you understand the work we're doing, Tristan. It was the reason I ultimately couldn't trust you to do the harder tasks to make this opportunity work."

"You mean, murder your companion and pin the blame on your enemies?"

Javen sneered. "Yes. I loved Ivana. Truly, I did. But she was just too tenacious and wanted peace. She didn't understand that peace will always be a temporary thing, and what we needed was to gain vampire dominance. With Were-shifters or even witches at the helm, our way of life and food supply could be compromised. They would combine forces and overpower us."

"What are you talking about? We aren't baby vamps. We know the score, and that has *always* been a risk."

"How long do you expect for us to last if that happens? Hmm? You think anyone gives a shit about our people? Vampires are hated everywhere. If we didn't make a move to keep us ahead, who would've helped us?"

"So instead of peace, you wanted to drum up loyalty within the vampire ranks to turn up the heat on your rivals."

Javen nodded. "First, we needed to take the wind out of the sails of our enemies. We knew that Ivana and Remelia were negotiating terms of a new truce. We didn't want her to take it that far, but, like I said, she was tenacious. Valette saw this as an opportunity to take Remelia and render the Green Girls helpless. We had Dashiell retrieve her and bring her back here. Of course, that wasn't enough. I knew her grimoire was just as powerful, and we couldn't risk another witch having the ability to use it against us."

"You sent me and Greg to collect it."

Javen smiled. "And that you did. This scattered them and made it totally plausible for them to get hostile. The Green Girls, after all, are naturally aggressive towards vampires. The dark against the light. Ivana by that time was starting to suspect we were up to something, but she couldn't tell what. She kept harping on about bringing the supernaturals together and all the work she was doing."

"You killed her and set up the witches."

Dashiell smiled and raised his hand. "Actually, that was me. After I handled Christophe, I was supposed to make sure the attack was fruitful. I warned The Three that putting you on detail meant they needed someone to make sure Ivana died. After all, you're the best protector The Three ever had. I took the high ground and watched the attack, and, sure enough, there you were being all badass and already getting her to safety."

He shook his head, chiding. "I had to think fast and slip into the church. Her death still had to appear as if a Were-shifter or a witch killed her. Heads versus tails, the witches won the toss."

Tristan growled as he pulled against the chains. "She was unarmed. Helpless."

Dashiell shrugged. "The moment she laid eyes on me, she knew her fate and accepted it. If it was any consolation, your name was the last words on her lips before I bled her out."

Tristan hissed.

Javen turned to Dashiell. "That is enough. It's almost time for the funeral. Get rid of them and make it look like an animal got them. It's time to throw Otto and his flea-bitten pack of mutts deeper in this mix. But first, I want to know if they talked with Otto and his men. Do what you have to do." He checked his pocket watch and turned to the door.

"Javen!" Tristan cried out as he paused to face him.

"Yes?"

"We're not done. Before Master Darkness comes for me, he's coming to you first."

Javen scoffed. "Bold words, former commander. Bold words." With that, he walked out.

Dashiell started to whistle and pop his gum. "Tristan, this would go a lot easier if you just told me what you know about Otto's plans."

"What makes you think I know anything? If memory serves, they ambushed us in that bar."

Takeshi walked past Dashiell and grabbed one of the various silver brands.

Dashiell watched the Yakuza vampire move behind Tristan and sighed. "True, but I did have a few vampires ducking for cover there mention you guys leaving the same time the Were-shifters fled. Coincidence?" He shrugged. "Maybe? Give me something so we don't have to do it the hard way."

Tristan spit his blood on the floor and looked up at Dashiell. "Don't have the stomach for it?"

He shook his head. "I'm not a monster, Tristan. I'm just a soldier. I took no joy in killing Ivana. Hell, I took no joy in killing those witches." He paused. "Well, a little, cause let's face it, those bitches are vicious. But you are different." He pointed behind Tristan. "But Takeshi, here...there's a reason Valette likes him so much."

Tristan yelled as Takeshi pressed the silver brand against his back and dragged it down his spine. It was going to be a long night.

~

REMELIA HEARD footsteps getting closer and slowly opened her eyes. "Please don't."

A laugh escaped Valette's lips as she watched the Supreme groveling at her feet. "Don't what, Green Girl? You know, I'm sure you feel a sort of emptiness by now, right? Can you feel it?"

Tears welled up in her eyes. She knew that emptiness and what it meant. "You killed them, didn't you? I feel their loss. Why?"

"Oh, come now. You had to know they were roadkill. It's quite pathetic how they can't make it without you. And now that the vampires feel victorious over the Green Girls, it will only grow. Then we'll have no use for you."

She looked over to Christophe, who was bound in the corner. From her angle, she couldn't tell if he was alive or dead. "Or you." A sinister smirk graced her demure face as she turned and walked towards the guards. "Make sure Takeshi leaves nothing of them recognizable. To our knowledge, Remelia disappeared off the face of the fucking planet."

"Yes ma'am," one of the guards replied as he stepped aside for her to leave. Valette stopped and turned to face Remelia once more. "Scratch that. Save me her head. I could use a souvenir from the war." Blowing a kiss, she walked out, and Remelia watched the door slam shut.

She closed her eyes as tears rolled down her face. This wasn't supposed to happen. Not like this.

Zoë, where are you?

No sooner than the thought entered her mind, a crash from above as the ceiling crumbled and a figure landed in a crouching position on the floor. She opened her eyes wide as the guards appeared rattled by the intrusion.

Standing to full height, Zoë's black feather wings tucked in and disappeared as she drew her sword and charged towards the guards. They both pulled their batons to defend against the strikes, and met her hit for hit until she swept one and beheaded the other. The guard laid still as her blade stopped at his throat.

"Please! I'm just doing my job," he pleaded. He looked to Remelia. "I didn't lay a finger on her! I swear."

Zoë glared at him. "Smart move. Where's the vampire Tristan?"

He swallowed. "He's downstairs. Takeshi has him in the torture chamber."

Her breath caught in her throat. "Thank you for that information."

"Wait—"

His voice was silenced by the swing of her blade. Shaking the blood off her sword, she sheathed it and ran to Remelia. Sliding onto the salt floor, she gently smoothed the hair from the Supreme's face.

"Zoë," she said with a soft smile on her face.

"I'm here, Remelia. Hold on, I'm setting you free." Moving to the wall, she searched for a control for the drain. Finally locating it, she turned the wheel to release the salt. She spun to see her sigh as she felt the pressure at her legs and sides slowly ease, and the salt became less compact.

Her eyes scanned the room and saw a body dangling in the corner tied in chains. Running across the room, she recognized Christophe and picked up his head. There were no signs of life in him, and the chains hooked into his mouth and gagged him. The silver no longer burned into his skin. The reaction had stopped.

Disgust on her face, she pulled at the chains. "Christophe? Hey!" She shook him. "Christophe!"

He was gone. Anger rose within her as she stared at his body. His own had let him die like a dog in some filthy chamber. He was a decent vampire, and he died horribly for nothing. None of it made any sense.

With a grunt, she pulled her sword and slashed the shackle that suspended him. His body fell against her as she lowered him gently to the ground. She turned to see Remelia climb out of the tank, a soft glow surrounding her as she was finally freed from her salt prison. She walked over to Zoë and placed a hand on her shoulder.

"This is why I chose you, Zoë. You see beyond your nature, beyond what you were taught. You, a Black Blood, should not mourn a vampire, but you do. You shouldn't care for a vampire."

Zoë looked up at Remelia.

"But you do. Don't you?"

"You took a gamble when you bound us together." Zoë stood up and faced her.

"More like an educated guess."

Zoë nodded. Pulling a dagger from behind her jeans, she handed it to her. "Here."

Remelia tightened her grip around the blade. "Thanks. Go help Tristan." She turned to walk out when Zoë stopped her.

"Wait, where are you going?"

The Supreme's eyes glowed blue. "Retribution."

TRISTAN COULDN'T FOCUS ANYMORE on any one object in the room. It always was his trick when enduring torture, but he was tired. The strength in his legs had already given out. Even Takeshi needed to take a break.

"You are quite resilient, Commander Castillion," Takeshi complimented as he pulled off his gloves. "Most vampires would not be able to take such pain."

A tired but dark laugh escaped Tristan's lips. "Glad I surprised you."

Takeshi walked past him and felt a presence close by. Spotting his katana braced upon the counter a few feet away, he got quiet and scanned the room for anything suspicious. Despite nothing apparent, the feeling didn't go away. Something was close and ready to strike.

With superspeed, Takeshi flipped over the counter, narrowly missing Zoë's blow, and rolled onto the floor where he grabbed his katana. Drawing his weapon, he established his fighting stance as he watched Zoë move in on him.

"Who are you?" Takeshi asked. He moved cautiously, side-stepping to keep his distance.

Zoë shook her head. "You worry yourself with details." Moving in, their blades collided and clinked as they engaged in fierce battle. Takeshi moved with speed, dodging blows until she kicked a chair at him, throwing his balance where she slashed across his side.

Hissing in pain, he gripped the wound and staggered back. With fury in her eyes, she circled him. Her sight cut to Tristan's motionless body, and the hate only escalated. "You like to torture, do you?"

"Only in the face of the broken can one truly see the soul of a man."

Zoë sneered. "How poetic." She felt the heat in her hand. "I'll remember to use that one day." Her eyes glowed violet as enthrallment seized him and pulled him closer.

Trying to fight it, he drew fangs and hissed, but the force was too strong. Her whispers tempted and haunted him, even convinced him to drop his sword.

Zoë smiled as he released it, watching it stick into the floor. Pulling him into her grasp, she growled as the promise of blood called to her. Grabbing his face, she tilted him and bit into his throat.

Sucking the blood into her, she continued to feel her strength multiplying. Takeshi struggled against her as he felt himself weakening. She was draining the life out of him. Just when he felt an inch from death, she pulled away and glared at him, his blood dripping from her mouth and jaw.

"Pity, I'm not that interested in seeing your soul." Her hand gripped his throat and picked him up a foot off the ground.

Roaring, she squeezed and crushed his neck, feeling his bones crumble like dust in her hand. She discarded him by tossing him across the room before running over to Tristan.

He hung against silver chains and didn't move. His body was beaten, bleeding and scarred as silver torture tools stayed embedded in his skin. Pulling them out, her heart dropped into her stomach.

"Tristan? Wake up."

She gently patted his cheek to rouse him. "Tristan? Come on." She froze as he slowly opened his eyes.

Tristan looked at her as if she was a mirage. Her charming, bloody face was a sight for sore eyes. But he had enough hallucinations for one torture session. "Get outta here."

Zoë shook her head. "You're coming with me."

She pulled her sword and stuck the shackle that held his hands above him, sending him leaning against her. Lowering him to the floor, she leaned him back and pulled all the chains off him.

"Save yourself, Zoë. The vampires are lost. You were right to hate us. You were right to hate me. Leave us."

"I can't do that." She stared at his once bright eyes then held her wrist to his mouth. "Now drink."

Tristan pushed it away. "No. Get Remelia and burn this place down."

"Listen to me. I have Remelia, but I need you. I can't do this alone." She bit into her wrist and let the blood trickle onto his lips.

The heady taste alone was enough to make him open his mouth. Pressing her wrist to him, she sighed as his lips created suction, siphoning her powerful blood into him.

Tristan found a peace he dared to describe in taking in her blood. It was fire and rain at the same time. It spoke volumes to her power. Her gift of strength was gracious, but what he really wanted was her.

He pulled himself up and released her wrist. He looked into her eyes as she wiped the blood from his lips. "Don't you listen to anyone, Black Blood?"

She smiled. His scars were healing, and the light in his eyes grew bright again. He was quite dashing when he wasn't half-dead.

"No. And you should be grateful of my rebellious behavior, vampire."

He claimed a gentle kiss on her lips.

"I am grateful." He stood up and looked around for his guns. "Where's Takeshi?"

Zoë pointed to the other side of the room. "He angered me."

Tristan saw his body limp on the floor. His neck looked like a string of cooked spaghetti. "Indeed. Did your beast do that?"

She shook her head. "No, it hasn't come out to play. Yet."

Seeing his holster and guns on the other table, he grabbed them and slipped it on.

"Remelia has been freed."

"Good." He looked around. "Have you seen Christophe?"

Her eyes softened as she looked down. "I was too late. He's gone."

Tristan slammed his fist on the table. He'd known Christophe for so long. He was trustworthy and fair, yet he'd died alone. "I'll make Dashiell pay for this. The funeral has started. There'll be at least 200 or so vampires between us and The Three. Does that worry you?"

A wicked smile grew on Zoë's face. She slowly shook her head. "Not at all."

THE FALLEN

The hall filled with vampires coming from all over to pay final respect to Javen's consort, Ivana. Mounds of lilies and mammoth banners flew high and adorned every area of the space. It was a farewell suitable for a queen, just as the people and The Three wanted it to be. Javen, Valette and Kostya sat patiently on their respected thrones like dolls as vampires touched the sleek black casket where the last of her remained. Her final coffin. Valette and Kostya turned to Javen, giving him a cue that it was time to speak. He straightened his tie and sash as he ascended the platform.

Tristan used his knife to quietly take out one of the guards near the hall's entrance while Zoë took out the other, breaking his neck. Laying their bodies quietly on the floor, they kept stealth as they moved to the other end. There were four more guards at the main door.

Zoë squeezed her body tight along the edge of the wall with Tristan right next to her. The guards were facing out, attentive and armed to the teeth. Apparently, The Three didn't want any surprises. *Well, tough shit. Cause they had one hell of a surprise to offer.*

Tristan turned to her. "If we trigger gunfire, the crowd will be on our ass and we'll have a hard time getting to The Three. It'll be pandamonium and we can't allow them to escape in the craziness."

She nodded in approval. "Agreed. You let me handle crowd control. First things first. Let's remove the guards. Quickly and quietly."

Tristan grimaced. "That's a long way to get to them before they sound the alarm, princess." He eyed her suggestively, hinting at an opportunity.

She rolled her eyes and sighed. *Seriously?* "Ugh, must I do everything, vamper?"

He raised an eyebrow. "You're the one with the great ass, Zoë. We can trade up if I get the gift."

"What about you? It's not like I can direct my enthrallment that way."

He shrugged. "I'll live."

She touched his chest, holding him back. "No, I have a better idea."

The guard jumped as they saw a curvy figure walk up the hall from the shadows. The clomp of her boot heels against the marble floor held a slow, methodical rhythm. They stood at attention. Probably more ways than one, but Zoë was still too far away to tell.

"The funeral has already started, and this is invite only," one guard said.

"Well, that's too bad. I've come a long way to pay my respects. I'm sure if you slip me in, no one would be the wiser." She continued closer with wide, reflective eyes. Just a little bit closer...

"Are they expecting you?"

She paused as she finally got close enough to do damage. "Not really."

Tristan only heard the swift sounds of a blade through both

air and matter before seeing one of the guards' heads roll past him down the slope of the hall. Running ahead, he saw the carnage left at her feet as she turned around to face him. An arterial spray of blood slashed across her demure, but dark face. "You all right?"

She wiped her face, only smearing the blood across her cheek like war paint for a Grim Reaper. "There's a side entrance that leads up to the catwalk. That's the best way inside without disrupting the herd."

A gunshot ruptured through the silence as Zoë flew back against the wall. She yelled as the white-hot blaze from the bullet burned into her chest. Tristan turned to find Dashiell smiling, holding a large caliber rifle. "Hurts like a bitch, doesn't it, bitch!"

Tristan aimed his guns at him, but darted between Zoë sliding down the wall, subdued.

"I gotta tell you, Tris, you hang with a pretty strange crowd. At first, I only thought Black Bloods were a myth. I mean, come on—a badass demon that eats vampires? Sounds like a bullshit boogeyman, right?" he scoffed. "That was my bad. I knew she was hot, and you were probably just the lucky guy fucking her. But after she nearly destroyed me and my crew, I figured something was up. So, I started looking in The Three's old armory. These blessed rounds pack quite a wallop." He inclined in head over to where she laid panting, bleeding. "Shake it off, cupcake."

Tristan's eyes looked of daggers. "Your shit is with me, so let's finish this."

Dashiell grinned. "You know, you are something else. Still the gentleman."

Tristan moved, and Dashiell cocked his gun. "If I put a shot to the head with a round like this, it's over for her. So, drop your weapons."

His eyes darted to Zoë, whose pained expression warned to decline. After a beat, he dropped both guns on the floor. "You and

I both know that only one of us is going to be alive by daylight, Dashiell. Don't prolong the inevitable."

Dashiell laughed. "For a morose vampire with obviously a death wish, I expected you to be a little less involved in these events."

"Shit changes."

"Indeed it does." Dashiell looked around and shrugged. "You know? What the hell, right? We can settle this the old way. I imagine it's just a formality, really. Then everyone knows you fell by my hand." He dropped the gun and prompted him to come. "That is, if you can handle an audience." He threw a dagger and missed Tristan, laughing as he went up to the side stairs into the rafters, taunting.

Tristan turned and leaned over Zoë. The wound didn't close, and she writhed in pain, her obsidian blood spilling out. "Let me help you."

Gritting through the pain, she pushed him away. "No! I'll make it! Go! Get that son of a bitch!" She leaned back in exasperation as he ran up the swirling stairs after Dashiell.

Her skin kept throbbing into a black hue, trying to heal, but it was no use. A blessed round couldn't be dug out or pushed out. When Black Bloods got hit with blessed rounds, they either did one of two things: found a man of the cloth or went home where the wound would heal. Panting, she tried to sit up. She wasn't ready to go home. She had a job to do, and Jay was too far away for another emergency call. It was time to put up or shut up.

Pulling herself slowly to her feet, she called to her hunger. That deep hunger that if not fed triggered something darker within her. Something more haunting and lethal. It was time to call her beast.

DASHIELL AND TRISTAN fought hand to hand, grappling, punching and kicking to inflict the greatest pain. Tristan caught Dashiell, flipping him over onto the catwalk. Jumping after him, he landed a punch. Then another. Dashiell pried away from his hold and caught Tristan with a jab. Running his tongue across his lips, he smiled. "That's all you got?" Dashiell growled and charged to him, releasing a series of blows that pushed Tristan against the rail. "Well, that was fun. Not as fun as it'll be to enslave that cute little Black Blood bangtail after you're gone. Now she has a taste for vampire cock, maybe she'll be my new entertainment after The Three give me a cut of enemy land." He stretched his body and advanced on Tristan.

But Dashiell paused as Tristan struck and ran his dagger forcefully into Dashiell's chest. "That's for Ivana." He shoved the blade deeper, a smirk of enjoyment on his face. "That's because you're a dick." He released Dashiell and let his body plummet to the bottom of the hall with a violent splat, alerting the vampires below.

To the screams and growls, The Three looked up to see Tristan on the catwalk.

Javen pointed. "That insolent bastard and traitor. Kill him!"

Everyone scattered at gun fire that rang out through the hall, including The Three. Guards, both house and Royal, came out of the woodwork. Javen turned as Valette grabbed his arm.

"We need to get out of here!"

He pulled his arm back and hissed. "I'm not going anywhere except up there to kill him! It's time he's finished!" He pushed her away and went to grab his sword.

Kostya and some of the guards sneaked out the back, moving with incredible speed to avoid the fray. "Hurry and get me the fuck out of here," he commanded to his guards. "Take me to my safe house immediately."

"Yes sir," a guard acknowledged as his eyes briefly turned amber. Walking down the hall to the exit, the guards finally led him to the limousine and opened the door for him to get inside.

Kostya hurried inside the back of the car, and paused when he realized he wasn't alone. Sucking in a breath, he peered up to see Otto sitting in the back with him. His legs were crossed as casually as were his bare arms.

"Hello Kostya."

Confused, Kostya looked around. "What the hell are you doing here, filthy *sobaka?*"

Otto smiled with full upper and lower fangs ready. He took off his shades. "Just contributing to the cause. Remember, I warned you long ago that if I ever got close to you, I would make you pay for the atrocities done against my shifters. The slaughters. The experiments. The torture." His eyes turned a menacing bright amber as he glared at his prey. "You're in my den now, little devil Kostya."

Kostya shook in the wake of his fate, but growled at the gall of the age old Were-shifter "Otto!"

"There's no sympathy for the Devil." With a blood-chilling growl, Otto ripped his shirt and instantly morphed into a Were-shifter. Vicious claws and teeth were the last thing Kostya saw as Otto's ravenous vengeance tore into him.

TRISTAN CLIMBED down to the bottom as the patrons spilled out the pandemonium and the guards remained. He pointed at the only remaining monarch in the hall. "I'm challenging him and him alone. But if you stand in my way, I will cut you down."

The guards stood like a sea between him and Javen, who stood seething at the podium. "You've got a lot of balls coming in here, Tristan!"

"I wonder if your royal guards would still respect you, knowing you fooled them into supremacy by having your own companion murdered," Tristan called out.

Some of the guards looked at each other.

Javen scoffed. "You are no longer of the royal guard, commander. You're delusional and toxic to our vampire ways. You're a traitor."

"And you're a liar." He gestured him to come. "You no longer have Dashiell to do your dirty work. If you want me dead, you have to work for it."

Javen looked at the group of guards and protection at least forty deep and replied with an arrogant smirk. "So do you."

Everyone's attention turned behind Tristan as the hall doors opened and a pair of bright violet eyes shone past pitch-black facial skin. Her fangs were longer than usual and belonged to a face that was fuming. The air around Zoë snapped and hummed with energy as she slowly walked in with a sword in each hand.

"Oooh," she cooed in an otherworldly, demonic voice. "Looks like you guys want to play. Hmm?" She rolled her neck and inhaled the scent of vampire blood in the room. "Good. So do I."

Javen stepped back in horror as he watched her. "Holy shit."

Tristan's hair rose on the back of his neck as the static in her presence was absolutely palpable. She was a Venus flytrap of a woman—deadly and gorgeous.

And lethal.

Zoë inclined her head to Tristan and tossed him the other sword in her hand and smiled. It was the first time he'd seen her beast, and she commended him for not running away. *Admirable.* "Need a path, cowboy?"

Tristan nodded.

"Kill them!" Javen ordered.

A wicked grin grew on her face as she twirled her sword in her hand. The room shook as her dark wings grew and extended on each side of her. With superior strength, one beat of them forced a wind through the hall that blew the guards back several feet.

Tristan took that opportunity to slash through the guards to leap onto the platform where Javen waited for him.

Not giving the guards an opportunity to recover, she readied her sword, centering herself. "I'm not finished yet." With a roar, Zoë advanced on the crowd and slashed through the fray.

～

VALETTE PUSHED past the swarm of vampires and out the back hall, trying to catch her breath. Javen and Kostya had to be somewhere in this chaos, but now was the time to seek some safety from the mayhem. Her long gown fluttering behind her, she moved faster, away from the screams of horror and death heard through the walls. What the hell was happening in there? She'd be damned if she stayed to find out.

It was Javen's fault this all crumbled.

"Leaving so soon?" A firm female voice broke Valette's concentration.

Turning around, her eyes focused on a woman with jet black hair and dark furious eyes. Her red dress still had salt embedded in the cloth.

Valette, calming after realizing who it was, scoffed and straightened her body to face her. "Remelia." She crossed her arms, shifting her hips. "What do you think you're going to do, little witch?"

"Something I perhaps should've done a long time ago." As she walked forward, her body began to glow. "You want my head?" She stopped and frowned, clasping her hands behind her back. "Then come take it. If you can, vampire whore."

Valette gripped the dagger behind her. "Little Green Girl bitch!" Anger rising, she unsheathed the knife and with a shriek, she ran charging towards Remelia. "Spell-bending slut! I'll see you dead like the others!"

"No, you won't," Remelia replied as she pulled her hands from behind her back.

With a swift strike of the silver hand-held scythe, Remelia cut her down. Now silenced, Valette staggered backwards. She gasped at the burning slash against her throat, bracing against the wall.

Remelia held the scythe up and smiled. "You've always under-estimated your enemies, Valette." Before the wound closed, she pulled her hand back, using magic to keep the wound open. Valette gagged as blood continued to spill out. "Your reign ended the moment you sent death to my daughters' door. The moment you killed and tortured your own." Valette couldn't speak, only held on for survival as Remelia walked up to her. "That is for Ivana and me." She dropped the scythe from her other hand and a white ball manifested into her palm. Valette's eyes widened in terror, gagging, shaking her head. "And yes, this for the Green Girls you've slaughtered." She pushed the white glowing ball into her mouth and walked away. *"Ab intus illuminet."*

With a shrieking, painful cry and bright light, Valette turned to ash behind her.

TRISTAN STALKED around Javen with his sword drawn. Both wouldn't take their eyes off each other. As the lightning struck, both of them ran and clashed metal to metal, fighting as if it was the end of the world. With a furious slash, Tristan hissed at the slice at his skin.

Javen shrugged. "I admire your bravery, Commander. But your age is only a drop in the bucket compared to me!" He punc-tuated his statement with another clash of swords.

Overpowering Tristan, Javen pushed harder against the blade until Tristan ground his teeth and used his power to shift him away and planted a solid kick to his face.

"Things change, *highness*," Tristan snapped.

Javen staggered back, and in frustration, swung high to try to take Tristan's head from his body. Ducking, he moved back and rebounded to engage tit for tat, the blades reflecting against their eyes.

Javen's face twisted in disgust. "You think the vampires will be able to make it without us? Hmm? When we formed The Three, there was nothing but a bunch of covens fighting for survival. Scavenging and hiding from humans. Is that what you want your people to be?" He swung his blade against Tristan's in a heated block. Tristan felt Zoë's blood deep within him, dying to be released. It scorched his veins and tensed his muscles.

Tristan looked at the ground below then at Javen before he moved in to strike. "You don't give us enough credit." Clink! Clink! He forced Javen back with each hit. Javen could barely keep himself protected, holding his sword with both hands. "If you haven't noticed, we're pretty resilient."

Javen swung and knocked the sword out of Tristan's hand and off the balcony. The last of The Three smiled and shook his head. "You're so noble, Commander. I hope you rest in peace." Javen raised the blade over his head and swung down with all his might. His eyes widened at Tristan catching the blade between his hands. The incredible strength from Tristan not only stopped the blade from contact but managed to shift it to the left. Javen's body shook with the effort of the fight, and he growled. "You son of a bitch! I am a king!"

With fluid motion, Tristan kicked the sword out of his hand, grabbed it, and sliced across Javen's throat. His surprised expression frozen, Javen fell to his knees, and his head fell beside him. Tristan looked down at his body and threw the sword down next to it.

"Long live the king."

WALKING OUT OF THE HALL, Tristan saw Zoë leaning against the wall, holding herself. Running to her, he caught her and cradled her as she fell. "Dammit, Black Blood. What have you done?" He looked her over and frowned as the wound was still open and bleeding. "Why did you lie to me?"

Zoë opened her eyes and sighed. "You needed help. I helped you. What do you want from me, vampire?"

"My name is Tristan."

She grunted with a smile. "Tristan." She closed her eyes as he smoothed her hair back. A gentle caress that once again felt so intimate and foreign to her. "Blessed rounds are a bitch to remove. I have to leave. I figured that if I couldn't plug the hole, I'd at least keep my feeding up to offset." She shivered in his arms.

"Did it work?"

Zoë looked up at him. "Saved your ass, didn't I?"

"That you did." Tristan picked her up into his arms and carried her out to the foyer, where there was a mix of vampires, Were-shifters and Remelia present. "How can we get you back?" he asked.

"Jay's." She started to lay her head against him.

"No, that's too far. You won't make it."

"Why do you care?" she mumbled against his chest.

Tristan didn't answer. He walked her over to Remelia, who turned in alarm. "What happened?"

"Blessed round. She has to go back. You pulled her from her plane before, can you send her back?"

Remelia looked at the wound, then at Tristan and nodded quickly. "Yes, I can." She opened the grimoire in her hand and looked around till she picked up a piece of stone from the obliterated statues.

Using the stone, she drew a symbol of The Fallen on the floor that served as a gateway and had Tristan gently lay Zoë in the center. She groaned, holding her bloodied area where the bullet struck.

He didn't know what to say, but he knew that silence was still the wrong answer. A kiss would be foolish, but to do nothing was wrong. But this was not meant to be. He stared into her tired eyes as she held her wound on the floor. Never had he seen a creature so amazing and brave as the one laid bleeding for protecting a vampire.

We don't fit. We can never fit.

He continued to think about that as Remelia chanted, the portal opened, and Zoë finally disappeared. Tristan stood there for a while quietly as Remelia closed her book. He turned and looked at her. "Thank you."

She smiled. "No, thank you. She will be fine on her plane where she can heal." She gently squeezed his hand. "Ivana was right. You are not like the others."

His attention shifted as he witnessed Otto and his Were-shifters leaving. "Otto, what are you doing here?"

Otto turned and nodded. "Ah, Tristan. I came to pay my respects to Ivana." He took off his shades to reveal his amber eyes. "And grab a quick bite. I did not hear from you on the witches; however, as providence would have it, Remelia is over there. I agree that it may be time to talk a bit more. Besides, it doesn't look like the vampires are quite ready."

Tristan looked into the old shifter's eyes. "Not yet."

Otto smiled. "Well, whenever the vamps are ready to get their shit together, let me know." He extended his hand and Tristan shook it.

"Yeah."

Otto tried to leave when he felt the pull of Tristan's hand.

"Enjoy that quick bite, wolf?"

With a devious smile, Otto shrugged. "A bit cold for my tastes, but you know what they say about revenge."

"Indeed I do, wolf."

Otto slipped on his shades and whistled for the rest of his men that followed behind him.

EPILOGUE

One Month Later

Tristan stood at the top of the gothic cathedral and watched the night life below him. Saints and sinners going about their journeys in the darkness. It felt different now. It had been about a month since The Three were removed from leadership, toppling a 500-year regime for the vampires. Since then, the vampires broke apart from one monarchy to several, resetting the leadership and fate of their kind. He was asked to lead and declined promptly. Some hated him for it. Some loved him. Either way, it didn't matter. It was his choice. Time would once again decide who was at the top. Right now, everyone had to regroup and rebuild. No one was better than the other. Maybe this was as close to peace as they would ever get. Otto and Remelia toyed with the idea of a public treaty and, of course, when they left, he laughed.

Most likely they would never get around to it.

Politics.

The recent events ruined him for meeting Mr. Darkness. He was quite the survivor, and going to ground didn't seem as tempting anymore now that change was on the horizon for the supernaturals. Ivana was right. There was hope in some of that change she wanted. He regretted not believing in it at first. But it took Zoë to drive it home. She believed in something better. In fighting for something, even when it didn't benefit her directly.

Zoë.

He looked out with a sigh. Her name kept coming to visit his thoughts, just like her image visited his dreams.

Perhaps he still wanted to tempt death. Why else would he grow feelings for a demon that killed his kind for work and play?

Walking into his home, he locked the door and went into the kitchen. Reaching into the fridge, he pulled out a bag of type A blood and started to drink. Leaning against the stove, he paused as he heard a faint sound above his head. Looking up, he listened carefully for another minute. Then, he heard it again.

Dammit. Just when I thought I had some peace...

Tristan pulled his gun and moved out the kitchen. He quickly moved up the stairs and braced against the door. Something had some nerve—to cross into his path after the past month he'd had would certainly face death. Taking a breath, he kicked the door open and went still as he found the source of the noise.

"What are you doing here?" he asked the half-naked Zoë laying on his bed. She wore a pair of red panties and bra that barely covered her. Her other accessory was a sully chain that secured her to the head post. A devious smile crept on her face as she watched him studying her.

She savored the way his eyes lingered on her. She burned for it and there just was no denying it any longer. "Believe it or not, this is my punishment for all the shit I've done a month ago. I've been grounded indefinitely. My only consolation: I got to choose where I'd be dumped."

As the words sank in, Tristan grunted in feigned suspicion. "And *this* was the first place you thought of?"

She slowly nodded. "Nudity was optional, of course."

Tristan sighed and leaned against the wall, still not taking his eyes off her. Her presence made him feel like he needed to check himself into rehab. Cunning, tempting, and terribly harrowing, Zoë was the woman of his dreams. But that was the problem. She wasn't a woman—she was a Black Blood Slayer, and her world did not include him unless it included also killing him. They survived the fallout of The Three, but he wasn't going to sell himself on the fantasy she could be his. From the time she crashed into his life, she'd made him wonder if he could imagine having a companion to help him embrace the darkness.

Not since Katya's death had he really entertained such a thing, but as he looked at her, craved her, Tristan couldn't help to smash that notion to oblivion for the sake of his sanity.

"This will never work, Black Blood. Our very different species alone is the writing on the wall." He pointed at her as he strode to the bed. "Predator." Then, he motioned to himself. "Prey."

Zoë sat up. "I'm more than that, and I know you are too." Her eyes brightened. "We can choose to believe we'll never change or that my attraction to you is just biology or—"

"Or what?"

She moistened her lips. "Or we can be honest with each other."

"And what's the truth?" he asked, staring at her mouth.

Zoë slowly crawled on all fours on the bed, a smirk on her face. "That our desire for each other goes much, *much* further than that." Tristan stopped at the side of the bed as she sat back on her knees. She gazed into his intrigued, mystic eyes. The proximity to him stirred her body. "Back home, I still could feel your presence," she purred. "As if you never left my side. Like a dark angel beside me, your aura clings to me like hot wax." She sighed. "I should feel threatened or afraid of it, but instead I find it…indescribable."

Tristan raised an eyebrow.

"You're different, Tristan. Let's not exhaust ourselves labeling what this is."

Because of him, she learned exactly why the Order existed. Everybody had a part to play, and it was too easy to choose one paranormal to hate, to victimize, or to fear. It was a crazy ride to be tethered to a creature like Tristan—a vampire who, underneath, had loyalty and strength unlike anyone she'd ever known. They were supposed to have killed each other, yet they didn't. Remelia must've been wiser than all of them to make such a decision.

Call her a fool, but she took it as a good sign.

Tristan nearly reached out to touch her face, he but clenched his fist instead. He couldn't escape the dangerous pull of his Mistress Darkness, it seemed. Behind a face like hers. Beside a fighter like her—he could very well die a lucky vampire. "We'll either try to kill each other or fuck each other crazy. That kind of polarization is dangerous."

She pulled against the chains and claimed his lips, letting him taste that fire she held for him. There wasn't a force above or below her that could compare to the magnetism that pulled her to him. Her dark companion. "There's plenty of opportunity to meet somewhere in between." She smiled as she kissed him. Then pulling back, she sighed at the feel of his hands rubbing and squeezing her flesh. Her skin was hot compared to his cool touch, and she yearned to be stripped down bare and taken like the spitfire demon she was created to be. His tongue stroked against hers and the wetness between her legs grew.

Oh, how she missed this. She missed the taste of him. Zoë didn't know how long she would be grounded, but Constantine made it clear that he would inform her when she was welcomed back. Suni refused to speak with her, but it was just as well. Connie was her superior and much easier to deal with anyway. The oldest Black Blood had his secrets, but she always found him fair. When Constantine hinted that the war was not over, she knew that Tristan would soon need her again. She whispered into his ear, "Are you looking for peace, vampire?"

"As much as I could get while Mr. Darkness takes his leave, Black Blood. If you're offering me peace in one of your valleys, then by all means, lead me there." His grin was wicked, promising even. As if he knew their time to rest would be brief.

Zoe hissed and licked his lips. "Take off these chains and we'll see."

With a pensive tilt of his head, Tristan stepped back and examined her. "I think I may like you this way." His bright eyes lingered over her like a hungry fox calculating his best method to attack. "Actually, I need to make an adjustment." With other-worldly speed, he climbed on top of her, snapped the chains at the headboard and took up the slack to pull her hands over her head in bondage before locking the links together. His hands slid down her arms, then broke the front clasp of her bra, allowing her breasts to spill into his hands. His thumbs rubbed her nipples to erection. "That's better."

Her back arched to him, intrigued at the sensation of being restricted to use her hands and granting Tristan dominion over her body. Who would've thought; her vampire fancied a bit of kink. "Hmm. This is interesting. What are you going to do to me?"

He raised one eyebrow. "That depends."

"On what?"

Tristan shifted beside her, long enough to gently pull her gauzy underwear off and toss it away. Resting on one elbow, his free hand slipped between the silkiness of her inner thighs. His fingers teased the little hairs, not yet breaching her sensitive folds. Heat radiated off her body as she waited in torture for him to finally touch her there. "On whether you're up for a little role play." He leaned in, running his fangs gently against the hollow of her throat. Her pulse escalated, sending her arousal into over-drive. She sucked in a breath.

"I'm listening…"

His tongue darted against her neck. "It's simple. This time, I'll be the predator." Then his fingers finally invaded the slick flesh at her core. "And you, prey."

A gasp escaped her lips as her body instinctively arched to his touch. She pulled at the chains, nearly forgetting they were there. She turned to meet his reflective eyes and smiled. "This could be tempting."

"You have no idea." His reply was more of a promise of what was to come, and she couldn't wait.

And though they didn't have all the answers and the fate of the supernaturals had yet to take shape, Tristan was thankful to have finally claimed some peace. Even if it was only for a short century.

And as long as it was with *her*.

ABOUT THE AUTHOR

A Paranormal Romance and Urban Fantasy author, Kharma Kelley has been enamored with all things that go "bump in the night" for who knows how long. She truly believes that finding humanity and beauty in some of the most seemingly unconventional places is part of the romantic psyche to her. A big fan of the Big Easy, Kharma tends to weave her proud Cajun heritage and values into her books. She enjoys reading other urban fantasy and romance novels and playing Minecraft in her spare time.

She believes there's something intriguing about strong women finding love in all the "wrong" places in the world of fantasy. Of angels, demons, ghosts, werewolves and the occasional blood sucker, all these paranormal metaphors are at the heart of what humans are and crave most...that we're all different, beautiful and a little bit weird—and just want someone to love us for who really we are."

Where You Can Find More of Kharma Kelley
Newsletter Sign-up
www.authorkharmakelley.com
Visit me on Facebook
Twitter: @kharmakelley